Gordon DeMarco was raised in Akron, Ohio. He came to San Francisco in 1967 to attend graduate school at San Francisco State College. There, he became a participant in the 1968–69 student strike and co-chairperson of Students for a Democratic Society (SDS). Since that time he has worked as a dishwasher, a chauffeur, a docker, a worker in a puppet centre and a supply teacher. He now writes full-time.

His other books include *Polish September* (on Solidarity) and *The Canvas Prison*, which stars Riley Kovachs and rebel actress Frances Farmer.

Pluto Crime

Edited by Ronald Segal

Murder in the Central Committee	Manuel Vázquez Montalban
The China Option	Nancy Milton
Morbid Symptoms	Gillian Slovo
The Waste Remains	Judith Cook
Junk on the Hill	Jeremy Pikser
Days Like These	Nigel Fountain
Dance Hall of the Dead	Tony Hillerman

'Is there anything inherently illogical in the concept of socialist – or, at least, politically and socially aware – crime fiction? Pluto Press, publishers of serious left-wing books, have inaugurated a crime list to prove that the two can mix . . . The first batch of pinko whodunits augurs well for the genre.' *The Times*

'Sturdily resisting the temptation to call the series Red Herrings, the editors begin promisingly with four quite different types of thriller, varied in their setting and in the way politics enters into the action, but all taking an intelligent readership for granted . . .' *The Bookseller*

'Meanwhile, the proof of the four titles currently issued is in the reading: not half bad.' *Sunday Times*

Gordon DeMarco

October Heat

Pluto Press
London and Sydney

First published in 1979 by Germinal Press, 209 Prospect, San Francisco, California 94110, USA

First published in Britain in 1984 by Pluto Press Limited, The Works, 105a Torriano Avenue, London NW5 2RX
and Pluto Press Australia Limited, PO Box 199, Leichhardt, New South Wales 2040, Australia

Reprinted in 1984 by Pluto Press.

Text designed by Claudine Meissner
Cover designed by Clive Challis Gr.R.

Set by Wayside Graphics, Clevedon, Avon
Printed in Great Britain by St Edmundsbury Press, Bury St Edmunds, Suffolk

British Library Cataloguing in Publication Data
De Marco, Gordon
October heat. — (Crime and conspiracy)
I. Title II. Series
813'.54[F] PS3554.E448

ISBN 0-86104-770-2
ISBN 0-86104-744-3

Special thanks to Nancy Huneke, Dorothy Reaven and Harry Clark for believing in Riley Kovachs and their vital contributions to this project.

To my mother and father for their three decades of constant encouragement and to the working class of San Francisco past and present.

1.

It was unusually hot in San Francisco for October. Even if it was Indian Summer. Hell, it was just plain hot, period. The papers said the heat would break soon, but the thermometer on the wall whose mercury had spurted past ninety before the morning dew had time to dry, knew nothing about it.

I had been spending the afternoon in my office in the Monadnock Building losing weight the easy way and listening to the first game of the World Series. Sweat beads the size of marbles rolled down my face and dripped onto my shirt while I tried to concentrate on the early edition of the *Examiner*. A breeze was only something to be rumored about.

The heat was exhausting; the Tigers had been humiliated by the Cardinals; and my rent, like the Vets Bonus, was long overdue. Otherwise everything was hunkey dory.

I was doing laps in the pools of my own perspiration when I heard a faint tapping on my office door. I didn't care for the interruption, but I was in a business that depended almost exclusively on tapping doors. I drew in a mouthful of stale air and acknowledged the tapper.

'I hope you brought the ice. I've got a couple of clean glasses and enough booze to last us until the sun goes down.'

A voice as weak as any breeze that might have been stirring down below on Market Street apologized. 'I am afraid I haven't any ice.'

'Well, the door's unlocked. Come on in and we can blow in each other's ears.'

The door opened and in glided a hundred-and-five pounds of the slickest gift-wrapped frail my tired, wet eyes had seen since Hector was a pup. She was a tall job with plenty of fahrenheit.

A small soft voice squeezed through a pair of friendly lips painted the color of an Oklahoma rose. 'Mr Kovachs?' I could have dissolved right there on the spot, but I fought it. 'Lady,' I said, 'You're looking at all that's left of him. Another fifteen minutes and you'd be talking to a puddle and a pair of suspenders.'

I pushed my chair back from the desk and wiped the salt water from my brow. She was the kind of woman that demanded a second look. Surrounding those lips was a pale smooth face draped by curly locks the color of tangerines. Her eyes were expensive jade and she smelled of lilacs. Her skin was white and flawless and reminded me of a rare wake robin I had once seen growing in Muir Woods.

She was wearing a designer-cut two-piece pleated suit of magenta crepe that modestly concealed a form that had more curves than the Coast highway. She was plenty easy on the eyes, the kind of dame who wouldn't sweat even if it were ninety degrees in the shade. It was and she wasn't.

She moved around the side of my desk and slid into the chair I reserved for my occasional customers.

'Mr Kovachs, I need your help,' she said in a tone that I've heard before, one that has occasionally cost me money.

'I knew I was in this steam bath for a reason. Now what seems to be the trouble, Miss, uh, uh . . .'

'Birdwell, Lana Birdwell.' She grew tense as she spoke and fumbled around in her handbag, withdrawing a scented hankie which she nervously dabbed at her neck. It didn't help her condition. 'I, I don't know where to begin.'

'It's not original, but may I suggest the beginning?'

'Well, you see, I was involved with a certain gentleman not long ago. I thought he loved me, but I learned he was . . .'

Her voice trailed off into her hankie. I took up the slack.

'The gentleman had a room-mate and a couple of tricycles in the driveway, is that it?'

'Something like that, yes,' she replied. Her eyes and the slight tightening at the corners of her mouth told me she didn't like my version, but that didn't stop her. A soft alabaster hand adorned with an elaborately tooled Indian bracelet gently rose to her forehead, palm out. 'I terminated our relationship and moved away from him, away from the shame, away from the guilt.'

'I am impressed Miss Birdwell, I really am, but it's just too damn hot for Bette Davis this afternoon. What say we skip right to those little things they call brass tacks. What's your beef and how does Riley Kovachs fit into the picture?'

For a second time she drew back, apparently miffed by my comments or manners, probably both. What did I care? My skin felt like warm cheese and my patience, like Judge Crater, had disappeared long ago.

'Well, Mr Kovachs!' she huffed the way high-class dames are famous for. Then she rose from the chair and started for the door. She paused long enough to say, 'I think I have come to the wrong person.'

'Hold the phone, Miss Birdwell,' I shot back, trying to redeem myself, realizing that cheesy skin or not, I hadn't worked in a couple of sevens and that it is bad for the reputation to drive beautiful dames from one's office, especially in my line of work.

She stopped in the middle of the room and waited for my next sentence.

'Please accept my apologies. It's this blasted heat that's got me all cranked up. That and the Tigers getting beat today.'

'I beg your pardon.'

'Skip it.' I motioned for her to come back and sit down. She returned to the chair with some hesitation and slowly inched her way into it like she was lowering herself into a tub of boiling hot bath water. 'You were saying you left your gentleman friend when you found out he was married.'

She straightened her skirt and dabbed her handkerchief at some imaginary sweat on her forehead and resumed her story.

During the next twenty minutes Lana Birdwell confided that her gentleman friend was Chandler Lane, the same Chandler Lane who owns the LA *Telegram* and other important chunks of the city of Los Angeles, including some of its more prominent citizens. Seems she was seeing him regularly until she found out that in addition to bags of money he also had a fulltime wife he had no intention of leaving. She blew town more than a month ago and thought she was through with him until a gumshoe picked up her trail here in Frisco a few days ago. She was afraid the dick was wise to her and might make her return to LA to settle accounts with Lane. She told me she was certain Lane was sore at her for running out on him and we both agreed Chandler Lane was not the sort one kisses off and gets away with it.

'I know this man has been following me, Mr Kovachs,' she said, twisting and pulling her hankie.

It was okay with me if she preferred to go through life as a rope of knots, but she was beginning to make me feel uncomfortable as well. I got up from my detective's chair and walked over to the little Kelvinator water cooler in the corner. I doused my handkerchief with half of what remained in the five-gallon jug and buried my face in it. I was a new man. Until the water dried, anyway.

'Suppose Dick Tracy puts a make on you and tells Daddy Warbucks that you're on the lam up here in Frisco,' I said, trying to get a line on her problem. 'What's likely to happen?'

'I dread to think about it, Mr Kovachs.' The fear was more in the way she kept mauling her handkerchief than in her voice. 'You see, there are some letters, some rather intimate letters and . . .'

'I see,' I interrupted, grabbing for what I thought might be the real reason what Lana Birdwell was doing going to pieces in my office. 'Lane thinks you might put the blast on him, sort of create an instant old age pension for yourself.'

'You are a very crude person, Mr Kovachs,' she shot back at me in a tone that cooled off the room a good ten degrees. 'However, I am in no position to stand on formalities. I am in a very desperate situation. I must have your assistance.'

I had to hand it to her, the lady had a lot of moxie. But I didn't let up on her. Professional reasons.

'And I ask you again, Miss Birdwell, what's your beef? Where's the problem? Why don't you just give the old creep the letters and be done with it?'

'I wish it were that simple, Mr Kovachs. You see, since I've been in San Francisco I have been fortunate to make friends with a wonderful man.' She paused a moment to allow her cheeks to turn red. 'Oh you must think I am a terrible person, Mr Kovachs.'

She pouted some and then rolled her eyes to tip me off she was embarrassed, just in case I missed it the first time. She sat there expecting me to jump in and reassure her that she wasn't really a terrible person, but she didn't know Riley Kovachs very well.

I looked out my window instead. The clanging of streetcars on Market sounded like a hundred hoboes beating on kettles. I popped two aspirin from the office bottle and waved my hand for her to continue with her story.

'This gentleman is a very prominent figure in the campaign for governor,' she said, without a trace of her former embarrassment. 'And as you must know, Mr Lane holds an extremely important position for the other side. If my past association with Mr Lane should become public knowledge, I am afraid it would cause a great embarrassment to my current gentleman friend as well as quite possibly creating a political scandal. You see, Mr Kovachs, returning the letters will not solve my problem. It is my identity and present whereabouts that must remain anonymous.'

I said 'Hmmm', and scratched my chin. Lana Birdwell raised her voice to convince me.

'If I am discovered, well, you know how vicious some men can be when politics is involved, don't you, Mr Kovachs?'

'I've heard something along those lines, yes.'

'Then you can appreciate just how delicate my situation is. It is absolutely imperative that everything about me is kept from Mr Lane, at least until the election is over. I know we have been less than cordial toward one another, Mr Kovachs, but I plead for your help. If not for me personally, then for the sake of decency and fair play in the election.'

'In California?' I choked.

'Please, Mr Kovachs, don't laugh at me, I am serious.'

'So am I. Look lady, I have been around the block a couple of times. And unless you've been living under a prickly pear in the Mojave Desert, you would know that already this campaign stinks like week-old fish. It's a smear job from the starting gate and I wouldn't be surprised if it gets worse. What you've got is pretty small potatoes. Just what the hell are you trying to sell me anyway?'

'I am not trying to sell you anything, Mr Kovachs, really I'm not.'

'Oh no? You come in here with a story that wouldn't wash in a high school drama class. You roll those big beautiful eyes at me like you are trying to make seven the hard way and swoon into your hankie every time the stock market drops a point. Then, just for insurance, you appeal to my patriotism. Well, let me tell you something Miss Birdwell. I don't care much for your impression of Helen Trent and as for my patriotism, I left that back on a rubber shop floor in Akron, Ohio, where I saw too many guys getting bloody noses for trying to organize a union. So, if you don't have a final act to this little play entitled *Now Here's the Real Truth*, you can pick your elegant self up from that chair and go audition for some other sap.'

Lana Birdwell sighed. She got up, but didn't head for the door. Instead she walked slowly to the open window the way a person might do who is about to say something difficult but doesn't quite have the courage to do so. She sighed again, this time out the window, pulled at her tattered mouchoir and walked back to her chair. She sucked in some confidence and spoke.

'You are absolutely right, Mr Kovachs. I have no right to treat you this way. I expected you to trust me without taking you into my confidence. I underestimated your intelligence and I am sorry. Forgive me?'

The way she said 'forgive me' stayed with me for a long while. With those two little words her moist lips became inviting little pillows that said 'kiss me' without saying anything at all. I became lightheaded for a moment. I wanted to say, 'Forgive you? Sure, baby, anything you say. Here's a hundred dollars and the key to my car. Do with them what you like. Do with me what you like.' That's what I wanted to say, but I didn't. I couldn't. When you've been in this business as long as I have, caution and suspicion are as valuable as a well-oiled revolver. Even more.

'Forgive you?' I said finally. 'I think I'll wait until I've heard some straight talk before I do any forgiving.'

'You are right, again, Mr Kovachs. It was presumptuous of me to ask such a question. I am sorry. I haven't lied to you, Mr Kovachs, not really. I may have held back some of the truth, but that's all. I can see now that you are an intelligent, honest man, a man a woman can trust. I can trust you, can't I, Mr Kovachs?'

'Miss Birdwell, if this country weren't in the middle of a depression I'd say I'm like money in the bank. But let's just say that if you deal with me you've got no other choice and I won't have it any other way.'

'Mr Kovachs, in a way I admire your frankness. I think . . .'

'Please, Miss Birdwell, flattery only makes my head swell up, and if I get a bigger head it means I'll have to buy a larger hat, Miss Birdwell, so knock it off, okay? All I want from you right now is the real lowdown on this cockeyed story of yours.'

'I'm sorry, Mr Kovachs, I . . .'

'And stop saying you're sorry.'

'I'm sorrr . . .' She coughed and blushed, then cleared her throat again. 'The only part I neglected to tell you is that when I left Los Angeles I borrowed some money from Mr Lane. Oh, I fully intend to repay him, but I was in dire need of funds at the time so I could leave town. Do you follow me?'

'Sure. He may toss a burglary rap at you, is that what you are worried about?'

'Yes, yes it is,' she said in a way that expressed great relief. 'Mr Lane is such a vindictive person and I can believe the man following me has been instructed by him to employ physical force, if necessary, to make me return to Los Angeles.'

'What about the letters? Are there any?'

Lana Birdwell looked at the floor while her face changed color again. 'Yes, some, but they are not in my possession. I don't think they are very important anyway. Mr Lane wants me for other reasons.'

'I'm beginning to get it. The snooper pinches you and hustles you back to LA. You're charged with burglary, maybe even blackmail, if Lane plays his hand right. The old boy has plenty of political drag. He owns the cops as well as the evening paper. You're arrested and he plants the story in the papers, page one, to read "Girlfriend of Sinclair Official Arrested on Charge of Burglary/Blackmail". A nice, tight scenario, that one is. It should make a great movie.'

'Then you understand, Mr Kovachs, how important it is for me to avoid detection and quite possibly a kidnapping?'

'I can chew on it. I assume your politician boyfriend knows nothing about any of this?'

'It would be most awkward for me to try to explain it to him. With the election only a month away he might not understand. So very much is at stake, both for me personally and for the campaign. I am praying this matter can be handled as discreetly as possible.'

'Um, and just what sort of discretion did you have in mind, Miss Birdwell?'

'Oh my, I'm sure I don't know, Mr Kovachs. I am not at all familiar with these things. I just assumed you would know what to do.'

'You know, Miss Birdwell, correct me if I'm wrong, but I can't help but get the feeling that you think this little meeting is a scene from the *Maltese Falcon*. Well, let me set you straight. I'm not Ricardo Cortez, and classy as you might be, you're not Bebe Daniels. I'm just a small-change dick. Humdrum is my middle name. Oh, I've been known to roughhouse with a husband or a boyfriend, but only rarely, and I'll confess that, on extreme occasions, that husband or boyfriend has punched out my lamps. Soon as I drop below 50 per cent in trading knuckles and lumps I'll know it's time to turn in my office key and get in the soup line down at St Anthony's. So far I'm ahead of the game, but I don't put the chill on anybody. If it's excitement you want, I'm sure there are a couple of dozen Little Caesars in this town with itchy trigger fingers who would jump at the chance to make a few bucks. At $20 a pop you should have no trouble in finding a gunsel to wipe out every third person in Oakland.'

I stopped and lit a Chesterfield. 'So, Miss Birdwell, that's both the long and the short of Riley Kovachs. There's no more to him than that. He's no glamor boy. He'll never make the movies, but his mother loves him. I figure being dull adds years to my life and I sort of like that arrangement.'

I was rough on her, but I had to be. I had seen and heard of too many nice guys with a private license ending up in the hospital or worse. And Lana Birdwell would have been very easy to be nice to.

'Oh, Mr Kovachs,' she apologized again, 'I've offended you. I certainly didn't mean to imply . . . I hope you don't think I wish you to employ violence on my behalf. Why, just the thought of prize-fighting makes me ill. I most sincerely don't wish you to endanger your safety.' She paused a minute, dropping her eyes lower than they were before. 'I was hoping that you could persuade this man – his name is Barnes, Duke Barnes – I was simply hoping that you could convince him to leave me alone. I am prepared to purchase my anonymity.'

'No gumshoe with broken arches draws breath who wouldn't turn mute for the right kind of dough. It should be a cinch to get our friend on a southbound bus.'

Lana Birdwell heaved her small shoulders. She began untying some of those knots. Riley Kovachs had taken the job and all was right with the world. In another moment, however, she went to piano wire again.

'How much money do you usually require for a job like this?' she asked in a voice that wanted to cut my fee by half.

'I get $20 a day plus expenses.'

'Expenses?'

'Expenses. You know, like chewing gum, half soles for my shoes and bribes. This guy, Barnes, might not scare away cheaply, but Chandler Lane's ex should be able to afford it.'

'I am afraid I don't have as much money as you might think, Mr Kovachs.'

'How much do you have with you?'

She reached into her handbag and pulled out a small leather billfold. She snapped open its metal clasp and peeked at her green.

'I have $65.'

'Not much, but it will get us started. Give me twenty.'

She pulled out two saws and laid them on the desk.

'I'll have more tomorrow, Mr Kovachs. Please be assured that I will pay whatever it takes to keep my identity from Chandler Lane.'

'Sure, sure. Where can I get in touch with you, Miss Birdwell?'

'I'd prefer to contact you, Mr Kovachs.'

'Oh, oh, here we go again. I thought I was "a man a woman could trust".'

'All right, Mr Kovachs, I guess I owe you that much. I am

staying with a friend out in the avenues. You can reach me at this number.'

She scrawled some digits on a scrap of paper and handed it to me.

'One more question, Miss Birdwell. I'd like the name of the man you are trying to protect.'

'Really, Mr Kovachs, I don't see . . .'

'Ah, ah, the name, if you please.'

'Dexter Hall.'

'Thank you, Miss Birdwell. I hope I can count on that as the truth.'

'Please believe me, Mr Kovachs. We started off on the wrong foot, but I hope that is all behind us now. It is very important to me that I have your trust. So very important.'

A slight pink returned to the top of her cheeks again and her fluttery eyelashes started sending signals that could have been picked up by the ships in the harbor.

'Miss Birdwell,' I said, 'you just bought yourself $20 worth of trust. It's good for the next twenty-four hours. Now, if you will excuse me, I'll begin earning my fee.'

A moment later she glided out of my office much the same way she had glided in. If I hadn't felt the slight breeze from the opening and closing of the door, I would have signed a statement that she just – what's the word? – wafted out my office the way the afternoon fog rolls through the Golden Gate. Silently, and without effort.

A dame like Lana Birdwell comes along once, maybe twice in a lifetime, I thought to myself as I started through the eight-by-ten of Barney Ross that was tacked on the wall. It took all the common sense I could rally to keep my head connected to my shoulders. She would have been easy to fall for, very easy indeed. The burning stub of a Chesterfield I had lighted several minutes before sent a painful message to my brain via my finger to return to earth. That and an uneasy intuition that told me to be careful of beautiful redheads who don't have sweat pores.

2.

It was late afternoon. Shadows were beginning to fall across Market Street. The burning white heat of the day was on the verge of being chased away by the typical soft cool of the San Francisco night.

I washed up for the fourth or fifth time since noon and put on a fresh shirt. I always keep a spare at the office. And lucky for me: I was beginning to smell like a bad joke and the shirt I started the day with was clinging to me like chewing gum on the underside of a moviehouse seat. I didn't exactly feel like a new man, but with a clean collar and sleeves I could tolerate myself a little while longer.

Lana Birdwell told me Duke Barnes was staying at a fleabag up on Ellis Street. She didn't exactly say how she came by that information or where she learned his name, and it bothered me some.

I stopped off at the Clinton Cafeteria, the one on Market near Sixth. I like to go there when I have the time and the money. It seemed I always had the former and I had just got twenty of the latter.

There is something about cafeterias. It's certainly not the food. At most of the places where I've pushed a tray, the pie tastes like the meatloaf. I think it must be the variety and the freedom to actually see what you are paying for. If a little tag says 'jello', you're getting jello. If it says 'macaroni', well, that's what it is. I like that and the anonymous feeling that goes with it. The items on your tray are strangers to each other, just like the people sitting across the table. A cafeteria is a place where you can be alone in a room full of people. No atmosphere, no music, no waiters pushing the chef's mistakes at you.

I took a table on the second floor near the big window that looked out on Market so I could keep an eye on the city.

The shops and offices were still letting out. The street was throbbing with life and clanging streetcars, but I couldn't miss the blank expressions on so many of the faces.

So I was two floors up and couldn't see the expressions on anyone's face. I could 'feel' their blankness and distance as they stood waiting for buses and streetcars in front of the Hibernia Bank where Taylor and Golden Gate meet Market.

They looked tired – worn out – probably as much from the skimpy wages they received each Friday as from their day's labor. They huddled in groups of two and three, shifting their weight from one foot to the other and staring into the pavement. They didn't appear to be in any rush to get home, a place which for some must serve as a cruel reminder just how little is really in those weekly pay envelopes.

A line was forming in front of the ticket window at the Fox. For two bits a person could park his cares at the curb until midnight.

What a lousy world, I grunted into my mashed potatoes. The hamburger steak wasn't listening and could have cared even less.

After downing a couple of cups of coffee almost as bad as my own home brew and burning a Chesterfield, I headed for the Pasadena Hotel.

The Ellis Street address was a typical transient palace. Sick and coughing men were sitting on ugly metal chairs in a cold and austere linoleum lobby waiting for things to get better. I walked over to the night clerk. He, too, was standard furniture for the kind of place the Pasadena had become. He had a certain look of snotty superiority scribbled all over his face. I knew we were going to have words.

'Duke Barnes in tonight?' I asked, not really expecting a straight answer.

He was bony, fiftyish, a man with a sneer sewn on his lips. Without moving his head, which was buried in a racing sheet, he slowly raised a pair of colorless eyes which lurked behind wire-rimmed cheaters, and fixed a stare on me like I had just crapped in his wheaties. He spoke with the shivering chill of a Taku wind.

'Who wants to know?'

I turned up my coat collar.

'J.P. Morgan,' I said. 'I want to make him a partner.'

'Very funny.'

'You see, I plan to buy this cockroach gymnasium and I need Mr Barnes to change a ten dollar bill for me.'

'Beat it bub, before I call the cops. We don't like wiseguys around here.'

I could see that gentle patter wasn't going to get me anywhere. I reached over the desk and gently brushed some imaginary dust from the night man's shoulders the way they do in the movies.

'Give me Mr Barnes's room number, junior,' I said, 'or I'll call the health inspector and have both you and this dive condemned.'

Junior just continued to sneer, although he had forgotten about the racing form.

'I don't give out that information, fella. Now hit the road if you know what's good for you.'

I stepped back, feigning fear.

'Gee, I hope that isn't a threat. You see, I just got my teeth capped and I can't afford to get beat up for at least a week. Doctor's orders.'

The clerk was extremely thick. 'Then I guess you know I mean business,' he boasted with borrowed confidence. 'Now take a hike before I lose my temper and have to get rough with you.'

I would have played with him a while longer, but I did have work to do. I reached across the desk again. This time I lifted him from the armpits until his feet left the ground.

'Look, junior, if you don't give me that room number in just three short seconds, you are going to make the papers as the first man to solo the Pacific without the aid of an airplane.'

'309!' he gulped, returning his counterfeit confidence with usurious interest.

'Thank you,' I smiled. 'I knew we could work something out. See how easy it is to be nice when you put your mind to it.' I walked for the stairs. A place like the Pasadena didn't have an elevator. I turned back to the night clerk before I reached the first step. 'Be sure that I get your address on my way out, junior. I want to add you to my Christmas card list.'

He mumbled something that would have embarrassed his mother and stuck his mug back into the racing form.

I climbed the three flights of stairs very cautiously. I half expected a dog-sized rat to appear and challenge my way. A couple of ten-watt bulbs kept the hall from total darkness. It was just enough to allow me to read the plastic room numbers tacked onto the doors and to reveal a worn, threadbare brown carpet and the faded and peeling yellow-ribbed wall paper. The place was as run down as an old man with anemia, but I could tell that not too terribly long ago the Pasadena was a joint with enough class not to tolerate someone like junior behind its registration desk. But like the men I saw in the lobby, somewhere along the line it had lost hope, and with it all self-respect.

From a room at the end of the hall, a man was coughing consumptively. I heard a toilet flush. I found number 309 and knocked. There was no answer. I would have left, but something told me to try the door. I did. It was unlocked. I turned the knob and slowly swung open the door. The room was dark, but somewhere outside its only window a silent neon sign flickered, spraying a rhythmic red glow over the entire room. It allowed me to pick up the general outline of things inside.

I saw no one. Once again I felt an imaginary elbow in my ribs urging me to go inside. I stepped in from the hall. The overhead light was burned out. I carefully worked my way to a small lamp on the night table in front of the window and pulled its chain. A dingy yellow light fell over the room.

There he was, lying on the bed. From the large, dark wetness on his shirt, I knew the Pasadena Hotel wasn't even a cheap memory for him. I touched his face. It was still warm. I had expected to find a stupid, brutish type with all the character of a bag of used diapers. But the man in the bed had an honest face. Duke Barnes hardly fitted the mold of an LA pug-uglie.

I went through his pockets. Nothing but a wallet and some change. There was a driver's license with his name written on it and some cards with LA addresses including one with Chandler Lane's moniker. That, a receipt for some auto repairs and an old laundry ticket from a place called Li Li Lin's up on Stockton Street here in the city were all that said the man lying on the bed had ever lived.

I got ready to leave. I picked up a working-man's jacket that was slung over the chipped black metal bedpost to cover him. Something fell from it and clinked on the floor. It was a key with a paper tag attached to it. I picked it up and instinctively put it in my pocket.

Before I left I took a last look around Duke Barnes's room. To that frozen tableau of death which could have been painted by one of those social realists, something didn't fit. It didn't smell like death in room 309 of the Pasadena Hotel. It smelled more like lilacs.

3.

I walked all the way to my South of Market flat on Frelon Street. I saw the distorted face of the dead man on every corner where people gathered. It made me uneasy. I thought I had experienced enough bad luck for one day, but when I opened my front door I knew I was in for another dose.

Sitting in my living-room on what I generically refer to as furniture were two mugs smoking cigarettes. From their ill-fitting suits and the unmistakable bulges under their coats I knew they were cops.

'Been to the movies, Kovachs?' said the smaller and less ugly of the two through a stub of tobacco that was potted in the corner of his mouth. He had a face that looked like it had been chipped out of a concrete block by a sculptor who wasn't too concerned with the end product. It scowled even when he relaxed, like maybe it held a permanent grudge against somebody, probably the sculptor.

I recognized him from a few years back when I was working part-time on the docks. He was in charge of a special squad of blue-coats that made raids on longshoremen in more than one of the pier-side rumbles that have become as regular as bran-eaters over the last few years. His name was Cahill.

Both cops got up from their chairs as if cued and showed me their buzzers. As if that were necessary. Cahill's partner was named Leery, a thick-browed type with a light bulb for a nose that had been in too many fights and looked like a relief map of the high Sierra.

'Gee, fellas,' I said, not knowing just what they expected me to do once I had inspected their shiny tin trophies. 'You caught me a little short, but put me down for a couple of ducats to the Policeman's Ball. Cahill, I understand that instead of live music this year you're going to bash some longshoremen for entertainment.'

'Cut the corn, Kovachs,' he snapped back. 'Where were you tonight, say during the last hour and a half?'

'I thought you knew – the movies. Saw *Flying Down To Rio* and a Hopalong Cassidy. You should go. The cultural experience would do you both some good.'

'Ever hear of Stanley Barnes?' Cahill growled.

'Was he in the Cassidy film or the other one?'

The square-jawed cop became excited. He hitched up his pants and jabbed a yellow, nicotine-stained finger into my chest.

'Look, smart guy, we know you were at the Pasadena Hotel tonight to see this Barnes. The night clerk will swear to it.'

'That weasel would turn in his mother for putting too much starch in his shirts.'

'Never mind that. You're in a bad way, Kovachs. You were the last person to see Barnes. Funny thing happened just about the same time you were there – he stopped breathing. Everything points your way, shamus.'

'I guess it didn't occur to you or your sidekick here – say, where did you get him anyway? Forget it, I don't want to know. I guess you couldn't figure that if I was going to put the chill on a guy I wouldn't trade brickbats with the desk man in front of half a dozen witnesses.'

Cahill was unmoved.

'All I know, Kovachs, is that you were at the Pasadena Hotel to see a man who turns up on a block down at the morgue less than an hour after you leave him.'

'You've been reading too many funny books, Cahill. Things aren't that simple, especially things like murder. Even you should know that.'

'Keep it up, wise guy, and you'll be telling your jokes to the audience we keep down at city prison for crumbs like you. You're a punk, Kovachs, a cheap, dime-a-dozen punk.'

He cracked all ten of his enormous knuckles just to show how much he loved me.

'Cahill, coming from you, that's a compliment.'

The Lieutenant spat out his cigarette and crushed it into the carpet. Then he took a disgustingly grimy gray handkerchief from his rear pocket and blew his nose like he was auditioning for a seat in the band at a Harlem jazz club. I ground my teeth together to keep my supper down.

'We're going to keep a close eye on you, Kovachs,' he said. 'One false move and I'll personally nail your hide to the City Hall dome.'

'Oh, Lieutenant, and I thought you didn't have a sense of humor.'

'Keep laughing, Kovachs. We'll see who laughs last.'

With that morsel of wisdom flushed from his system he nudged his mute friend and they started for the door.

'By the way, Cahill,' I said as they were leaving, 'who told you I was at the Pasadena tonight? Was it the night clerk?'

'We got a tip from an anonymous caller.'

I shut the door after them. The air cleared almost immediately.

4.

Riley Kovachs, so-called private eye, stood in the middle of his rooms with a dozen eggs hanging from his average face. An anonymous tip! Who could have tipped off the cops? That one was easy. The tough one was why?

I dialed Lana Birdwell's number. There was no answer. I hung up and dialed again and came up with the same result. I turned on my radio. Listening to it allowed me to think better. Or so I rationalized. It was my one possession, the only thing I owned that had any real value. It was the very latest in audio engineering – an eight-tube Philco with four-point tone control, shadow tuning, rubber-floated chassis, patented inclined sounding board and an electro-dynamic speaker. All this and in dark walnut too. I tuned into the last few minutes of *Amos'n'Andy* and went into the kitchen to burn a pot of coffee. A few moments later I returned to the living-room where I drank the scorch and smoked a couple of Chesterfields while waiting for the other shoe to drop.

I must have dozed off, for when the phone rang I could hear the late-night sounds of Vincent Lopez purring from the electro-dynamic speaker.

'Kovachs here,' I said, clearing my throat.

'Oh, Mr Kovachs, I hope I didn't wake you.' It was Lana Birdwell. 'I called to tell you that something terrible has happened. Mr Barnes – the man who has been following me – he, he's been murdered.'

'Yes, I know. I was there just after it happened. How did you find out?'

'I, I just heard it on the radio a few minutes ago. I thought you, I mean . . .'

'I didn't kill him, if that's what you are thinking. I told you I don't go in for the rough stuff.'

'Oh, Mr Kovachs, I am so relieved.'

'I bet you are.'

'I beg your pardon.'

'Let's cut out the baby-talk, Miss Birdwell. I went to see Duke Barnes tonight as per instructions. When I got there he was dead. So I went home, and who do you think was waiting for me in my own living-room? The police, that's who. They said they had received a tip about Barnes's murder, an anonymous tip. And you didn't hear about the killing on the radio because the newscast was too early to have that information. Am I making myself clear, Miss Birdwell?'

'I, I think you are accusing me of informing the police.'

'It could be much worse than that. Where were you between 6 and 8 o'clock tonight?'

'Really, Mr Kovachs, I don't like your manner. It is regrettable that a man died, but I only called to tell you that our business association is terminated. I have no further need of your services. I didn't call to be accused of murder. Good night, Mr Kovachs.'

The phone went dead. I reached into my pocket for Lana Birdwell's number. I dialed. This time there was an answer, but it wasn't Miss Birdwell.

'I'd like to speak to Lana Birdwell,' I said.

'Who?' a man's voice asked, incredulously.

'Lana Birdwell.'

'No one here by that name, buddy. In fact there ain't no dames here at all. Just me and Herbie.'

'And where's here?' I asked. I had that sinking feeling I sometimes get.

'This here's the package-room at Rincon Annex Post Office. Say, is this one of the guys on the day shift? Is this a rib?'

'Yeah, pal, it's a rib. Not a very good one, but it's the best I can do at this hour.'

I put the receiver back on the hook and started at it for a long minute. What a sap! I knew I was being played for a fool by the Birdwell dame when she first came into my office, but I thought I had cleared that up.

I walked over to the window and looked out into the darkness. The glare from a table lamp threw my reflection back at me. I spoke to it. 'Kovachs, if you were half as smart as you thought you were, you would . . . Oh, hell, skip it.' I got taken for a ride by a class dame, that's all. It happens every day – to other guys. But I thought I was smarter than 'other guys'. I would have lumped it and put it in my coffee it it weren't for two things. First, the police had tapped me as a murder suspect and, second, I couldn't chase the image of a pathetic, dead Duke Barnes from my mind. I didn't like the first and I couldn't just let the second drop without doing something.

5.

Riley Kovachs was stumped. Not that that was unusual, but this time the mug's skin hung in the balance. And his reputation, such as it might be. Lana Birdwell was a fake. No use driving all the way out to the avenues to hunt for an address that was sure not to exist. What else did I have to go on? I sat slumped in the stuffed corduroy staring at the lit end of my Chesterfield, watching the ash grow bigger, when I remembered the key that fell from the dead man's jacket. I dug it out of my pocket. It looked like it could fit a trunk or a locker. The paper tag attached to it had a date stamped on it – 1 October. There was also the number '32' and some tiny pencil writing that looked to be names or parts of names.

I could make out the letters 'AI'. It was all Chinese to me, but it was the only thing I had. It wasn't much to sleep on, but there was nothing to do until morning.

I spent most of the next a.m. running from the bus terminal on Seventh to a couple of banks and gynnasiums and finally to the Southern Pacific depot down on Third and Townsend. There my luck changed.

I took the key to the small overnight lockers and hunted out number 32. I stuck the key into the small lock. It fit snugly. I looked around to see if I was being watched. I felt everyone in the station was staring at me, including a wino sleeping on a bench fifty feet away. I tried to act casual. I reached inside my coat and pulled out a tailor-made and gave it heat. I took a couple of drags, casual drags, before I turned the key.

The door opened and inside lay an envelope. I took it out. It was addressed to Duke Barnes. I stuffed it into the side pocket of my coat and walked away. I caught a bus back to Market and walked a block to the Monadnock Building.

On the way I stopped at Young's cigar stand across the street from the Palace Hotel to get an *Examiner*. I wanted to read about the opening game of the Series. Granny Rice was covering it personally. I was sweating like an Iowa hog in the midday sun, but I was so preoccupied I didn't notice it until Jackie, the old white-haired elevator boy at the Monadnock, brought it to my attention.

'Just race a cable car up Powell, Mr Kovachs, or are you getting back from a fraternity initiation?'

'Ah, Jackie, the Fred Allen of the elevator set. The answer to both your questions is negative.' I cupped my hands around my mouth and whispered in his ear. 'I was out at Land's End looking for a body and I got too close to the surf.'

Jackie's eyebrows went to upper case. 'Yeah? Whose body you looking for?'

'Yours,' I smiled, 'And I have a feeling I'll find it there any day now.'

'Very funny, Mr Kovachs, very funny.'

Jackie became grumpy and didn't talk to me during the rest of the trip. The elevator wheezed asthmatically as it climbed slowly toward the seventh floor. I dropped my eyes on the afternoon headline – 'Hauptman Hit By New Witness'. I'm against kidnapping just as much as the next fellow, but it looked to me like that poor sucker was taking a bum rap, a real bum rap. And after Cahill's tea party the night before, I felt like we were brothers in a frame.

Jackie brought the car to a routine jerking halt and let me out a foot below the floor, which was also routine. I readjusted my hat which had been knocked over my left eye and climbed out.

'Give my regards to Portland,' I saluted.

Jackie gave me an I'll-get-you-next-time smile as he shut his gate.

I walked into my office and threw the newspaper on the desk. I started to reach into my coat pocket for the envelope, but I stopped and looked at my watch instead. I cleared my tonsils with a low, barely audible yelp. It was past one o'clock and game two had started at eleven. I hurried to the old Atwater-Kent I kept around the office for just such occasions and flipped it on. I hunched over the dark box waiting for the tubes to warm up and the sound to come on. I wondered how the 'Schoolboy' and the Tigers were doing. Finally, I heard Graham McNamee's voice.

'It's been a pitcher's duel all the way down the line. Rowe has pitched superbly, but so has Hallahan, and he has the lead, 2 to 1, as we go into the bottom of the ninth inning here at Navin field in Detroit.'

That was just dandy, I fumed. The Tigers were just three short outs from going down two games to none. On their home field! I shut off the radio, but turned it back on before the sound died. After all, it was the Series. I decided to agonize through the last three outs and hope against the odds that the Tigers could get something going.

I walked over to my chair and sat down. The first batter came to the plate. I put my back to the radio and swung my chair toward the open window. I propped my feet up on the sill and tried to absorb the tiny breeze blowing in. It was still dreadfully hot.

I reached inside my coat and pulled out the envelope addressed to Duke Barnes and tore it open. I removed the contents and spread them on my lap. But my concentration lay elsewhere. The Tigers had a man on base. There were maybe half a dozen pieces of paper in the envelope. One had a professional letterhead. 'Antelope Investments' was printed along the top. There was a little figure of an antelope separating the two words. Some of the other pages had names and some addresses, but there didn't seem to be any particular organization to the documents.

I nearly jumped out of my chair when Walker's foul pop was booted by Rip Collins. Then Walker singled to left on the next pitch. Cochrane's boys had a chance. I put the Barnes papers on the desk. They would have to wait until the game was over. I had just begun to rise from my chair to turn up the volume on the radio for what was shaping up to be a nail-biting climax when I was startled by a low, dull pain at the base of my skull. It surprised more than it hurt. I turned in the direction of the pain and saw one of the biggest and ugliest louts this side of a carnival road show standing over me. In his right hand was a sap the size of a small tree. They were a matched pair. He struck me again, that much I know.

After that it was dream time. I remember seeing Walker running around the bases in slow motion. The grass on the playing field was growing greener and higher and Walker was running slower and slower. I was there, too, pulling blades of grass out by hand from the area between third base and home – to permit Walker to run faster, I suppose. Then the crowd began cheering. The noise grew louder as every one of the 30,000 faces flashed before me. The roar was deafening. I hid in the waist-high grass near the pitcher's mound where I found the entire Tiger ball team huddled together. Only it wasn't grass anymore. It was an opium den on Grant Street. Mickey Cochrane passed me a hashish pipe and asked what a good pair of dress shoes cost in San Francisco.

Over in the corner, sitting on a pillow and wearing oriental silk pajamas, was General Hugh Johnson sucking on a water pipe. Out of the pipe was coming not smoke, but blue eagles. That was jake with me until the eagles popped like soap bubbles releasing dozens of slippery black serpents. At that point I must have decided that it could only get worse, for I mercifully slipped away into an inky, mindless void.

6.

I awoke to the buzzing sound of my radio and Jackie, who was slapping my face.

'Who won the game?' I asked reflexively.

'What game? Say, you okay, Mr Kovachs? I heard your radio and didn't see no lights on in your office,' Jackie said as he continued patting my face.

'The World Series! Who won the game today and quit slapping me, will you?'

'The Tigers in twelve,' he answered quizzically. 'Gosling singled to drive in Gehringer. Hey, what happened to you anyway? That's a pretty nasty bruise you got on your forehead.'

'Some mug sapped me,' I said, stating the obvious. 'Maybe he had his bankroll on the Cardinals.'

I pulled myself together as I wobbled over to the water cooler. A cold wet handkerchief to the golfballs on the back of my head helped a little. I looked in the small mirror above the cooler just to convince myself I was really in my office and not in some smoke shop in Chinatown getting spooked by the NRA chief blowing snake bubbles.

I asked Jackie if he had seen the ugly galoot who tapped me enter or leave the building. He shook his head. But then Jackie wouldn't notice King Kong playing checkers in the lobby.

'Okay, Jackie, thanks for bringing me around. You can go back and terrorize your passengers, now. I'll be all right.'

'Sure, Mr Kovachs, but if you get stiffed again don't hesitate to call on old Jackie,' he said with a grin as he backed out into the hall. In his eyes we were even for the day.

I sat in my chair massaging my lumps, trying to figure out why they were there. I froze. The Barnes envelope. I looked on my desk. It wasn't there. I rifled through the newspapers, cigarettes, magazines, unpaid bills and the other things that clutter a modern detective's desk. It was gone. Stolen! What could have been on those pages? I said out loud. Whatever they contained it was important enough to contribute to one man's death and cause another to be knocked goofy.

I drew hard on my mental powers, such as they were at that moment, to recall what I had seen on those half dozen sheets of paper before that goon pulled my plug. I remembered the name 'Antelope Investments'. I tried to come up with an address or a phone number to go with the name. Nothing. I seemed to remember seeing a name on one of the pages that impressed me at the time as the handle of a well-known public figure. I reached into the well, hoping to come up with a make on it, but the bucket came up dry. I realized that it would have to come another time, preferably when the sexton between my ears ceased his bell ringing. The only thing left for me to do was to return to the dead man, Duke Barnes.

7.

There were still a few specks of light in the warm October sky as I passed through the rear door to the Hall of Justice. I walked to the morgue to get the police sheet on Barnes. I had a friend working the second shift who could be trusted.

'Good evening, Benny. How's the boy?'

'Well, cut off my legs and call me shorty, if it isn't Mr Kovachs. Long time no see, Mr Kovachs. What brings you to the hotel?'

'Benny, I'm trying to run down some dope on a stiff who got in the way of a blade in a dive up on Ellis, a guy named Barnes, Duke Barnes.'

Benny looked puzzled. 'Hmmm. When did the unfortunate incident take place?'

'Yesterday afternoon. I'd say between four and six.'

Benny was still stumped. He scratched his ear and stared at the wall. He opened a book that logged all the corpses, a book he liked to call his 'guest register'.

'Barnes, Barnes, Barnes,' he murmured running a forefinger up and down the pages. 'Sorry, Mr Kovachs, there's no one named Barnes staying with us. You sure about the time?'

'Positive. Look, Benny, he's got to be here. You've got the only morgue in town. He was a young guy, about 30, sandy hair, good looking . . .'

Something I said must have struck a responsive chord, for Benny interrupted me with an 'ah ha' snap of his fingers.

'Sure! I know who you mean. Cops brought him in yesterday evening. Name's not Barnes, though. I mean it was Barnes, but it really isn't.'

'Whoa, hold still a minute, Benny, you're not making any sense. What do you mean it was Barnes, but it wasn't? Let's try it from the top and slowly.'

'Okay, Mr Kovachs. It was like this. The cops brought in this customer yesterday like I say. It was 7.30. I just got back from dinner so I'm sure about the time. I logged it in the register. Here, look for yourself.' Benny started to push the log book toward me, but drew it back before I could take a look. 'It wouldn't do any good to show you, Mr Kovachs. I erased it – Barnes's name, not the time. You see, about two hours after I checked him in I get a call from upstairs. It was Homicide telling me I should change the tag from Barnes to Blodgett, Ira Blodgett. Says it was checked out and that's his real name and that someone would be by in a few minutes to make a positive ID.

'Well, I hardly hang up the phone when a homicide dick comes down. I don't know his name. He was a big guy with a puss like a cement block.'

'Cahill,' I informed him.

'Yeah, I think that was it. This Cahill comes in with a priest, name of Windy. I show them the goods and the priest says it's Ira Blodgett all right. Says he knows him from the docks. Then this afternoon Father Windy comes by again with a couple of boys from the funeral home and they claim the body.' Benny paused a moment to summarize everything in his mind. 'That's just how it was, Mr Kovachs. There ain't no more to it than that.'

I thanked Benny for the news and walked back into the night. I flirted with the idea of going upstairs to double check Benny's facts, but I didn't think I'd be any too welcome there. Besides, I knew my constitution would never forgive me if I were to see Detective Lieutenant Cahill two days in a row. My lead was now Father Windy. I went to look him up.

8.

Father Windy was known around town as the 'waterfront priest'. I don't think anyone knew for sure whether he was a real minister since he didn't operate out of a church, but he wore a turned-around collar and ran a little mission on Spear Street just off the Embarcadero.

I had never met the man personally, but I knew first hand of his work from the time I spent unloading ships. His door was always open to anyone for coffee and sandwiches and a place to flop. He was respected from Fisherman's Wharf to the Army Street Terminal as a friend of longshoremen. He was a one-man social service, looking after the families of stevedores who got laid off or hurt on the job, and was always writing letters to the papers complaining about the way the shipping bosses were treating the men. During the General Strike he ran a soup kitchen and first aid station out of his mission. Word has it he was right in the thick of the fray during the Battle of Rincon Hill and mixed it up pretty good with the police.

I parked on Howard Street and walked over to Spear. It was dark and lightless. A small naked light above the door half way down the street was all that prevented me from passing the store-front tabernacle. A sign – a piece of hand-lettered cardboard tacked on the door – said 'walk in', so I did.

A half dozen men were huddled around a black wood-burning stove, drinking coffee and smoking cigarettes. They looked like some of the boys from the open road, fresh in from some distant hobo jungle. They were speaking in low voices which bounced off the bare wood walls of the large room. A few metal chairs stacked against a long table in a corner was the mission's only stab at furniture. The rough pine floors gave the place the appearance of an industrial warehouse. In a sense, I philosophized, it was a warehouse – for the human spare parts of American society.

There was nothing original in my thought – I probably heard or read it somewhere – but it struck me at the time as something that said a lot about the downhill way things were going for too many people.

The men didn't drop a beat in their conversation as I walked past them to a door at the rear of the large room. Father Windy's name was scratched on it. I knocked and was told to enter by a deep robust voice I recognized from many dock-side rallies as belonging to the padre in question.

I stepped into an office that made mine look like the executive suite at the Mark Hopkins. To say that it was a little cluttered was like saying there was a little dust in Oklahoma. The floor was piled ankle-deep with newspapers and magazines including, I could tell, dozens of copies of *New Masses*. A sagging bookcase made from cheap pine clung tenaciously to one wall. The other walls were plastered with posters and hand-bills of all sizes, announcing past longshoremen's meetings. Some I had seen around town during the strike. Next to the bookcase was a severely dented dark-green metal three-drawer filing cabinet that looked like it had been used for a floor by a troupe of Spanish flamenco dancers. It, too, sagged badly. The drawers were jammed open and erupting like Lassen's lava with file folders and newspaper clippings spilling over on to the desk next to it. Behind the desk sat a man in clerical garb smoking a cigarette and poring over a tattered San Francisco street directory.

'Father Windy?' I asked. 'My name is Kovachs. I'd like a word with you.'

'Kovachs!' he shot back, looking at me like I had just admitted spending the night with the Virgin Mary. 'So, you're Kovachs! The bulls told me you have something to do with Ira's murder. What are you doing here?'

I took up his challenge. 'Hold the phone, Father. I had nothing to do with Duke, I mean Ira's death. I've been set up by someone to take the rap and the cops are believers. Seems like they convinced you, too.'

Father Windy's fire was uncooled. He rose threateningly from his chair. He just kept going, heightwise, that is. He was the kind of guy who didn't have to stand on a chair to see parades. The lines on his leathery, fifty-year-old face tightened. A long and sharp finger stabbed at me.

'Kovachs, Ira Blodgett was a decent man, a goddamn decent man! He was good for the union and he was my friend. The cops are just bullshit to me, but I saw their report. It said you are a private snooper. I figure maybe it's worse. Maybe you're a Pinkerton or a WMA fink. I don't like snoopers and I despise Pinkertons and thugs for the goddamn Western Maritime Association. You get my meaning, Kovachs? In my book you're worse than a rat on a rice ship and if you had anything to do with Ira's death, anything at all, I will take personal responsibility to see to it that you get the chair. Do you understand me, mister?'

I did and I was just thankful that the lashing I received came from Father Windy's tongue and not the business end of the fleshy hammers growing out the end of his wrists. He could have easily licked his weight in dockside rowdies and still had enough energy to eat the metal plating off a freighter. I would have rather tangled with a colony of gibbons at the zoo. But for some foolish reason I felt too cocky to just stand there and let him push my face in. I dug my heels into the floor and came back at him.

'Look, Father, don't come on with that tough guy stuff with me. You can pound me into bread dough; we both know that. But that mouth of yours should be used to blow on your coffee instead of jumping to wrong conclusions. Now, if you will loosen your collar and get some of that blood in your neck to start serving your brain, I'll give you the lowdown on the late Ira Blodgett. Or would you rather drop-kick me over the Ferry Building?'

I looked directly into the priest's eyes. They were nearly drowned with rage, but it was momentary. A blue, relatively serene luster returned to them by the time I had made my proposition. Too, the lines on his face started to melt and the veins in his neck, which had been guitar strings waiting to be twanged, returned to normal. He seemed almost relaxed. I said almost.

'Forgive me, Kovachs,' he said in a tone that was normal for him. 'I had no right to stick the needle in you like that. I'm just as sick as hell over Ira's death. He was a fine man and a friend. I think some anti-union thugs were hired to kill him. The cops told me you were their prime suspect and I . . . oh, hell, Kovachs, tell me what's on your mind.'

'Much rather do that than get drop-kicked over the Ferry Building,' I grinned. Father Windy smiled and I sighed sincerely. 'Yesterday I was hired by a screwy redhead who said she was Chandler Lane's ex . . .'

'The newspaper tycoon?' Father Windy interrupted.

'The same.'

'A right-wing bastard if there ever was one.'

'Yeah. She told me the old boy had put a tail on her and she was afraid of being privately extradited to LA. The tail, she said, was a guy named Duke Barnes and would I please go up to his hotel and kindly ask him to beg off. Looking back, I should have smelled a rat, but she is the kind of dame that makes you forget the word "no", if you get what I mean.'

Father Windy smiled knowingly. He was not a man without experience. I continued.

'I went up to see Barnes at his hotel and found him stretched out for the last time. Someone had stuck a knife in his ribs and wanted me there to take the rap.'

Father Windy broke in. 'Did you find anything in the room that looked like Ira put up a fight?'

'That's the funny part, Father. I think whoever killed Ira might have been known to him. There was no physical sign of a struggle and the look on his face was one of surprise rather than fear.'

'Then the murderer just killed him and left? I mean the room wasn't burglarized or ransacked, was it?'

Father Windy was driving at something.

'No, Father, the room hardly looked lived in, let alone turned over. You suppose maybe your friend was killed for something he had in his possession?'

Father Windy backed off. He rummaged through the effluvia on his desk and came up with a rumpled pack of Camels. He shook one out, tapped it on his wrist, struck a match with one hand and with the same motion put fire to the tobacco and blew out the match. The smoke rushed from his mouth and nostrils and began twisting its way toward the ceiling like ivy up a tree trunk.

Despite his flamboyance, Father Windy was a cautious man in many ways and we had reached the point where we had to begin investing a little trust in one another if we were to continue. There was a slight, uneasy silence before the cleric spoke.

'I should say I don't know what you mean, Kovachs, but I won't. I'm going to lay some of my cards on the table.'

'Why not play a full hand?' I said, trying to encourage him. 'I'll tell you all I know. You see, I've a personal stake in finding the killer, too. Until I come up with someone, I'm number one on the cops hit parade.'

I think Father Windy could buy that. He looked ready to show his hand. I played mine first.

I told him of finding the key in Blodgett's room and the locker at the train station which contained the documents. When I told him I was sand-bagged and the papers stolen less than six hours ago, he jumped from his chair like he was sitting on cut glass.

'Jesus H. Christ!' he boomed in a voice that could have been heard in the vespers at Mission Dolores. He pounded the desk with one hand while the other crushed out his cigarette with a force that could have broken a bowling bowl. 'That just about clinches it, doesn't it? Those dirty bastards! Those dirty lousy WMA bastards!'

Father Windy began pacing around his office – which wasn't easy – like a large fox in a small cage. His huge chest rose and fell with each noisy, hyperventilated breath he took and his nostrils grew grotesquely larger, looking like dark hairy caves. His face was a purple picture of rage. I took a chance and spoke.

'Father, for what it's worth, I have an idea how you feel. When you're ready, why don't you tell me what connection Ira had with the WMA? Maybe we can come up with something.'

Father Windy stopped pacing. He clasped his enormous hands together and pressed hard until his knuckles turned the color of ivory. He took a deep breath, unlocked his hands and lit another cigarette. He sat on the edge of his desk and spent the next twenty minutes tell me about the longshore strike. He spoke in partisan terms of the hard-bitten attitude of the Western Maritime Association, the main employer of the dockers, and the conduct of the police. He described in harsh detail the Battle of Rincon Hill which everybody called 'Bloody Thursday'. It was during that day of pitched battle between longshoremen and the police and National Guard for control of the waterfront that two men were killed. Father Windy's eyes grew moist telling of the brutal savagery that reigned that day. I was moved by his commentary, but I didn't see what it had to do with murder at the Pasadena Hotel until he said that one of the slain men was Ira Blodgett's best friend.

'After Howard was killed,' he continued, 'Ira was a changed man. He was very bitter. He had a fire within him, Kovachs, a fire that wouldn't be banked, if you know what I mean. He appointed himself a one-man committee to get the killers of his brother longshoreman. He wanted to go beyond the cops who had pulled the triggers to the big boys upstairs who were responsible for the whole thing. He said he was going to follow the trail of blood wherever it led him. Those were his words.'

Father Windy stopped talking for a moment. He drilled a stare into my eyes that almost hurt. 'That's why he was murdered, Kovachs,' he resumed. 'He must have found something on those WMA bastards.'

My attention to detail, such as it might be, picked up the inflexion of the padre's 'must'. I threw it back to him.

'Does that mean you don't know it to be a fact?'

'A fact! A fact! Hell, Kovachs, it's as plain as that silly-looking tie you're wearing. The WMA runs this town. They and the SP and Nob Hill boys. Everybody knows that. They own the police and the newspapers, too. That's no secret either. You read the papers, don't you, Kovachs? Remember how they screamed red anarchy and demanded military force be used to put down the strike to protect their goddamn private property? Bullshit, I say! Everyone on the docks knows the WMA was behind the cops. But Ira wanted the hard proof. He wanted to name names and see them made to pay for the killings on Rincon Hill.'

'Slow down, Father,' I said, squeezing in when he dropped a beat to catch his breath. 'I don't have any trouble with what you're saying. I swung a hook a few years back so I have a pretty fair idea what goes on down on the docks. But as strong as you feel about this, we are dealing with a murder, and it can't be treated like another political speech. Like it or not, we've got to work with the facts, the cold, hard, facts.

'Ira Blodgett was a longshoreman, a union man – fact; Ira Blodgett was conducting an investigation into the killings that took place on Rincon Hill – fact; Ira Blodgett had an envelope full of documents of an undetermined nature that was placed in a Southern Pacific depot locker – fact; Riley Kovachs found and removed that envelope with a key he found in the dead man's hotel room – fact; the same Riley Kovachs took the envelope back to his office where he was knocked unconscious and the envelope stolen – fact.'

'Okay, Mr Sherlock Holmes,' Father Windy said, stepping in impatiently. 'What do all these *facts* tell you? I'll tell you what they say to me. They say Ira was getting too close to some WMA big wigs and they hired a goon to kill him.'

'Perhaps, but we don't know anything for sure until we learn what is in that envelope. Does the name Antelope Investments mean anything to you, Father?'

'Never heard of it. Say what's this got to do with anything?'

'Antelope Investments is the only name I remember seeing among Ira's papers before the lights went out. There was also the name of a radio or movie personality, somebody big, somebody I should remember but don't.'

Father Windy rubbed the salt and pepper stubble on his chin, trying to come up with something that would throw light on the subject. He lit another Camel.

'Like I said, Kovachs, Ira and I were friends, good friends. I know it's corny, but I thought of him as a son. But there was a private side to him that nobody could penetrate. His investigation was like that. He wouldn't tell anyone just what he was doing. You know, I think he knew it was dangerous and clammed up to protect his friends. The only time he talked about it with me was a little more than two weeks ago. He had just returned from LA. He told me the responsibility for Bloody Thursday went higher than any of us had imagined. But that was all he said. He never mentioned it again.' The priest dropped his eyes and gazed blankly into the ashtray by his elbow.

A few minutes later I left Father Windy. I tried to size him up as I walked back to my car. I could see how the power boys in the city, especially the WMA, could fear such a man. He was a human earthquake capable of rearranging the shape of people and things that got in his way. He was a man boiling with rich and conflicting emotions. He was full of fury and at the same time a deep sorrow at the death of his friend. He was ready to singlehandedly storm the ramparts of the capitalist system and, yet, though he hid it well, I suspected he was more than a bit frightened by the events of the past two days. I thought Ira Blodgett must have been a lucky man to have had him for a friend.

9.

It was well past midnight when I returned to my flat. Somewhere howled a cat in heat sounding like a hungry infant. Benny Goodman competed for the night on a nearby victrola.

The streets around Fourth and Brannan, which should have been empty at that hour, weren't. The working-class neighborhood which I call home was never what you would call prosperous. Its citizens have always struggled to make ends meet. The recent economic difficulties, as the government like to call the Depression, made the struggle a mortal one for many who live 'South of the Slot'. I could feel their restlessness, their anxiety of not knowing what was coming next, each time I saw the streets populated the way they were that night.

I walked up the decaying steps of the decaying Victorian where I paid a guy too much rent money not to fix things. I went into my flat which was also decaying and flipped on the Philco. I tuned in KJBS's Night Owl program. It was the only thing on at that hour.

I went into the kitchen and made myself a drink. I returned to the living-room and flopped into my favorite easy chair, propped my feet up on the wooden crate I told company was a pine ottoman, and opened the evening *Examiner*. A drink with some hair on it and perusing the daily blat after a hard day of getting my brains scrambled was a small but humbly welcome joy.

What a world! General Smedley Butler was knocked off the air for saying 'lousy' and 'hell'. Seems he was criticizing the VFW. FDR held a meeting between the captains of capital and labor insisting on a truce that would 'restore industrial peace'. Fat chance. Billy Green attacked the 'reds' at the AFL convention being held downtown while the militants lowered the boom on Roosevelt and his pro-business administration. And Charles Ponzi was being deported to Italy as a pauper. Things just aren't the same anymore.

I was reading a story about Hugh Johnson's teary resignation from the NRA when the phone rang. I was as spent as last week's pay and turning the pages of the paper was all I could handle. If the phone had been any more than an arm's length away, I might have gone to bed wondering who had rung me up in the middle of the night. But it wasn't, so I didn't. I picked up the receiver and put it to my ear as is my wont in those situations.

'Kovachs?' the voice on the other end asked in a way that demanded an immediate response. It was Father Windy.

'Yeah, Father, what's up besides you and me?'

'Remember when you asked me about Ira's papers?'

'Sure. You rang up a no sale.'

'Right. But you said there was a name you couldn't come up with, some bigshot.' He paused then asked, 'Does the name Jackson Berg help your memory?'

I sprung from the chair as if someone told me I had just won the Ten-O-Win at the Embassy. 'That's it, Father, that's the name.' Jackson Berg, president of United Movie Studios, the grand poobah of the film industry. He and Zanuck run Hollywood. That was the name I had seen. 'How did you come up with it, Father?' I said, pacing back and forth as far as the telephone cord would allow.

'Purely by accident. I was reading the newspaper after you left and spotted Berg's name in connection with a big film extravaganza on the movie page. Then I remembered Ira dropped his name in our last conversation. I don't recall the context, but I remember him saying that he should be watched, you know, like he was trouble.'

'Father, I was almost up to the comics when you called, trying to find an angle. I was just chewing water, but this might be the lead we're looking for. I'll get back to you if anything develops.' I sank back into the chair and was about to hang up when Father Windy growled into my ear.

'Kovachs!'

'Father?'

'Be careful. We've already lost one good man too many. I'll say one for you tonight.'

'One what?'

'A prayer, my boy, a prayer. I *am* a priest you know.'

Father Windy laughed. My face muscles were too tired to do even routine and involuntary things like smile back. I wanted to, however. I thanked Father Windy for his words and hung up.

I had a desperate craving for a Chesterfield, but I was too drowsy to do anything so physical. I pushed the last of my drink over my tongue and worked my way out of the armchair. I traveled the twenty paces to the bedroom where I passed out on the bed just about the time I sat down and began untying my algonquins.

10.

I must have dreamed about Lana Birdwell, for when the sun landed a haymaker to my eyes, waking me from the snoring dead, she was on my mind. Not the Lana Birdwell of the soft pouting lips and well-turned calves, but the Lana Birdwell of the big lie. I sat in bed fighting a losing battle with the relentless sun, reviewing what I knew of the redheaded temptress. One thing stuck in my throat like a hull from a piece of undercooked popcorn – Dexter Hall. Unlike Duke Barnes, a phantom phone number and a fairy-tale sob story, Dexter Hall I knew to be the real McCoy. That is, he existed somewhere in the real world.

He was one of those slick USF Law School graduates on the make who could always be found around the power boys when the democrats were in City Hall. From time to time the *News* carried stories about his good work for the county party. All the papers called him a bright young man with a future. He made the headlines in the spring as one of the first big names in the party to jump on the Sinclair bandwagon. I couldn't comment on whether or not he was committed to EPIC and Sinclair's brand of progressivism, but from a distance Dexter Hall looked like the type who was loyal and dedicated to whoever's political star was on the rise. That made him the rule to a system that had few exceptions.

It made sense to start the morning with Dexter Hall before running to LA to snoop around movie lots.

The sun filled my flat, giving it hope. I put the kettle on the stove, thinking my luck might change. I rooted around the Shelvador looking for something to mate with the grounds and came up with a couple of sinkers that were hiding behind a head of lettuce that looked a lot like last year's model.

With breakfast in the past tense, I walked out into the South of Market morning. The sweet anise smell of fennel that grew tall and free in all the vacant lots tickled my nose. The sun glistened through a big blue sky that didn't have a care in the world. Cotton-white billows of cumulus clouds lying on their elbows were there to keep it that way. It was too early to tell if the heat wave had returned to the Livermore Valley where it belonged, but the previous day's intolerable hot was just a faint recollection.

My Plymouth once more beat the odds and got me downtown, which was uptown from where I lived. I parked on Jessie near the Mint and walked to Taylor Street at Market where the Sinclair people had their headquarters. The place was a large sprawling storefront energized by a sea of human salmon swimming up rivers of desks, typewriters, paper, telephones, and mimeograph machines. It had the steady hum of machines and voices that attends most campaign centrals and was busier than boot camp the night before general inspection. Young, intense women with fingers flying over typewriter keys; middle-aged men, shirtsleeves rolled up like doughnuts, gulping coffee, talking on telephones and waving their arms while they waded through mountains of paper piled on their desks; and dozens of young kids scurrying about like chipmunks on cold marble, toting bales of paper, trays of coffee and boxes, some empty, some full.

I stood and watched this activity for a long moment. On the walls were many larger-than-life posters of the candidate – Upton Sinclair, the socialist turned Democrat, who turned the state upside down when he won the party's nomination for governor. The posters announced in bold letters that the candidate was to speak at a rally in Union Square in a few days. That explained the hubbub that was putting my eyes through a rigorous morning calisthenic.

I walked over to the reception area. A young woman with a telephone headset was working a switchboard that had more lights than the City of Paris Christmas tree. Her hands were a blur of motion. She plugged and unplugged the board with the speed of a vegetable picker after the rates had been dropped.

I could see real beads of sweat ringing her forehead. Her Claudette Colbert hairdo was paying the price. She had a pleasant face, although it was beginning to tarnish a little with age and maybe one political campaign too many. She had that unmistakable look of idealistic dedication about her that told me she was a volunteer. I could have stood in front of her all day if I had wanted to and she wouldn't have noticed me. A man could have raised a family while waiting to be asked what he wanted. I had to force myself on her attention.

'I'm here to see Mr Hall,' I crowed.

'I'll ring his office,' came a reflexive reply. She didn't bother to look up. 'Who's calling please?'

'Riley Kovachs.'

'A Mr Kovachs to see you Mr Hall,' she said to her microphone. She returned to me. 'Mr Hall won't be free until possibly late this afternoon. If you like, I will schedule an appointment.'

'Forget it, doll, I'll take my chances some other time.'

It was evident that I wasn't going to see Hall by traveling through the proper channels; not in that political fun house anyway.

I smiled at the receptionist as I turned to leave. She caught it and smiled back. It was the kind of smile that said, 'I'm committed to my candidate, but what have I got myself into?' 'Keep up the good work, honey,' I comforted. It was the least I could do.

Getting to Dexter Hall's office was no more problem than boarding a streetcar at rush hour. There are a lot of people that have to be climbed over and stepped on to get aboard, but no one really cares where you are going. I located Hall's office by asking directions from one of the young proles running about doing the dirty work. I pinned a 'Sinclair for Governor' button to my lapel, grabbed a handful of campaign literature and peeled my way through the swarm to the second-floor balcony where Hall's office was located.

I didn't bother to knock. I entered the small and remarkably tidy quarters and marched over to his desk. He was sitting back in his chair. From the way the phone hugged his ear and the distant look on his face, I imagined him to be wrapped up in some critical conversation. He stared right at me. He had no choice because I had planted myself squarely in front of him. Despite this he refused to acknowledge my presence and that got me sore.

I reached inside my coat and pulled out a notepad. I jotted a message that was guaranteed to win recognition, if not favor, from the assistant campaign director. I held it up in front of his pale unfocused eyes. It read: 'Lana Birdwell is up to her shoulders in an unsolved murder. Put down that damn phone and talk to me. Signed R. Kovachs, private investigator.'

At first he stared right through the note as he had done me. However, his eyes soon swelled up three times their normal size. He snatched the note from my hand and examined it up close. Convinced that it was probably legit and all the words were spelled correctly, he glared up at me like I had just handed him the bill of sale from selling his kid sister to a white slavery ring.

'Something's come up, Fred. I'll call you back,' he said abruptly, before dropping the receiver onto its hook.

He rose from his seat and walked quickly to the door. He took a key from his pocket and locked it. He gave me another dirty look on his way back to the chair. He sat down, took a paper clip from a small tray on the desk blotter and began bending and unbending it nervously. I just stood and watched.

'Now,' he said, clearing his throat in a vain effort to recapture the composure he had commanded only two short minutes before, 'what's this about a Miss, uh, uh . . .' he looked at my note, 'Miss Birdwell?' He was a terrible actor.

'Relax, Hall,' I said. 'I didn't come here to shake you down. For all you know, I might be a friend.'

'I'm afraid I don't know what you are talking about.'

'Look, Hall, you and I both know more than a little something about Miss Lana Birdwell, so you can kill the Wallace Beery routine. You couldn't buffalo a buffalo. Lana Birdwell claims you as her boyfriend. Let's start with that.'

'Kovachs, is it?' I nodded. 'Mr Kovachs, I don't know what your game is. Despite what you say, for all I know you have been sent by the opposition to make trouble for the campaign. It would be like them to do just that. I don't care who you are or who sent you. I'm in no position to take chances.'

'I like that,' I said rallying all the sincerity I could, given the circumstances. For a moment I could see it his way. If you're involved in political campaigns you have to have a pretty fat account at the First National Bank of Mistrust. Since it was common knowledge that the Sinclair campaign had seen more mud than Big Sur during the winter rains, I could understand how suspicion had been elevated to an art form.

'I can appreciate your position,' I continued, 'but consider the sauce a guy finds himself in when a beautiful dame struts into his office all tears and lilacs and wets his shoulder with a sob story about a romance gone sour and the ex putting a salt shaker on her tail to bring her back to LA – in ropes if necessary.'

'Mr Kovachs, I don't see where this is taking us,' Hall clucked impatiently.

I raised a finger. It bought his silence.

'Hear me out, Hall. It may be to your advantage, not to mention that of your candidate.' I told him the rest of the story about Lana Birdwell and the murder of Ira Blodgett at the Pasadena Hotel. 'You figure in this in at least two ways,' I concluded. 'First, you know Lana Birdwell better than anyone in this town and second, the killing of the longshoremen is not an unconnected coincidence.

Miss Birdwell has a lot to say on the subject, but she hasn't leveled with me since she walked into my office two days ago. And now she's taken a powder.'

Hall must have been persuaded he would have to talk to me whether he wanted to or not, for he dropped his act abruptly, like a hobo's bundle from a moving boxcar.

'Very good, Mr Kovachs,' he said in a way that brought back some of the over-confident, socially arrogant manner of the man I had seen when I first entered his office. 'You may look a bit unsavory, if you will forgive my frankness – I would suppose most men in your line of work are – but your thinking is of a sharper quality than that of most of the people we have working around here. And I like that.'

He was relaxed now. He reached into the top drawer of his desk and plucked out an expensive looking briarwood pipe. He loaded it with a shag from a handmade leather pouch he took from the same drawer. Then he struck a long wood match and momentarily disappeared behind a swirling groundfog of yellow-gray smoke. The sweet, moist smell of raisins mixed with cherries fresh from the tree gathered about the room in thick layers.

'I haven't seen Lana for a couple of days,' Hall squeezed out of the corner of his mouth that wasn't chewing the pipe. 'I'm a bit worried about her, actually. She's checked out of her hotel and left no forwarding address.'

Dexter Hall was worried. Worried that he might himself be dragged into a murder investigation and worried that publicity of same would do injury to the campaign, not to mention his career. After that, I guess he was worried about Lana Birdwell.

'I'm interested in finding Blodgett's killer for personal reasons,' I said. Hall looked puzzled.

'And what are those reasons, may I ask?'

'Well, you see, the cops think I killed Blodgett and are working very hard to come up with something to make it stick. A date with the electrician at Quentin would mean that I couldn't stay around for the rest of the Depression, and I don't want to miss all the fun.'

'The Depression may not last as long as you think if Mr Sinclair is elected and we put the EPIC plan into action,' Hall riposted, ignoring my crack, preferring instead to plug his candidate.

'I wouldn't hold my breath, but the point is this. I'm not interested in making points for either side. I want Ira Blodgett's killer so I can clear myself and because a waterfront priest I know says Blodgett was a good man.'

Hall took a deep breath and let it out. It seemed to say, 'To hell with killers and killings; at least this isn't going to be a shakedown.'

'My sentiments, also, Mr Kovachs,' he said. 'Above all, this matter must be contained.'

'I don't think you understand, Hall. Above all, the killer of Ira Blodgett must be found.'

'Yes, yes, of course,' he agreed. His embarrassment was slight. 'What can I do? What can we do?'

'You can begin by telling me what you know about Lana Birdwell.'

Hall didn't hesitate. He began speaking freely of meeting her a month ago and falling hopelessly in love. She told him she had just come from Seattle and was seeking work as a fashion model. Hall appointed her to a job working with the campaign treasurer at a modest salary until she could find the right job. They had seen each other nearly every day until three days ago, when she just dropped from sight.

When I reminded him of the story she had served me, he responded like the faithful beau.

'She never mentioned Chandler Lane or anything about living in Los Angeles. Quite obviously, Mr Kovachs, I am astounded by all this, but it's plain to see that she kept this part of her past from me, if indeed what you are saying is true, to protect me and the campaign. I believe you suggest another motive. Am I correct?'

'Anything is possible. All I know at this point is that Lana Birdwell has lied to one or both of us in spades. That alone should be enough to lift some eyebrows.'

'I'm convinced you are mistaken.'

'I'd like to hear that from her. Can you get in touch with her?'

'I'll try, Mr Kovachs. I'm sure Lana can clear up this whole matter to everyone's satisfaction.'

'If you can find her.'

Dexter Hall, always the political animal, would not tell me any more than he could safely afford to make public. But then, that went with his job.

11.

Hall assured me he would spare no effort to reach the Birdwell dame by afternoon and would have her contact me immediately. I returned to my office to wait for her call and to catch the third game of the Series.

I stopped at Mead's Cafeteria on Sixth Street for an early lunch. In good times the street had more than its share of derelicts, but the boys had been joined in recent years by folks from Bernal Heights, Hayes Valley and the Sunset, family people who used to be home-owners. It was a spectacle. Sixth Street had become a grand boulevard of broken dreams. Every now and then Jessie and Stevenson, the alleys that crossed Sixth between Market and Mission, were staked out for blocks with mattresses and household goods and even an occasional cooking fire which was always surrounded by hungry kids. During those times, usually the first of the month, that area just South of Market Street – the foot of Nob Hill if you wanted to stretch a point – became an urban edition of those hopeless settlement camps known as Hoovervilles.

And every now and then, usually a few days following the first of the month, the blue-coated protectors of the city of Saint Francis would stroll down the sidewalks, three and four abreast, and casually kick, club and otherwise demolish whatever stood in their path. They would not discriminate between a cardboard couch and a child's head.

I lunched on boiled beef and carrots, but I left my plate half full. I couldn't eat while kids with dirty faces and empty bellies pressed their noses to the glass window, not to beg, but to keep the memory of food current in their young minds. I'm not one of those enlightened liberals whose heart bleeds for every humanitarian cause and social injustice, but I can't tolerate being made to feel like a Bourbon prince just because I have the scratch to afford a 35-cent meal. I didn't even finish my coffee. I left, promising myself I wouldn't return to Mead's until recovery or infinity, whichever came first.

I reached the Monadnock Building some minutes before noon and took the back stairs to my office. I wasn't in the mood to trade verbal rabbit punches with Jackie.

I opened my window to chase away the hot stale air and read my mail, which included a 'final warning' from the credit department at Magnin's for an unpaid $4.35 bill for a hat I bought back before Montgomery Street became a lovers' leap.

I turned on the game and suffered through two hours of uncomplicated agony and frustration. Cochrane's nine knocked Paul Dean all over the lot but couldn't deliver in the pinch. Eight stinking hits they had and all they could muster was a single thin run. The Cards touched Tommy Bridges for enough hits to push across four tallies.

It was still early afternoon. I killed a couple Chesterfields and two rolls of cherry life-savers, waiting for Lana Birdwell to call. An article on the flora of San Bruno Mountain in the latest issue of *Pacific Naturalist* helped pass the time. At 3 p.m. the phone rang.

'Kovachs here,' I said authoritatively.

'Mr Kovachs, this is Dexter Hall – from the Sinclair campaign.'

'Jesus, Hall, I know who you are. What have you got for me?'

'I contacted Lana like I promised. She will meet you this evening at 9 p.m. on the steps in front of Coit Tower.' I didn't like the sound of his voice.

'I wanted to talk to her myself before I start traipsing all over town. How do I know there won't be a dead body and the cops waiting for me at Coit Tower?'

'All I know is what I'm telling you. This is how Lana wants it. She insisted I call you and deliver this message. She sounded very strange, Mr Kovachs. She wouldn't explain her disappearance for the past three days. She said I had to trust her, which I do, of course, but it was the way she said it that bothered me. I think something may be wrong.'

'That makes two us us, bucko.' There was a worried timbre to Dexter Hall's voice. It sounded more genuine this time. Either that or he had just returned from lunch with his acting coach. 'Okay, Hall, the message has been delivered. I'll be at Coit Tower at 9 o'clock. Assuming Miss Birdwell is also there, we may get some answers to a couple of difficult questions. Where can I reach you?'

He was instantly obliging with his home phone number.

'Mr Kovachs, I'd like to make you a formal business proposition. I want to retain your services to clear Lana from whatever predicament she may be in. How much . . .'

I cut him off at the neck.

'Look, Hall, this isn't an election. You don't just go around buying people out of what you call predicaments. Besides I'm working to clear Riley Kovachs and I can only handle one client at a time.'

'I'm sorry. I didn't mean to offend. Outside of political circles, I guess I am very awkward.'

'No apologies needed. I'll share any information I can get from your girlfriend. For that there is no fee.'

'Thank you, Mr Kovachs, thank you very much. I'll be waiting for your call.'

I walked down to the arcade to get an *Examiner*, to see what Granny Rice had to say about the debacle in St Louis. I was walking away from the smokestands when my eyes picked up a couple of familiar backs stepping into the elevator. It was Cahill and his monkey. I didn't have to guess twice to figure they were going as far as the seventh floor. And I didn't think they were going to the dentist down the hall to get their teeth cleaned, although they both could have used it. I stood in the shadows until Jackie closed the door and I saw the floor indicator jerk upward. I hit the front door and walked out onto Market, where I got lost in the traffic.

12.

I spent the hours until dark driving around the southern part of the city. I didn't want to hang around downtown or my flat and take a chance of being pinched by Cahill. Too, I wanted a chance to sort things out, and when I wasn't snuggled up with my Philco, I found I could clear the straw from my brain by taking a drive in my Plymouth. Something about being the master of machine and environment. 'A nuts and bolts extension of the ego,' I heard a Cal professor explain once.

I drove out of Howard to South Van Ness and over to Dolores via Seventeenth Street. I continued down Dolores to Army, slowing down along the way to admire the palm trees and study the Victorian architecture. From Army I went twisting around the narrow and semi-paved streets of Bernal Heights. I used to live on the hill at Coso and Mirabell before Wells Fargo took over the mortgage and raised the rent. That was a couple of years ago. Had a view from my front room that almost made being down and out tolerable. I used to sit at the window and watch the fog coming over Twin Peaks in the late afternoon. Sometimes it would ooze slowly, while other times it rushed down the slopes to swallow Noe and Eureka Valleys. It always reminded me of volcanic lava – airy, cotton-candy lava. Some days it would be a fine gray-white steam that was everywhere. Other times it was a sturdy 200-foot wall of dense vapor that would pour over the two mounds like molasses from a jar.

I stopped at the top of the road where Coso becomes Stoneman and looked back over my shoulder. The fog was there like clockwork. It had slithered its way into the valleys and was still coming. It would be night before it crossed Mission Street. I continued on to Folsom where I turned right and down-shifted the Plymouth skyward to Bernal Heights Boulevard. I drove around the Hill a couple of times to catch up on the view and the wild radish which owned a good portion of the northern slope.

Following a meal of enchiladas, rice and beans at the Mexico City Grill on Mission Street near Twenty-fourth, and a couple anise-flavored cookies from an Italian bakery in the next block, I was ready for Miss Lana Birdwell.

Night had fallen by the time I pushed my heap up Telegraph Hill Boulevard to Coit Tower. It was not yet a quarter to nine. No sign of the Birdwell dame. I put a penny in one of the tourist telescopes and scanned the waterfront. The *Pacific Princess*, *Manila Bear* and *La Paloma* were unloading at the closer piers. Lights burned into the holds where white-capped men were unloading tea and rice from the Orient. Things looked normal as vanilla ice cream. Across the inky wet lay Alcatraz and the new federal prison. A stiff wind which is sucked in through the Golden Gate, the fog and the churning icy waters which battle the rock twenty-four hours a day, make escape only a dream to those hundreds locked in stir.

The shutter clicked and the telescope went dark. I looked at my watch. It was two minutes before nine. I walked over to the steps leading up to Lilly Coit's monument. Still no Lana Birdwell. I shook out a smoke and lit up.

A moment later a huge figure in a dark top coat and a hat pulled over his eyes was standing in front of me blocking my view of Marin County. He was as tall as two city mailboxes and built the same way. He looked familiar, but I didn't want to know for sure. He asked me for a light. I got that sinking feeling and my heart began to throb like a love story in a woman's magazine as I dug into my pocket for the match. When I struck it I saw the gun in his hand. It was a very unfriendly looking .45.

'You shouldn't smoke those things,' I said pointing to his gat. 'They say it's bad for the lungs, especially if you inhale.'

He jammed the steel hard to my ribs. They always do it the same way, always hard to the ribs. Probably get it from some Hollywood directors who heard gangsters do it that way.

'Shut up, crumb bum, or it'll be your lungs that ain't feeling so good,' he growled.

The sound came from somewhere between a thick neck and a

pair of neanderthal eyebrows that grew out from under his hat. I was eager to oblige him.

'My mother always said for good health, drink lots of milk, eat all your vegetables and never argue with the business end of a gun. Now what can I do for you that will prolong my life a few more minutes?'

'Get in the car,' he spat, waving the gun in the direction of a long sedan with its parking lights on.

'Sure, be glad to.' I started walking. 'Say, did anyone ever mistake you for a redwood?'

'Shut up, wise guy, and keep moving.'

He jammed his metal persuader into my ribs again. I almost blacked out from the pain. The rear door of the car opened as we approached it. The lofty gunsel shoved me inside. I was blindfolded immediately so I couldn't tell who was throwing the party, but it sounded like we were at least four, judging from the different voices I heard. I didn't hear much before one of their number jabbed a needle full of hop into my right arm. I thought I heard someone speak the word Grundy. After that it was Mickey Cochrane and opium den time again.

I woke up on a cot in a room darker than the inside of a boot. My head was pounding like it had spent the last few hours as a drill bit in a bituminous coal mine. The rest of me was just wobbly and almost formless. I felt like I had gone the limit with Max Baer at the Cow Palace. I tried to get up. The rushing of food halfway up my windpipe reminded me who, if not where, I was. At that moment the most pressing problem in my life was to come up with a scheme that would get me from the horizontal to the vertical.

I called on my arm muscles to hoist me, but they were about as useful as a toothless winch lifting an overload of coffee sacks from a deep hold. I dropped to the floor and practiced crawling around on all fours to get my bearings and test my strength. I was painfully slow getting the former and I flunked the latter. It seemed as hopeless as a quadraplegic training for the decathlon, but I didn't have another choice. Some minutes or hours later I became a biped again, though I'm not sure how.

As I stood on my own two feet, my brain started working again and told me I was in trouble. It told me I didn't know where I was, who my hosts were, or what was going to happen to me. As for why, instinct told me that Ira Blodgett had a lot to do with it.

I saw a thin thread of light squeeze under the door to the room in which I had just relearned the meaning of *homo erectus* the hard way. I heard voices coming from beyond. One of them was female. I walked slowly and carefully to the door and pressed an ear to it.

The voices were talking about the Lindberg kidnapping. How appropriate I thought. Some of the words were lost in the wood, but I heard enough to know they were trying to figure out the consequences of what they had done to me. And well they should. Folks in the Bay Area have become pretty touchy on the subject ever since the snatch and murder of that San Jose department store owner's son last November. Self-appointed citizens lynched a man for it – actually strung him up.

'We'll keep him here until next Thursday, then release him. He doesn't know anything yet and we don't have anything to gain by killing him,' I heard a reasonable voice posit.

'And I say we bump him off. The sooner the better.' I recognized the voice. It belonged to the human *sempre viren* with the trailing eyebrows.

The voices debated my fate a few more minutes before a third voice, that of the woman, ended the discussion. 'It doesn't matter what we think,' she said, 'it's up to Mr Grundy to decide.' A murmuring of agreement followed.

'Okay, but we should give him another needle,' a small, high-pitched male voice contributed. 'He will be coming down in a little while.'

I knew the needle they were talking about had nothing to do with mending socks. I returned to the cot and stretched out, feigning unconsciousness. There was but one way out and I tried not to dwell on the consequences should I fail.

Five minutes later a key clicked in the lock and the door opened wide. The figure of the giant redwood was illuminated by the light behind him. In his right hand was a hypo the size of a Louisville Slugger. I could see him like noon. He, on the other hand, was peering into total darkness and I knew it would be a moment or two before his eyes made the adjustment.

He lumbered over to me carelessly. I could see the stupid, vacant grin on his face as he leaned over the cot to put the poison into my veins. My right hand shot out and grabbed the hand holding the needle and jerked the wrist back toward its owner. At the same time I looped my other arm around his massive head and pulled it down toward me with every bit of strength I had.

His total surprise left him not only speechless, but as weak as a kitten with a heart condition. His small brain had not yet figured out that his body was under attack and delayed in calling out the muscles to repel the assailant. I pulled the head and the needle toward each other until contact was made somewhere on the neck. I could feel the sharp steel slowly enter the ropy flesh. He made no sound. I emptied the syringe and he collapsed on top of me like a tent full of rocks.

I squirmed under the weight, trying to pry his unconscious bulk from my chest. It wasn't as difficult as lifting a manhole cover with your pinky, but almost.

I squeezed out from under the load and got to my feet. The door was still more than half open. I went to it cautiously and allowed one eye to peer into the lighted room. Only it wasn't a room, but a foyer, and it was empty. Looking further, I discovered that ten paces away was a thick, elegantly stained oak door that looked like it might be the main entrance. I studied its lock for a moment then sprinted for it. I grabbed the latch with one hand and the knob with the other and turned them both. Success was instantaneous. The door swung open onto a quiet street. I excused myself without formality. I even neglected to say goodbye to my hosts, whoever they were.

13.

It was late by the time I found my way back to my flat. I pushed my way through the front door and made a beeline for the kitchen. I needed a strong drink with plenty of hair in it and a pot of strong coffee. I made some of both. I kicked off my shoes and slumped down in the easy chair. I propped my feet on the ottoman and made a mental summary of the day's events, which included the address of my recent captivity. For the moment I stashed it away as a place in Pacific Heights where they put up kidnap victims.

I decided to call Dexter Hall and apply the screws to his thumbs. I poured a couple of fingers of bourbon into a cup of the gritty hot stuff I tried to convince myself was coffee and dialed his number. The fifth ring found somebody home.

'Yes, hello,' a sleepy voice rasped.

'Hall?' I demanded to know.

'This is Dexter Hall. Mr Kovachs, is that you?'

'Yeah, this is the Late Riley Kovachs. Say, Hall, your girlfriend is more fun than home-made fudge.'

'I'm sorry, I don't understand your meaning,' he said between yawns.

'Well, let me make it real simple for you. Someone lied to me again. Instead of meeting Lana Birdwell and having a quiet adult conversation about murder, I got muscled into a car by a palooka who could pass for King Kong's bigger brother, shot so full of dope I could have been mistaken for a jazz musician, and taken to a place in Pacific Heights where people I didn't know debated my continued existence on this mortal coil. Then just to fight the boredom, I stiffed the gorilla and beat it back to my place. Someone set me up again, Hall.'

There was a long silence on the line, followed by a stunned, quivering voice.

'What is going on? This is incredible. You were drugged? I'm sure Lana . . .'

'You can store that one in your ice box. Look, Hall, either you set me up with a phony meeting with your girlfriend, in which case what I'm telling you is old stuff, or else our little redhead has fibbed to us again.'

'I've told you the truth, Mr Kovachs, believe me. I relayed to you exactly what Lana told me to say.'

'Points the finger at your Lana, then, doesn't it? You know, this thing is getting out of hand. My body can take only so much punishment. But I'm nowhere if I don't talk with her. She's the only person who can clear me, clear up this whole thing. If you know where she is, man, tell me!'

'I don't. I swear I don't know where she is.' Hall was approaching hysteria.

'Well, find her! And when you locate her, I want you to tell her that I know all about Antelope Investments and Jackson Berg and if she doesn't want me talking to the wrong people she had better see me in person.'

'Jackson Berg?' Hall repeated quizzically. 'What does he have to do with any of this?'

'Never mind, just deliver the message.'

'Very well. I was just curious, that's all. I'm always interested in what the opposition is doing.'

'Opposition? What the hell are you talking about?'

'Jackson Berg. He's the chairman of the opposition's campaign finance and publicity committee. Goodnight, Mr Kovachs. I'll deliver your message.'

The second click was my brain. I wouldn't know a piece of information if it lived under my tongue. Jackson Berg – big-time movie mogul, mentioned by Ira Blodgett as a person to be watched – holder of the dough for the party running against Sinclair! Father Windy would march on Hollywood with less information.

The doorbell rang. I crushed a smoke in an ashtray and put Jackson Berg on a back burner. I went to the door, wondering what new outrage I could expect. I unbolted the door exercising considerable caution.

It was Lana Birdwell! Before I could utter a sound she pushed her way past me to the middle of the living room.

'Mr Kovachs, before you get angry with me please allow me a moment to explain.'

She darted to the window and furtively peered around the yellow-paper shade onto the street below.

'Angry?' I said with a tinge of sarcasm in my voice. 'Why should I be angry? Just because I've been framed for murder, slugged, robbed, kidnapped and drugged in the past forty-eight hours is no reason for a person to be angry. I figure I'm unlucky, that's all.'

'Please, Mr Kovachs, don't humor me. I'm in trouble.'

'She's in trouble!'

'Yes, and I think I may have been followed here.'

'Couldn't be Duke Barnes, we've already used him. Besides, he's dead, remember?'

'Mr Kovachs, please!' She moved away from the window to the couch where she sat down and nervously took a cigarette from her handbag and even more nervously attempted to light it. 'I don't know if you will ever believe a word I say again.'

'Probably not, but since I'm up and not all that sober, why don't you give it a try.'

'You must believe me, Mr Kovachs. I had nothing to do with what happened to you tonight. They forced me to decoy you. I had no choice. They are very desperate people and I'm terribly frightened of them.'

'Back up a bit,' I said. 'Who made you do it? Who are they?'

'The Committee, Mr Kovachs. They forced me to act as their intermediary to lure you into a trap. You see, after Mr Barnes was killed I panicked. I thought I might be suspected. Then I received a telephone call from a person who said the Committee knew all about the murder and if I didn't do exactly as they wished, the Committee would see to it that I was turned over to the police.'

'And what is this committee?'

'The name for some organization. I think it might be connected with the mafia. I don't know anything more about it.'

'If it's the outfit, you probably wouldn't. Just what did they tell you to do?'

'I was told to arrange a meeting with you. At Coit Tower. I know I shouldn't have, but I was so terribly frightened. I thought if I did this one thing for them I could be free of them and suspicion of murder.'

'Thought you'd throw that suspicion in old Riley Kovachs's lap, is that it?'

Lana Birdwell's face lit up pink. She sprang from the couch and looked in the direction of the kitchen.

'May I brew us some coffee, Mr Kovachs?' she said seductively, trying to change the subject.

'Sure. If it'll clear your conscience, go ahead.'

While she was in the kitchen I tried to sop up what she had just spilled down my front. It was plausible all right and just cock-eyed enough to be true. Frightened dame plays ball with the mob in order to remove herself from any suspicion of murder. Could be, but why would organized crime want to hang the Blodgett killing on me? That part didn't make sense. What about Jackson Berg and Antelope Investments? What, if anything, did they have to do with any of this? Nothing seemed to fit. Scooping liquid mercury off a glass floor with leather mittens was easier than getting a grip on this caper.

Lana Birdwell returned with two steaming hot cups of a beverage that reminded me greatly of fresh-brewed coffee. It had been so long since I tasted a first rate cup of the aromatic black stimulant that I had almost forgotten what satisfaction it can bring. I went to the cupboard in the kitchen and brought back a package of Lorna Doones. I took half and offered the rest to Miss Birdwell. She took two. It was time to talk again. I went first.

'Who is Lana Birdwell?'

'I beg your pardon,' she said, choking on a cookie.

'I said who is Lana Birdwell? You know the beautiful redhead who tells Riley Kovachs all those big ole fibs.'

'Then you don't believe anything I've said to you?'

She looked crushed.

'I'm not saying. Maybe I would if I knew who you are and what the hell you are trying to do to me.'

She flashed an uneasy smile.

'You're cute, Mr Kovachs. I could really go for you. Oh, I've known men more handsome, but none with your intelligence. And those eyes . . .'

'Leave my eyes out of this, damn it! Let's talk about Lana Birdwell or let's talk to the cops.'

She flashed her baby-blues, which were green, in a way few women can. Her eyelashes began to flutter like roll-up window shades and her mouth turned into an encouraging little oval that began to give me ideas. I felt the temperature in the room rising and it wasn't coming from the steam heater in the hall.

'You come on like such a bully, Mr Kovachs, but you're an old softy underneath it all, really you are. But to answer your question. I'm just who I said I was that first day in your office. I *was* involved with Chandler Lane at one time and have been running and hiding ever since I left him. I've had to protect myself, Mr Kovachs. I have had to protect myself all my life. You see, I was raised in a small Jesuit orphanage near San Bernadino where I was taught to take care of myself at a very tender age. If I didn't look out for my interests, no one would. Perhaps that explains my behavior. I know I have caused you some problems, Mr Kovachs, and I am truly sorry, but I was only trying to protect myself.

'With the moves you've got, lady, you should be in the ring,' I said, doing some protecting myself.'

It was a rather simple story that Lana Birdwell had, but it sounded preposterous. Yet, I couldn't totally discount it. What reason would she have to lie to me? If I were a big time operative at the Continental Detective Agency, I might be able to understand. But I had always been small time. In a negative way I could almost be flattered by all the smoke that was being blown my way. All I really knew was what Ears Palermo, my old boxing coach, had taught me when I was training to become the champ of all the thirteen-year-olds in northeastern Ohio. And that was to keep your hands up in front of your face at all times. I never made champ, but it was sound advice. The stakes in this ring were considerably higher and it didn't require any coaching to know that once I dropped my guard, the bout would be over and somebody would be standing over me, waving a towel in my face. I didn't want Lana

Birdwell or anybody else counting me out.

'Why did you come here tonight, Miss Birdwell?'

'Won't you ever call me Lana . . . Riley?'

She was still doing tricks with her eyes.

'Sure. Lana, why did you come here tonight?'

'I never know when you're making fun of me and when you are serious.'

I believed that. I don't think any dame could answer that question about me, but I found it healthier to keep it that way.

'I came here,' she continued, 'to explain and to see if you were all right. I didn't know what those awful people might do. I know this is terribly bold of me, but I was worried about you and I wanted to, to . . .' She stopped stammering and slid over to my end of the couch in a way that would have made them forget Sally Rand. I was surprised but not displeased. 'Kiss me, Riley Kovachs.'

I did. It wasn't hard.

She was unbuckling her things when I broke from a long clinch. I was no prude. I was just following Ears's advice. I felt that a night in the sheets with Lana Birdwell would send me down for the long count in more ways than one.

'At this very moment,' I said holding her at arm's length, 'there are two things in this world I want. One is for the Tigers to sweep the Cards and the other is to make love to you.'

She started to speak. I put a finger to her lips. 'Don't say anything. First, I never sleep with clients or principals in a case. At least until the case is completed. And, second, I don't chip on another man's girl.'

'But Dexter . . .' she tried to squeeze out.

'I said no talking. It's got to be my way or nothing at all. If this thing turns out right and I'm not crocheting doilies at San Quentin and Mr Dexter Hall drops from the picture, we can pick up the pieces where they are right now. But not until then. You might be the best thing that ever happened to me. If you are, well, you'll still be around a few days from now. If not, I'll know that too. Now put yourself together like a good girl and go home while I'm still strong.'

She did exactly that. The protest was in her eyes. That and a hurt, but they would both go away. She sniffled some while putting on her shoes and dolling up her face. I would like to say that I bit my tongue and tried very hard to think about the fourth game of the series, but I won't. One thing only occupied my thoughts. For what it's worth, I remained strong. Weaker men, happier men, would have melted dead away.

She gave me a phone number, again, and left. She didn't say goodbye. A dead silence hung in my flat like a valley fog. It was 2.30 a.m. I should have taken some satisfaction that I had done the right thing, but I didn't.

14.

It was a sleepless night for me, but that goes without saying. I stared at rainspots on the ceiling for the worst part of five hours, thinking about what might have been. I chewed the sheets until well past dawn, when I decided to call it a night, or rather a day, and got up.

I was dressed and out of the flat in less time than it takes a bald man to comb his hair. It was not yet 8 o'clock when I got to the Monadnock Building. Jackie hadn't even reported for work yet. I climbed the seven flights of stairs, stopping on each landing to gulp for air, reminding myself to get down to Alex's Gym and start skipping rope before it was too late. By the time I reached the seventh floor my head was sending tom-tom signals of pain to all parts of my body. On the brighter side, the pounding replaced Lana Birdwell in my thoughts.

I had only been in my office a few minutes, just long enough to scan the headlines of the morning *Chronicle* and read the articles on the game when the phone rang.

'Mr Kovachs, is that you?' a small voice asked.

'Yeah, it's me, who is this?'

'Pitts Langley. You probably don't remember me, Mr Kovachs,

but you done me a favor once.'

'Sure, Pitts, of course I remember you. How are you?'

Pitts Langley was a little old fellow who lived on the waterfront. Some said he actually crawled into the warehouses on the docks at night to sleep because he didn't have a place of his own. Used to be a merchant seaman. He helped Burnette Haskell and Danielewicz organize the sailors' union way back in the 1880s. Anyway, I helped him out a couple years back. A shyster boat salesman had taken his life's savings for the purchase of a miserable old tub that would have sunk in wet cement. The old boy had been putting away money all his life to buy a boat of his own, and this crook with dollar signs for eyeballs came along and took it. It was a great personal pleasure to shake down that rat.

'Well, Mr Kovachs,' Pitts said, 'folks down on the docks is plenty sore about Ira Blodgett's murder. I got it straight from the feedbag you're working on the case. I don't want to hurt your feelings none, but the feedbag says you're not getting anywhere.'

'It's my head that hurts more than my feelings, Pitts, but your feedbag's got it right.'

'Well, Mr Kovachs, I think I can make the sleddin' a little smoother for you if you're interested.'

'Pitts, I'm interested in anything that will put me on the right track. Can I meet you to talk?'

'I'm at the Red Jack Lunch down on Fourth and Mission Rock.'

'I can be there in thirty minutes.'

'Better make it twenty, Mr Kovachs. I don't think I've got too much more time.'

I hung up, swept my smokes from the desk, locked my office and raced down the back stairs to the arcade behind the lobby and out the side entrance. My headache had disappeared. I wondered what information Pitts had. What did he mean when he said he didn't have too much more time? I hurried to a Mission Street garage where I paid a guy by the month to leave my hubcaps alone. It was only ten minutes from there to the Red Jack. I made it in eight.

The Red Jack was a pierside cafe located just off the China

Basin. A person wouldn't know about it unless he was part of the waterfront. Its specialty was coffee. You were taking chances with the food.

I walked in and sniffed the air. The smell of cooking fat nearly anesthetized me. I saw Pitts sitting at a table in the far corner of the cafe. He was cradling a large pink crockery mug. His eyes caught mine and motioned me over. I placed an order for a cup with the counter man. He poured it right there and I carried it hot and dripping to Pitts's table.

The little man had aged since I saw him last. He looked like he hadn't slept in a while and could have used a hot shave. A white stubble matched the color of the thin stringy hair that covered the top of his sea-browned head. Despite the rags he wore on his back, Pitts was no bum. His eyes always burned with a pride that distinguished men in his profession. His body may have been twisted up some by Father Time and years of back-breaking labor, but his eyes told a different story. And Pitts was a fighter. Everyone on the docks knew that. From the early days of the Seamen's Protective Association, when sailors were indentured slaves, right down to the present, Pitts Langley had fought to scrape out a life for himself. Lesser men would have given up and been carried away to the county home. Those proud eyes, however, looked troubled.

'Sit down, Mr Kovachs,' he commanded politely, while extending a hand in greeting that felt as rough as lime slag. His grip was that of a man half his age.

'Good to see you again, Pitts. How have you been?'

He waved a hand in front of my face.

'No time for small talk, Mr Kovachs. I've got something for you that I want to get off my chest before it's too late.'

I tried to interrupt and ask what he meant, but again his sailor's hand demanded my silence.

'It's like this. Ira Blodgett was onto something big. I know that for a fact. I guess you know he was trying to get the goods on the people who was behind the killings during the strike. He left me some papers to hold for him a while back. Figured I was safe. Nobody'd suspect an old coot like me.' Pitts winked at me. 'Well, I can't see so good since my glasses broke a couple years back, but I took a look at some of those papers he give me.'

'Did you see the name Antelope Investments, Pitts?'

He was irritated by my interruption.

'I seen that name, but I don't know nothin' about it. What I do know is that somebody connected with the Ku Klux Klan, maybe the whole Klan itself, and them Hitler boys, too, has a direct pipe into this governor's election. And that ain't all. There's this guy name of Grundy who's organizing them into a gun-totin' militia to run the reds and labor organizations out of the state. They've got big money behind them, too.'

I literally shouted, 'My God, do you know what this means?'

The counter man turned away from the eggs he was frying and looked over at us. Pitts reached across the table and put a hand over my mouth. He looked around and crouched down even farther in his chair. His head was only a few inches from the top of the table. He spoke in an impatient whisper.

'Sure I know what it means. The right-wingers are everywhere and they're up to no good. That's the other thing I want to tell you. Before Ira come and took his papers, I remember seeing something else. It was a date – 9 October. It is important, I remember that. Something big is supposed to come off here in the city on that day. Something that Klan guy is going to do.'

'What is he going to do, Pitts?'

'That I don't know, Mr Kovachs. Like I said, my eyes ain't so good since my glasses broke. Maybe it was there and I couldn't read it. Maybe I just can't remember, I don't know. But it's something big, Mr Kovachs, it's something big all right.'

I could tell that Pitts was angry at himself for not being able to come up with the details. He stared into his empty coffee cup looking for help. It must have worked. He slapped the table and scooted his chair closer to mine.

'There's a guy in LA,' he said, 'a guy named Blinky Rizonetti. Ira told me about him once. All I remember is that he runs a shoeshine stand in front of one of the movie studios. I'll bet he knows something, Mr Kovachs.'

I wanted to buy the little man another cup of coffee. I knew he would refuse any offer of food. He declined the coffee, too.

'No thanks, Mr Kovachs, I got to be going.'

'I'll give you a lift, Pitts. Where do you want to go?'

'No thanks again, Mr Kovachs. It's better if I go alone.'

In a few moments the old sailor's mysterious behavior was explained. We walked out of the Red Jack. Pitts stopped on the sidewalk and pointed to a partially visible ship tied up at Pier 48.

'The *Coast of Normandy*', he said wistfully, but not specifically to me. 'I used to ship out on her. That was a long time ago.'

He stood for a long moment just staring at the old square rigger. I figured he was remembering the days long ago when ships had sails and he was young and strong. I was only partially correct.

I heard a car squeal around a corner. I looked to the sound and saw a large black sedan make a wild turn onto Third Street. It was the same car that had taken me for a ride the night before. As it drew closer, I saw the big subaltern – the human redwood tree – behind the wheel. He was racing right for us.

Then in that period of time, only an instant really, when everything seems to stand still forever, I knew what Pitts meant by not having much time left. I reacted and dove under the bus stop bench on the corner where we stood. As I dropped to the ground I reached out to grab Pitts. He shook me off and remained standing like a statue transfixed on the *Coast of Normandy*. He was unaware of, or unconcerned with, anything else in the universe. The car roared down the street at us.

Three seconds or less. That's all the time it took. After that – quiet. Pitts lay on the sidewalk. The old man had the look of quiet peace on his face. His eyes were open. Even in death they retained the rebellious pride they possessed in life. Pitts Langley's long struggle was at an end.

'Goodbye, Pitts,' I murmured softly. A crowd began to gather. I went back into Red Jack's and dialed the Seamen's Union to come for him. There was nothing the cops could or would do.

15.

I walked the waterfront for an hour before returning to the Monadnock Building. When I got to my office, Cahill and his sidekick were waiting for me. I didn't even bother to open with a verbal jab. Quasimodo grabbed me and pushed my face into my own wall and searched me.

'Kovachs, seems everywhere you go people get killed,' the lieutenant said with an obscene grin.

'Go catch a fish, Cahill.'

'Look, punk, we've got plenty on you. Witnesses saw you with that little pier rat that was iced down at the Red Jack Lunch.'

'You're corrupt Cahill, you know that? That "little pier rat" as you call him was twice the man you think you are.'

Without a word, police Lt Cahill rushed me, throwing a wild punch that landed on my jaw next to an ear. I reeled back and crashed into the wall. It felt like the Hyde Street cable car had been rerouted over my head, but I retained consciousness.

I came off the wall and instinctively began charging my assailant. I stopped almost as soon as I started. Cahill loved it. He was little more than a barroom brawler with a tin badge and he was spoiling for a fight. He egged me on.

'Come on, punk. Come on and hit me, you commie-lover. Come on, right here on this "corrupt" jaw.'

I backed off. I was not about to give Cahill and his 200-pound accomplice the satisfaction of splattering my guts over my own office and then dragging the remains downtown and throwing me in the clink on an assault charge. I pointed a trembling finger at him instead.

'Make that three times the man, Cahill.'

I turned and staggered toward my chair. Cahill's partner, who was by this time salivating profusely at all the excitement, rushed me and deposited a cement fist in my bread basket. I doubled over but refused to cough or throw up. I wobbled a few steps to my chair and sat down. Cahill swaggered over smugly and sat on the corner of the desk. He struck a match and lit a cigarette. He made a point of throwing the match on the floor.

'Kovachs, you're not so tough. Just a cheap punk, a dime-a-dozen punk.' He leaned over, sticking his face in mine. 'Now listen good, you lousy red sissy. We know that Langley had information about the Blodgett murder that he passed on to you. You're too stupid to cooperate with the police and give us that information. I'm not even going to waste my time trying to drag it out of you, though I would like nothing better. The DA's office is preparing a warrant for your arrest, a material witness warrant. It will be ready this afternoon. I could take you now, but they want me to go by the book. I'm warning you, Kovachs, it'll go hard on you if you skip. We'll add criminal charges if you do.'

He put out his cigarette on a magazine and leaned back. He grinned broadly, exposing a set of teeth the color of the yellow pages.

'So you see, Kovachs, you're in a whole lot of trouble. Be a good soldier and be here this afternoon when we come back.'

Cahill was flushed with the feeling of victory. I could see it in his ruddy face. He had me and he knew it. He could have broken an arm slapping himself on the back, he was so proud.

He got off my desk and walked to the door, trailed by his drooling sidekick. He spoke to him but it was purely for my benefit.

'You know, Leery, I always find that the cheaper the punk the easier the job, don't you?'

The other cop grunted and they both smiled, if you can call it that.

'Cahill,' I called as he was stepping through the doorway.

He stopped and glared back.

'Yeah?'

'The big shots who run this country are like a giant pus wart on the lives of decent people, but you, running around loose with the law tattooed on your knuckles, you and your kind are worse – you're a goddamn syphilis.'

He slammed the door, cracking the glass, but I didn't care.

I attended my wounds at the water cooler and poured a drink that could have got up and walked out of the office under its own power. I sat in my chair and looked at nothing. I thought about Pitts Langley. I wiped my eyes after a while. 'Kovachs,' I said out loud, 'Cahill was right about one thing – you're not so tough.'

16.

The only place I could go and still be out of Cahill's reach was Father Windy's mission. It was a little past one when I got to Spear Street.

Father Windy wasn't in. Just a couple of fellows down on their luck sleeping in blankets in a corner and a man in a longshoreman's cap reading a newspaper were the only signs of life in the usually busy mission.

Father Windy's office was unlocked and I allowed myself to enter. I climbed over and stepped around newspapers, magazines and crates of books and papers. In a way, if you knew where everything was in the little cubicle, it could prove to be a very cozy place. The sun was streaming in through the skylight and warm yellow rectangles gave the office personality. I wanted never to leave.

I began my wait, looking through Father Windy's collection of books and magazines. I didn't think he would mind. Mostly political literature – Marx, Lenin, Trotsky and some volumes of Jack London, like *The Iron Heel* and *The Class Struggle*. There was a mountain of magazines in that librarian's nightmare. Everything from the *Saturday Evening Post* and the *New Yorker* to *New Masses* and the *Daily Worker*. I took *The Iron Heel* and a couple issues of *New Masses*.

After an hour of articles on proletarian art, the uprisings in Spain and three or four chapters about the remarkable Ernest Everhard, I grew tired. I tossed the magazines on Father Windy's desk. Who could remember where I originally found them? I overshot the mark and the magazines slid off onto the floor, carrying with them a quantity of the flotsam that covered the desk. Father Windy probably would never have noticed, but I walked over to pick up the clutter anyway. I just grabbed with both hands and scooped up as much as I could and placed it all back on the desk.

A solitary piece of paper fluttered harmlessly back to the floor. I bent over to pick it up and placed it on top of the pile. I walked away from the desk on tiptoe. I didn't want to start an avalanche.

I stopped in my tracks. Something was wrong. The piece of paper. I returned to the desk and picked it up again. There in thick bold type was the letterhead – Antelope Investments. It was a letter to Father Windy. I read it twice.

Sept. 28

Dear Father Windy

We are looking forward to your visit next week. We hope to show you the parcels mentioned in your letter of Sept. 24 as well as our operation here.

Please call in the next few days with your specific travel plans. Someone will meet your train and bring you to AI headquarters.

Sincerely,
Moody Pugh

My mind went blank for a moment. I couldn't digest what I had read. Father Windy connected with Antelope Investments? The Klan? Was this another betrayal? All these things charged through my brain, nearly causing it to short circuit.

Was I the fall guy in a big set up, with Father Windy, Lana Birdwell and/or Dexter Hall doing the setting? I had to ask the question again – why me? And again I came up with the same answer which was no answer. Suddenly Father Windy's office wasn't comfortable any longer. It was time to go to LA and see about Blinky Rizonetti, Jackson Berg and Antelope Investments.

17.

Cahill wasn't waiting for me when I went home to pack. Nor did I see any plainclothesmen in baggy suits holding up street lamps. I threw a shirt and some shaving gear into an old scuff-brown suitcase which had once been kicked down the slopes of Mt Shasta. Or so it looked.

I tossed the suitcase in the back seat of the Plymouth and drove out to Bernal Heights again. I hoped Cahill could find somebody else to push around until I got back.

Steve Busby lived on Prospect just off Virginia. He was an old friend who owed me a favor. He was home and I was able to collect. I had him drive me to Palo Alto where I wanted to catch the 8.48 to LA. I didn't want to run into Cahill or any of his flunkies at the SP depot in the city.

I slept most of the way South, although I remember getting out at a stop in Fresno for coffee and a pack of butts and a fat lady tripping over my dogs somewhere near Bakersfield. All else was as dark as the night in my memory.

The 'Lark' was scheduled into LA at 6.53. I woke with first light an hour before. At six the sun decided to take a chance on another day and began climbing carefully over the peaks of the San Bernadino Mountains.

Its rays burst through the lower passes first, sending beams of light like rifle shots down into the dry brown valley communities that drape LA like junk jewelry. The blinding gold danced off windows, the hoods of automobiles and power lines and into my eyes, causing me to squint. In a few hours the playful post-dawn star would become angry and beat a relentless tattoo through a cloudless sky and bake the earth. But before all that happened the train pulled into LA, which is another world entirely.

Los Angeles is changing. The past twenty years have seen the movie industry boom and reshape the once yawning town. It is an exciting place, LA is, but it is tarnished some by pretension, garishness and a whole lot of insincerity, which are all properties of its major industry. I read a story in *Black Mask* by a new writer who said LA used to be 'a big, dry sunny place with ugly homes and no style, but good-hearted and peaceful'. Now, he said, it is a 'neon-lighted slum'. I think he has something there.

I got off the train and grabbed a taxi in front of the station. I told the hackie to take me to United Movie Studios. Like too many big-city cabbies, he was a quipster and I was his breakfast.

'United? Let me guess. You've been signed to replace Clark Gable.'

I saw the smirk on his face through the rear-view mirror.

'Is everybody in LA a wise guy or are you with the Jack Benny show?' I countered, still wiping the winkers out of my eyes from the ten-hour train ride.

The driver, who from my position in the back seat was only two ears, an inch of black curly hair, a yellow cap and a voice that whined like a loose fan belt, wouldn't give up.

'Nah, you ain't pretty enough. Let's see. You're Irving Thalberg disguised as a bum. Maybe you're . . .'

I had my fill of this character and declared breakfast over.

'Say, mac, where does a fellow go for a good time in this town, other than the back seat of your cab, of course?'

It was weak, but asking cab drivers for the lowdown on local hotspots was like telling your grandmother you want to see the family album again.

It diverted his attention long enough to get him into a self-perpetuating monologue during which he described all the weird things that pass for entertainment in Los Angeles. From prostitution any way you want it, to illegal gambling, cock and pit bull fights and dirty movies, LA had it all. By the time he finished his spiel we were idling outside United's main gate.

'Thanks just the same, pal,' I said through a triumphant grin, 'but I'll just get out here.'

'Two bucks-five,' the driver grumbled, realizing he had been duped.

I took two singles from my wallet and a buffalo from my pocket and tossed them on the front seat.

'Keep the change,' I said.

I heard him spit out some uncomplimentary oaths as I walked away, but he didn't come after me. His kind never do.

Over the main studio entrance was an embarrassingly oversized arch of wrought-iron with gold phosphorescent letters that spelled out the words 'United Movie Studios'.

Fifteen steps away was a small sign – 'Rizonetti's Shoeshine Studio Two Chairs No Waiting'. It wasn't nearly as fancy as its name. There were two elderly naugahide chairs mounted on wood blocks. Behind them was a mirror mounted on a wall next to an autographed picture of Jean Harlow. Under the picture was a calendar with a picture of an orange grove. The calendar was held up by a large brown nail. The whole outfit was more or less portable. Its dirty plywood walls had metal hinges in two places, so it could be folded around the chairs at night. If it had wheels, it could have been rolled away.

I climbed up into one of the two empty chairs. A smallish man with a round face and balding head appeared from nowhere and started cracking a shine cloth. An incessant distracting facial twitch, probably the result of a nervous disorder, told me how the man came to be called Blinky.

'Yes sir,' he beamed, 'what'll it be today?'

'I'll take a shine and some information, Blinky.'

'Shine's ten cents, information's more.' He was all business.

'How much more?'

'Depends on what kind of information you want and how hard it is to get.'

'Something's happening up in Frisco in a few days, something big. I'd like to know what it is. Ira Blodgett said you might know.'

He stopped shining my shoes and raised his head. He looked at me suspiciously.

'What the hell you talking about, mister? Ira Blodgett's dead. Leastways that's what his priest told me.'

'I know, Blinky. I'm trying to find his killer.'

'How do I know I can trust you?'

'You don't, not for sure anyway. I went to see him the day he was killed. I got there too late, but the cops don't think so. They peg me as the killer. So I'm looking for the killer to save my own skin, if that means anything.'

'It might.'

'Ira was putting together some dope on the people responsible for shooting his friend during the strike and I figure he stumbled onto something too big for him to handle. I know he spoke to you before he died. You must have given him some hard sauce because he mentioned your name to a friend.'

Blinky resumed shining my shoes. His rag popped like a rawhide whip. He waited until he could see his face in the toes of my shoes before he spoke.

'I don't know nothing, really. I just told the kid that Mr Berg stopped by for a shine a couple of weeks ago. He was with this politician I seen him with before, a man named Mason. He's a senator or something. Berg says to this Mason that everything was going smooth and that the boys were ready for the big day. Said something about "fixing that commie's wagon". I don't know who he meant, but from the way they were talking I figure it had something to do with politics. Meant nothing to me, but the kid wanted to know. He picked my brain for everything I knew about the old man.'

'Anything else, Blinky?'

'That's everything, honest. I know a guy what's in the movies, though. He knows plenty. The kid talked to him. I can call him and see if he'll talk to you.'

'How much is all this going to cost me, Blinky?'

He finished with my shoes and looked up into my face.

'Ten cents total,' he grinned.

'How come? You don't know me. Why stick your neck out for a stranger?'

He folded up his cloth and carefully laid it on the empty chair. He drove his eyes into mine.

'I didn't know Ira very well. Met him only one time. But I liked him a lot. He was a decent kid and I think it's lousy someone went and killed him. If you're after his killer, mister, for whatever reason, you're an ace in my book.'

'Thanks, Blinky, thanks a lot. I'll stop by later to see if you've made contact with your friend.'

I slid down from the chair. I reached into my pocket and came up with a couple of singles. I pressed them into Blinky's palm and walked down Sunset to look for breakfast.

I read the paper while stuffing my face with French toast in a place where respectable people dined. It had been a while. About all I could handle, other than the French toast, was the coverage of yesterday's game.

The Tigers were in pretty bad shape. They had scored only six runs in the first three games while the Cardinals had thirteen and everybody in Detroit, from the front office on down to the bat boy, was sore about it. They said Greenberg's big bat wasn't carrying the team the way it should. Cochrane said we could expect some surprises in game four. Something to give the Tiger bats more pep. Maybe he planned to change his lineup. He had to do something, but he couldn't afford to bench Greenberg.

I took a bus downtown to rent a car. Nobody can get around in LA unless they have a car. I knew that much about the town. I got the oldest bucket of bolts on the lot – a '28 Studebaker – from a place on La Cienega. I drove around a while before finding a $2 room at a motor hotel out on the Coast highway. I thought it might come in handy if I wanted to do something special later on, like get a real night's sleep.

I returned to Blinky's shine parlor about 11.30. He told me he had arranged a meeting with his friend.

'Come back at 8.30 tonight,' he said, shoving a small card into my hand. 'Here, take this, it's a studio pass. It'll get you onto the lot. Walk back past the western set to Studio C and go to the red trailer. Charlie says he'll be waiting for you.'

'Blinky,' I said genuinely, 'I must say you are a most efficient fellow. Don't take this the wrong way, but I hope for your sake as well as mine that you're on the level with me.'

'And vicey versey,' he came back, smiling good-naturedly. 'I'm taking my chances with you, too.'

'Touché, Blinky,' I said touching the brim of my hat.

I put the pass into my wallet and patted the slim leather for good luck. I said goodbye to the little shine man and walked to where the Studebaker was parked. I wanted to take a drive out in the valley to look at some property.

18.

Waves of heat rippled skyward from the valley floor. My mouth was as dry as an insurance policy. But in places where there should have been desert there grew green grass that belonged on a golf course. Scarlet bougainvillea and purple and rose fuchsia paid tired-looking stucco one-storys compliments they didn't deserve. Carpets of sea fig and rows of tropical palm gave the area the look of a Busby Berkely movie set. For all I knew, maybe it was.

I had no easy time locating Antelope Investments. The information in Ira Blodgett's envelope was only a dim recollection and Moody Pugh's letter had a post office box for a return address. But I pooled this scrap of information with the telephone operator and struck paydirt.

I found it tucked away on a small back street in Burbank in a pink stucco and steel job. The building directory in the lobby said Antelope Investments was located on the second floor.

I walked up a flight of cement stairs that looked like it had been poured yesterday. On the second floor were a number of unfriendly doors with opaque half-glass. Only one had any identification, and this was a small sign – 'AI walk in'. I straightened my tie, took a hankie to my shoes, turned up the brim of my hat and opened the door.

The office had the personality of a soda cracker. Two chairs, an anonymous potted plant, a bare metal desk that looked like it had just been unpacked, a door to an inner room and a window were all that was holding up the floor. On the desk was a little hand-printed sign that read, 'Ring Bell'. I pressed the button next to it. I expected an over-sized rabbit to come hopping out from behind the inner door.

Instead a man appeared. He was tall and thin, probably forty-five, and was wearing a blue pin-striped suit with a monogrammed red silk handkerchief drooping out of the breast pocket. His hair was the color of engine oil, which must have been what he used to slick it down. He had it pressed flat, straight and close to his head like he was afraid it might get up and climb off if he gave it any breathing room.

Narrow eyes that pierced if you let them were planted deep in sockets on either side of a nose that could have carved a roast. A thin black line of hair ran horizontally a quarter inch above a taut lipless mouth. He spit a chilly greeting from behind teeth that looked like they had just received a fresh coat of paint.

'Yes, may I help you?'

I grabbed his hand and pumped it like a bumper jack.

'Sure hope so. Name's Buhl, Milo Buhl. I'm real interested in buying some of that beautiful California land that you got. Thought I'd like to try my hand at growing oranges or lemons. Heard you boys got some good land for that sort of thing.' I was whistling in the dark, but I hoped he didn't know the tune. I thought if I could keep talking long enough I might strike it rich. 'I'm from Ohio, Mr, uh . . .'

'Mr Pugh,' he said reluctantly.

'That's right, Mr Pugh. Glad to meet you. Like I said, I'm from out in Ohio. Sold the hardware store in Medina and me and the missus headed west to seek our fortunes in the golden state.'

Pugh looked at me like I had two heads, but I didn't let that stop me.

'Hated to leave Ohio, you know,' I said, 'but business fell off and I didn't have no choice. Fine country, Ohio, good country for white, Christian Americans.'

Pugh tried to interrupt me as I knew he would, but I talked right through him.

'Well, we ain't found our fortunes yet, me and the missus, that is. Been kind of down on our luck you might say. Met a fellow up in Frisco last week, though, said you boys could show us some of them choice properties and maybe even include us in on some old-fashioned fun, if you know what I mean.'

I winked and nudged him in the side. Mr Pugh was not amused.

'I am sure I have no idea what you are talking about, Mr . . .'

'Buhl, Milo Buhl. From Medina, Ohio. Like I said, Mr Pugh, this fellow said maybe you could use a good old hell-raising Klanner like me.'

'And just who was this fellow, as you call him?'

'Don't rightly know, Mr Pugh. A minister of some kind or another, I think. He said anytime I was in Los Angeles to look up ole Moody Pugh at Antelope Investments. You are Mr Moody Pugh, ain't you?'

'Yes, that is correct. You said you were a member of the Knights in . . .'

'Ohio. Medina, Ohio. Ran a whole passel of communists out of the rubber shops in Akron a couple months back. Maybe you heard about it. Those damn reds like to have taken over Akron before we showed them who was boss.'

Moody Pugh's eyes were working overtime giving me the once over. He scratched the stiletto he had for a chin.

'Excuse me for a moment, Mr Buhl.'

He disappeared through the side door. I heard him dialing the telephone. Five minutes later he returned. He was smiling; smiling as much as face would allow.

'Mr Buhl. I think we have some parcels that will interest you. Unfortunately our salesman is with a client at the moment. However, if you will return this evening we can discuss our, shall we say, land development ideas for the state of California.'

I gave him a little wink like it was a secret between just us two.

'Sure thing, Mr Pugh. I'll be here with bells on.'

'Shall we say 8 o'clock?'

'Sure, let's say 8 o'clock.'

We shook hands and parted. I don't think either one of us was fooled by the act, but I got what I came for.

Antelope Investments was likely a front for the Committee. I figured it must have connections in some pretty high places which would explain its secret and phony front. It all sounded pretty simple. Too simple. However, there were many things that weren't. Lana Birdwell and Father Windy were still big question marks, and I knew that if I didn't keep my eyes wide open I could very easily end up in the nice guys hall of fame with Ira Blodgett and Pitts Langley. The only qualification for getting in was being dead. Jackson Berg was another mystery, and him I hoped to learn about from a man named Charlie.

All this bounced around between my ears as I drove back to LA through a heat that could have raised blisters on a box of dirt.

19.

LA is two different cities. By day it is hot and tiring and normal. But something happens when the sun goes down. A tawdry neon smoke blankets the city, drawing out the denizens of the night like moths to the proverbial flame. They say at night LA is exciting and fearful and more than a little unreal.

I spent the afternoon holed up in a downtown gin mill sipping tonics and listening to the fourth game of the Series. Cochrane shuffled the batting order to give the Tigers more punch. Greenberg was dropped to sixth! But the Tiger skipper must have known something, because his boys slugged across ten runs, crushing the Gashouse nine 10 to 4. Frisch made the bone-head move of the Series when he sent Dizzy Dean into the game in the fourth inning to run for Davis. All that happened to the best pitcher in baseball was that he was knocked out cold when he caught Rogell's throw to Greenberg on the skull in a routine force play. Now, instead of getting ready to pitch the fifth game of the Series, the 30-game winner was in the hospital counting stars. But, then again, knowing old Diz, he could probably twirl a two-hitter from a stretcher.

I remained in the bar quenching my thirst until 8 o'clock when I drove out to United Studios to see my contact. I had the cold vision that I might find Moody Pugh and his cronies waiting for me with a hemp necktie on some back lot.

I reached into the glove compartment and checked my gun. I

hadn't fired the damn thing for more than two years and then only to break up a back yard triangle between a couple of rambunctious toms and a she-cat.

I parked the car on Santa Monica and walked to the main gate. Blinky's shoeshine parlor was locked up for the night, but a bank of blazing blue lights made sure no one forgot what the main attraction was. I strolled up to a burly, thick-lipped security guard and flashed him the pass Blinky had given me. I started to enter the grounds when he called out.

'Hey buddy, let me see that pass again.'

I returned and humored him. He took the small card in his puffy catcher's mitt hands and examined it closer than a gem merchant looking for flaws in a diamond. He pushed back his hat and scratched his head.

'It looks legit, but I dunno. Where you goin'?'

'I'm supposed to meet some people at Studio C,' I answered, trying to sound like a regular studio joe. 'They want me to look at some sets. The director wants some changes made.'

'At night?' the big cop harrumphed skeptically.

I shrugged my shoulders and stretched out my hands.

'What can you do? You know how these Hollywood directors are. Most of them are little dictators and the rest are just plain screwy.'

He guffawed and slapped me on the back.

'Don't I know. They shoulda married my wife.' He bellowed with laughter and waved me on to the studio grounds.

Still chuckling loudly, he called out after me, 'Don't let them keep you out too late now, ya hear.'

I turned and gave him a playful wave.

I had never been on a movie lot before. In a way it looked like a military base. The long low buildings – some, ribbed metal huts; others, cheap wood – looked like temporary and hastily erected airplane hangars. They were stretched out before me in no particular direction.

Then again, it was like something I had never seen before. It was a walk through time and fantasy. Off to my left was a dimly lit set that looked like the main street of Dodge City, back when people punched cows for a living. Several hundred yards away was a group of building facades that must have been a New York tenement. Still further along was a small rural village surrounded on three sides with papier mâché mountains and skies painted on canvas.

It was all make-believe, but then who could say for sure what was real anymore? The Night of the Long Knives back in April, those strange rumblings coming from Moscow and Mr Adolf Hitler. They seemed just as unreal as Shirley Temple's latest film.

I made a couple of wrong turns poking my way through Jackson Berg's vast and deserted fairyland before I reached Studio C. Its main set looked like the interior of an enormous factory of some kind. Giant gear wheels dominated the sound stage. It was poorly lit, which allowed me to stumble over thick dark cables that slithered along the ground like lamprey eels.

Lights were burning in the long fancy red trailer where Blinky told me I would find the man 'what knows plenty'. I took a deep breath the way young boys do when they go up to the girl's house on their first date. I knocked on the door. A man in loosely fitting trousers and a wrinkled white shirt with the sleeves rolled up appeared. Since there were two steps up to the trailer's door and I was standing on the ground, initially my eyes came only to the man's chest. I raised them to speak.

'Blinky told me I can find a man named Chaaa . . .' I didn't finish my sentence. The face of the man standing at the door belonged to Charlie Chaplin. You could have knocked me over with a feather. My mouth fell open as if the pins in my jaws had been removed. Chaplin covered my embarrassment.

'I see Blinky didn't tell you I would be here.'

My mouth closed. I forget if I used my hand, but I regained the ability to speak and words started jumping out.

'Oh, he told me all right, but when he said a guy named Charlie, I didn't think he meant you.'

Charlie Chaplin smiled. I'm sure he has encountered ten thousand like me – dumbfounded, incoherent, an all-round fool. But then I recovered after producing a couple of self-conscious compliments like 'I thought you were just swell in *City Lights*.' After that it was back to business.

He invited me inside and we sat across from each other at a small kitchen table, although there was no kitchen as such in the trailer. The miniature house was long and thin, as I suppose most trailers are. The walls were covered with autographed pictures and other personal mementos. Its main living area was furnished with a couple of inexpensive easy chairs, a refrigerator and a movie projector on a metal stand next to the door. Canisters of film were lying everywhere and a number of books and magazines stuffed a mahogany bookcase that stood shoulder-high against the back wall.

'Riley,' he said. 'I'd like to call you Riley if it's all right.' I automatically nodded my permission. 'I insist you call me Charlie.'

There are few people in this world that you meet for the first time and five minutes later you feel at home with them – like you've known them for a lifetime. Charlie Chaplin was one of those people. His voice was trusting and his manner open. It had been a while since I had talked with anyone who didn't look at me like I was a dish of yesterday's ice cream.

'Riley,' he continued, 'I don't know you and you don't know me, but we both know something rotten is going on around here. Blinky told me you were investigating the murder of that longshoreman from San Francisco. I met the kid when he came here about a month ago and I knew him to be on the level. Blinky says you're okay and I trust his judgement implicitly. If this were a just world, people like Blinky would be running the film industry instead of the rats we have now.'

He stopped talking and offered to get me a beer. I accepted.

'How about a sandwich to go with that beer?' he said, his head buried inside the small refrigerator. 'I'm going to throw some roast beef and mayonnaise on a couple of pieces of bread. There's plenty to go around.'

Again I accepted. I figured he wanted to take a moment to size me up before taking me into his confidence, as much as he wanted a snack. I would have done the same thing. I looked at some of the photographs that hung on the wall while he made the sandwiches. I noticed that several of the pictures were from labor demonstrations. One looked particularly familiar. Chaplin told me it was the longshore strike and the photo had been snapped on Bloody Thursday moments before the police opened fire on the picketing workers. The picture was signed by Harry Bridges and inscribed, 'To Charlie Chaplin, labor's great friend in its hour of need.' I returned to the table where Chaplin had set the beer and sandwiches. He talked as he ate.

'I don't know how much you know about what has been happening around here, Riley, but it's pretty damn ugly. Berg has imposed a reign of terror on the industry. He is forcing actors and the other workers on the lots to pay into his campaign chest. It's nothing short of extortion!'

'How much is he skimming?' I asked, wholly ignorant of what he was talking about.

'He's demanding we give a day's pay. Now, I'm making a lot of money and it doesn't hurt my pocketbook. But that isn't the point. What I oppose is an employer being able to force the workers to make political contributions as a condition of employment, and to a cause many of them oppose. It's tyranny. It's fascism!'

Chaplin's face became red. He was agitated. The friendly little clown who had won his way into the hearts of an entire generation was now smoldering with indignation. I asked him how Jackson Berg was able to get away with this injustice.

'Blackmail! That's what it is – blackmail! Most people don't know the film industry is run by fear. People are literally frightened twenty-four hours a day that the almighty god Berg will reassign them, cut their contracts or simply fire them. If a person wants to work around here, he is wise to keep his mouth shut tight and not upset his royal majesty. Keeping one's lip buttoned is the most popular participation sport on the lots.

'Hell, even those who play the game and keep silent have been thrown out of work. That's why he is able to get away with it, Riley. When you hold absolute power over scared and unorganized subjects – well, you know – it's the Dark Ages.'

Chaplin told me that some of the actors and writers were beginning to stand up to Berg's despotism. People like Dorothy Parker, Nunnally Johnson, Jean Harlow and Jimmie Cagney had refused to fork over even one dollar of their salary to finance Berg's candidate. At this Chaplin took some small satisfaction. We began a second beer. He had much more to tell me.

'It's movie time,' he said, popping up from his chair and going to the projector.

He began threading a small reel of film. I had no idea what this had to do with anything, but I went along with him. He asked me to pull down the screen that was rolled up like a window shade against the far wall of the trailer. When he finished loading the projector, he flipped off the lights and the show began. He said I might find it interesting. I did.

We saw a five-minute segment from a United Movie newsreel. The subject was the gubernatorial campaign. Following testimonials from three or four well-dressed citizens who swore the acting governor was the best thing to happen to California since steam beer, there were scenes of dark, unshaven, surly-looking men in dirty clothes. They spoke with Russian accents and said such things as 'Upton Sinclair vill make Caleefornia a paradise for zee poor peyeples' and 'I vill be coming to Caleefornia if meester Zeenclair vins da election.' There were also shots of hundreds of hoboes jumping off a train as it pulled into a depot. Off-camera a band was playing 'California, Here I Come'.

In the final moments of the film, Jackson Berg himself came on the screen. Speaking from his plush executive office, he addressed the movie audience:

> The gubernatorial election in California is the most important political contest since the Civil War. At stake is our American way of life and the free enterprise system which has made this country great. The governor is pledged to defend these things we Americans hold so dear. His opponent, on the other hand, despite some fine-sounding words and lofty ideals, is being manipulated by forces both inside this country and overseas, and if elected will be helpless to prevent an alien ideology and an alien way of life from taking control of our state and plunging it into total ruin.
>
> We of the motion picture industry are keenly aware of this

threat and wish to inform the citizens of California that, should the governor be defeated in the coming election, United Movie Studios, as well as the other major film companies, would be forced to relocate our industry in the friendlier environment of another state.

We at United respectfully call upon the good people of California to go the polls on election day and cast a vote for democracy. Your vote will help keep America strong as well as keep the motion picture industry the vital part of California that it has been for nearly a quarter of a century.

The film ended with an elaborate orchestration of 'The Star Spangled Banner' played against a sky filled with the Stars and Stripes and the Bear Flag of California. Chaplin turned on the lights.

'Well, what do you think of that little number?' he asked rhetorically.

'Offhand, I'd say Jackson Berg won't ever be accused of having a crush on Sinclair.'

'To say the least. The bastards claim they will move everything to Florida.' He swallowed the last of his beer. 'Riley, you can see just how serious Berg is about this election. And it's not just him either. It's all the big-shot executives. There is a saying around here that as Jackson Berg goes, so goes Hollywood. These tinsel-town moguls are using every dirty trick in the book to defeat Sinclair. Hell, they won't stop at destroying free elections.' He paused and then added as an afterthought, 'Such as they are.'

Chaplin got up from his chair and started pacing the length of the trailer, pounding his fist into an open palm.

'Actors being blackmailed, fake newsreels being cranked out right under our noses and being distributed in every theater in the state – from Alturas to Chula Vista – I tell you, Riley, the movie industry is corrupt and it could very well buy itself a governor. There will be many more Bloody Thursdays if Jackson Berg gets his way.'

Charlie Chaplin may be the world's greatest master of the trick fall and the art of clowning, but there was nothing funny in what he was telling me. With this new information, pieces which had sat on the table staring dumbly up at me were beginning to come together in a giant jigsaw puzzle. I didn't like the picture that was taking shape.

I told Chaplin about Antelope Investments, Moody Pugh and the Committee. He had never heard of any of them, but wasn't surprised to learn of their existence. He promised to keep an ear to the ground.

I related what Pitts had told me about 9 October. Chaplin shrugged. He had no knowledge of the date in terms of the campaign. Then he thought a moment. The lines on his forehead scrooched together. He put a forefinger to his chin and then started talking about Tom Mooney.

Chaplin told me he was a member of a committee of actors and writers who believed in the imprisoned labor leader's innocence. Last month a group of them traveled to San Quentin to visit him. Chaplin said he was greatly impressed with Mooney's knowledge of the shenanigans surrounding the campaign.

'He must have a very special grapevine,' the actor said. 'He knew things that even we were ignorant of. He warned us to keep a sharp eye on the opposition and the extremists of the right wing. He said they were capable of just about anything.

'He wasn't specific about anything, but I have a feeling that he knows a whole lot more than he told us. I'd say it would be a wise idea to get to Mooney before the ninth. He just might know something. Harry Bridges – he's the man to get you in to see him.'

We talked for another half hour, during which time we each killed a third beer. I would have stayed longer, but we both had work to do. Chaplin was due on the set at 7.30 to work on his new movie and I had to spend more time with that puzzle before hopping a northbound freight. We shook hands and said goodnight.

I retraced my steps as best I could remember toward the main gate. I got to the guard's shack to find the laughing flatfoot asleep and snoring loud enough to peel paint from a stone wall. I walked out into the night and was swallowed by a blinking blue dust.

20.

It wasn't early, but I was too worked up from my meeting with Charlie Chaplin to go straight to bed. I wouldn't say I was high, but a couple of goofballs would probably have had the same effect. I drove around aimlessly before stopping at an all-night hash joint in Westwood. Nothing special about the place. All cafes in LA have a 30-foot plastic hamburger on the roof.

I got the early edition of the morning paper on my way in. I spent the next hour reading Chandler Lane's *Telegram*, drinking coffee and picking at a piece of custard pie that had a crust like the rubber liner of a mason jar.

A particularly nasty editorial against Sinclair jumped off the opinion page. Under the heading, 'Bolsheviks and Bums Threaten Invasion', the publisher called Sinclair 'Moscow's stooge', and huffed, 'If elected, he will transform a free and prosperous state into a Soviet slave camp.'

What interested me even more than the bad smear job was the existence of Jackson Berg's name. Lane quoted him several times in the five-hundred-word editorial. I recognized the words from the newsreel. What a neat operation. Together, Berg and Lane had tied up two-thirds of the communications media. No wonder their class was able to stay on top. The only question I had was – who's tying up radio?

The clock on the diner wall ticked 1.45 through a plastic cover turned yellow and almost opaque by a generation of grill spatter. I paid my tab, promised the counter man I wouldn't return, even to pay off a bet, and walked out into the warm southern California night. The atmosphere was thick and I found it difficult to breathe. The smell of greasy hamburgers had eaten most of the oxygen. I drove the three or four miles to the El Rancho motor hotel, the place where I had paid a guy two bucks for a bed. Red lights spelled out 'vacancy' on a motel sign that stood out like a smart-alec dare to travelers driving down the Coast highway. It seemed redundant to me. The El Ranchos of the world always have vacancies. There simply aren't that many guys like Riley Kovachs, husbands on the lam or traveling knife-sharpener salesmen to pay cash money to fill up such dreary places.

I parked in the space in front of my room. Except for an occasional somnambulist pushing two tons of metal and rubber down the highway, the only sound was the surf. I thought maybe it was too quiet.

Many years ago, I trusted everybody, probably even politicians. But I've become a suspicious sort in recent times and I always try to remember to take those extra little precautions that insure one's life, especially when I'm out of town on a case and always when the caper takes me to LA. When I left the motel earlier, I stuck a bent bookmatch in the jamb of the door. Any detective magazine will tell you that if it was still in place when you returned from wherever it was you went you could breathe easy. On the other hand, if it had slipped from its place, you were warned and, with any luck, prepared.

I shined my pen flashlight into the corner of the door. No bent match. Someone had been in my room and I knew it wasn't the maid. The El Rancho was the kind of dump that if there were a maid, she'd only come around on pay days.

I stopped and sniffed the night. Murder was in the air. I could smell it.

I returned to the rented Studebaker and once again removed my .38 from the glove box. I took off the safety and tiptoed back to my door. I placed the key in the hole, but it wasn't necessary. The door was unlocked. I cracked it open two inches and stood to the side, out of harm's range. Nothing stirred.

Then taking my gun in both hands, I went into a crouch and squared off. I kicked the door the rest of the way open with a mighty force. It flew around to the rubber stopper on the base-board inside the room and bounced right back with an equal force to slam shut in my face. I stared at the grain of the wood for a moment before I tried the procedure once again, using less leg.

No one was inside the room. I should qualify that and say there were no pipe-toting skull-breakers waiting to make an omelette out of my gray stuff. I should qualify it even more and say there were no living persons in the room. There was a dead one, however.

He was propped up on the bed in a sitting position. His face was covered with ugly dark welts the color of beef livers and his right eye was a bloody brown hole. The face was so swollen it was almost unrecognizable. Almost.

It was Blinky.

I closed the door and put my gun away. I made a sound something like air escaping from a punctured innertube. I wanted to put my fist through the cheap plaster wall and scream until my voice went away, but I didn't. Despite the previous murders and mayhem, for the first time, I felt like throwing in the towel and declaring the other guy a winner by a technical. I stood trembling for only a few moments, but the feeling was devastating while it lasted.

The deeper I got into the case and the closer I came to understanding it, some innocent somebody turned up dead. I might have swallowed easier if the stiffs were cheap, low-life punks, although I don't wish even them a permanent snooze. But Ira Blodgett, Pitts Langley and Blinky Rizonetti were innocent victims. Their only crime was doing their own small part to make the world a little better place for everyday folk. And for that they were sent west.

It was a grim lesson. It told you that if you stick your neck out for whatever reason – to fight for the little guy, to put something more than a lousy plate of beans and spuds on your supper table, to say a loud 'no' to the kind of unemployment that is planned in corporate boardrooms to boost profit – you are inviting pain and suffering and maybe a bullet or a knife in the ribs as your reward.

It was that lesson that I had learned before and it made me sick then, too. It brought back memories of the days when I was a part of the drive to unionize the rubber shops in Ohio. I was there when the tire workers were crushed. And there were other memories, less personal, but more recent – Hitlerism in Europe, for example. The murders in Toledo, Minneapolis, and the Frisco Longshore Strike – I had them to think about, too. I knew, standing there over

Blinky's body, that I was wallowing in political pessimism and more than a pinch of self-pity.

Most of the time I am an optimist in these matters and believe that one day the workers overseas will bury the Third Reich so far underground a coal miner won't be able to find it. I also look to the time when American workers will have their own labor unions. That is my true belief, if anyone is interested enough to ask. But at that moment, with a dead little shoeshine man on my bed, I was something less than an optimist . . . about a lot of things.

I forced myself to get a grip on more pressing matters. It didn't take a degree in sociology from Stanford to know that I was in more trouble than a mastodon in La Brea's tar pit.

I had a dead man in my room and if it was anything like the Blodgett killing, the cops were probably already on their way. And the police in Los Angeles do things a little differently. They don't even bother to trade insults with you the way Cahill and his boys do. They throw you in the can and let you rot until someone remembers you're there. And they have very poor memories. Cahill would be a soft-hearted sentimentalist in the black-and-blue world of Chief Ed Simmons. The city of Los Angeles, in addition to earning a national reputation as a union-hating and union-busting paradise, thanks largely to Chandler Lane's thirty-year vendetta, has the distinction of having one of the more corrupt police forces in America. A few years back the Payne Committee blew the whistle, finding it to be up to its badges in everything from gambling payoffs to civil rights abuse that would have made Attila the Hun turn green with envy.

With that kind of track record, I had no chance of convincing Simmons's ramrods I had nothing to do with Blinky's death. If they hadn't already been tipped off by the Committee or some dolled-up redhead with green eyes, the bully boys would only have to dial Frisco to find Cahill with an arrest warrant in his fat hand.

I had to get out of LA pronto, but there was one more thing I wanted to do. I hoped I would have time before the nets dropped on me.

21.

I drove up and down the Coast highway from Santa Monica all the way to Point Dume and back down past Redondo Beach for three hours or more. I needed to keep moving, and it gave me a chance to sort things out. A half-dozen Chesterfields, a couple of egg salad sandwiches washed away with a quart of coffee I picked up at a coastside diner near Malibu, helped me.

I knew I would leave LA with many things still in the air, but with a little Magyar luck I thought I might be able to tie a ribbon around Antelope Investments and the Committee. It wouldn't do to drive back to Burbank to explain to Mr Moody Pugh I wasn't able to attend his meeting because I was on a movie lot talking with Charlie Chaplin about dictators and right-wing smear campaigns. He might not understand. No, I had other ideas, and a Mr Cal Grundy figured prominently in them.

I turned off the Coast highway onto Hawthorne Boulevard and returned to LA. Hawthorne turned into La Brea in Inglewood and I took it into town.

Daylight had come about an hour before I realized I could turn off my headlights and quit worrying about spooks lurking in the shadows of the night. I drove to a beanery near downtown for a cup of coffee, a cheese Danish and an address. The coffee was old, the Danish lied about the cheese, but there was an address. In fact, there were three of them. I gambled that my man was the Cal Grundy who owned Grundy's Used Automobiles. It seemed to fit that the boss of a weekend army would be a gypster pedaling junk cars.

I gave the coffee a second chance it didn't deserve before heading out to the address on Wilshire.

It was already approaching 9 a.m. The Santa Anas were blowing in from the southeast. The cool dewy morning of only an hour past was being kicked out of the way by a heat that within two hours would lie in thick horizontal ropes you could almost climb.

Cal Grundy was open for business. Cheap, brightly colored plastic flags covered nearly everything in the lot that wasn't moving. Large signs filled the spaces where the flags gapped. They told you how honest Cal Grundy was, what a great deal he would make for you, how low his prices were and what a swell bunch of cars he had. They packed all the sincerity of a Hoover campaign promise.

The signs and flags had another purpose: to cover the metal zombies Cal Grundy sold to trusting folks. He called them cars. The few decent looking jalopies were prominently placed, but under the fanfare of flags and signs were wrecks held together only by their paint, which on most of them bubbled badly.

I parked a block away and walked to Grundy's lot. A shiny young fellow in a suit whose jacket was misinformed about the length of his arms stood at parade rest next to a '22 Buick. The pants matched the jacket, coming to just above the ankles. But he was scrubbed clean and looked untarnished by the deception he was a part of. When he spotted me looking in the direction of the Buick, he literally flew at me.

'Yes sir!' he squawked, coming to a stop on a dime. He bent over to catch his breath and then straightened up. 'What can I show you today?' He made a sweeping gesture toward the Buick that would never see 1935. 'This Buick here is a proud little beauty, ain't, I mean isn't she?'

'Slow down, son, you're trying too hard,' I said attempting to prevent the kid from having a thrombosis. 'I hope you can take a friendly little suggestion or two.'

The young man nodded quizzically.

'First, you're not likely to sell lollypops to little children by charging at people like a runaway bus.'

His bright toothsome smile dropped. He knew he was doing it all wrong, but he didn't like to be reminded about it. He recovered as best he could from my unsolicited advice, probably remembering that his high school business teacher had taught him that the customer was always right.

'And what's your other suggestion?' he asked, taking a very audible gulp.

'Quit! Get an honest job. You're too nice a kid to be hustling condemned machinery to honest citizens.'

His face dropped into his bow tie.

'Then you don't want the Buick?'

He was so wound up trying to make what was obviously his first sale that he didn't hear a word I said. If I weren't asking to see under the hood or how many miles the tires had, I might as well be speaking Hungarian.

'Now, I didn't say that,' I assured him. 'I just said this is a rotten business for a decent kid like you.'

He stepped back and raised his eyebrows. He heard the first part.

'Then can I show you this Buick?' He hurried around to the driver's side. 'This baby only has 96,000 miles. It's got freewheeling, too.' He opened the door and climbed in. 'And just take a look at this interior.'

'Kid!' I shouted.

He jumped, bumping his head on the sun visor. He looked at me through the windshield and crawled out.

'Yes sir? Something wrong? Maybe you'd like to see something a little more up to date. I have a Chevy over here that . . .'

'Kid!' I repeated.

'Sir?'

'Is Mr Grundy in?'

'Yes sir, but please don't report me. This is only my second day on the job and Mr Grundy told me if any customer complains, I'm out on the street.'

'Relax, kid. I don't have any complaints.' I put my arm around his shoulder. 'You're doing just fine.'

'Really?' he asked.

He probably didn't believe me, but just wanted to hear it repeated that he was up to snuff.

'Really. Now run along and get Mr Grundy. Tell him it's sort of important.'

The young man scratched his head for a moment. He then turned on his heels and dashed off to the office which was located at the rear of the lot. I would have gone myself, but I thought it more conducive to my health if I were to meet Mr Grundy *al fresco*, away from closets full of blackjack artists and drawers with hair-trigger revolvers.

A few minutes later a man emerged from the office and came strutting toward me. He was a good ten paces away when he extended his right hand for me to shake.

'Hi there. Cal Grundy here. Billy said you wanted to see me.'

He was tall and Protestant and was wearing a smile wide enough to build a fire in. He was fortyish and very athletic looking, the sort who pressed barbells instead of reading books. He was ruggedly handsome, but in an evil sort of way. He looked like a man whose hobby was turning young girls into women. He might have played half back for UCLA at one time.

I thought he looked straight-forward enough to be just what all those signs said he was. But there was something about him that made me believe I had made no mistake. Maybe it was his conspicuous military bearing – he stood stiffer than a plasterer's overalls – or perhaps it was that baleful grin that hung out below a thick, slow-witted brow. Anyway, I had come to play poker, so I began playing my cards.

'The priest said you were looking for good men,' I opened, trusting that was the right card.

His grin did a sort of double-take and his wrinkled forehead showed me that he was puzzled.

'And just what priest was that?'

'Up in Frisco. Goes by the name of Father Windy. He said your outfit could use some muscle.'

Cal Grundy didn't say anything, but his mind, such as it might be, was working overtime.

'Father Windy, Father Windy.' He looked up in the sky trying to remember where he had heard that name. He and Dexter Hall had the same acting coach. 'And just what kind of muscle did this Father Windy say I might be looking for? As you can see, this is a used car lot and we don't have much need for muscle, except every once in a while to collect a bill from a deadbeat.'

He laughed out loud.

'I don't know,' I said, shrugging my shoulders, 'maybe I've

come to the wrong place, but Father Windy said you could use some men to help put the kibosh on the reds.'

Grundy wasn't convinced, but the way he was asking questions was a tipoff he could be had. He, on the other hand, thought he was putting me through the third degree.

'What does this Father Windy look like?' he asked pointedly.

I described the waterfront minister down to the number of lashes on each eyelid. Cal Grundy was pleased. And that was the toughest question he could come up with.

'I still don't get it why he sent you here,' he continued slowly. 'You should be talking to the bunch in Frisco.'

'Oh, that's easy. I'm tired of Frisco and am thinking hard about moving down here. Got a job, too, if I want it. United Studios offered to hire me on as a carpenter at $50 a week. Father Windy thought you could use some inside men at the movies. Sort of keep an eye on the Bolshies.'

Grundy liked that even more. He asked me a few more questions about Father Windy and, satisfied with my answers, confided that the good prelate was his inside man on the waterfront. He shook his head from side to side.

'We took a big chance with Jim Windy. You know he's got a left-wing reputation and is tight as two tits with some of the top communists up there. But he come to us a while back and said he was throwing in the towel with the Russia boys. Said they weren't for freedom no way. Just wanted to take over and control things for the mother country.

'We didn't believe him at first, but he's given us some damn valuable information. And he had a little snoop who was nosing around in our business taken care of just last week. Some in the Committee still don't trust him, but I'd say if he was willing to go as far as he did with that sneak, he's a good enough man for me.

'And being friends as he is with the top reds, he can clue us in on their every move. He's real friendly with the EPIC clubs, too. I'd say a man like Jim Windy is money in the bank, wouldn't you?'

I nodded agreement. What I didn't say was that the bank I thought Father Windy was with had just gone bust. I made a mental reminder to congratulate him on the Academy Award winning performance he gave me the next time I saw him. That and breaking his jaw would allow me to live with myself.

Cal Grundy may have been a dandy commander for a vigilante militia, but he was a tyro when it came to security. I could have been William Z. Foster and probably slipped by him. He rigged up that toothy grin once again and was slapping me on the back and touching my coat while he continued dropping secrets in my ear. He hadn't even asked my name.

'Yes sir, anybody Jim Windy sends to me gets my personal attention. Course we'll have to check you out. Just routine, but we can't be too careful, you know.'

I bluffed him.

'Yeah, well maybe you should call Windy right now if you don't believe me,' I said, feigning indignation.

Grundy put his arm around my shoulder in an attempt to reassure me.

'Hey, buddy, don't take it that way. It's nothing personal. Hell, Father Coughlin could walk in here carrying a stack of bibles and we'd still run a check on him. I'm sure everything will be all right, but we got to be careful. You know how it is.'

I sulked a moment or two before making up with him.

'Yeah, I guess you're right. I just get all steamed up when a man doubts my word. I guess that's why they call me Smoke – because of my temper. Hell, Cal, I never did introduce myself. Bellew's the name – Smoke Bellew.'

Jack London would never forgive me for the theft, but I was feeling heady with my con.

'Real glad to know you, Smoke,' he said, grabbing my hand and pumping it like he was trying to draw water.

He couldn't keep his hands off me after that. He was the sort who talked with his hands – always nudging you, poking you in the ribs and so on. Nothing queer about it, many people are that way. I don't care for it, though, it makes me nervous.

Cal Grundy forgot about calling Father Windy for the moment. He wouldn't have had to go that far. A crosstown call to Moody Pugh would have been enough, but Grundy wasn't that bright.

Grundy took me into the front seat of the '22 Buick the kid tried to sell me and continued talking. The man was overjoyed at having a fresh new recruit.

'You'll have to meet the Executive Board. They have to pass on all new members. You'll be a cinch, Smoke.'

I couldn't figure what made Grundy so screwy about me. He certainly didn't have the wits to be putting a reverse con on me. He was the kind of mug who would have had a hard time keeping up with Lum and Abner in a conversation about the weather.

We smoked a couple of cigarettes and drank from Grundy's hip flask for nearly an hour. He was a quick drunk and a politically belligerent one. He insisted on stuffing my hat with his philosophy. The guy had been a Jew- and Negro-hater since childhood. He grew up in the Klan the way most people are brought up Methodist. It was only recently, however, that he had taken up hating communists and labor unions. He was quite serious when he said Adolf Hitler had set an example he felt compelled to follow.

'He's getting a bad rap in the papers. Hell, everybody knows it's the communists and Jews that are responsible for the mess the world is in. And they stir up the niggers. It's a fact. Look at what the reds did in Germany after the war – strike after strike; revolt after revolt. Almost bankrupted the country. Would have, too, if Mr Hitler hadn't come along to save it.

'The same exact thing is happening here in America, Smoke. Look at what those revolutionists done in Toledo and Minneapolis. I guess I don't have to tell you about what happened in Frisco, do I?'

He smiled and poked my ribs. I returned both. He staggered on, draining both his flask and his heart.

'But we're in a good position to stop 'em before things get too far. We got Mr Hitler's example to follow for one thing. I tell you, Smoke, the way he done in them godless reds and took over the unions – why it makes me so proud I could bust. Hitler shoulda been an American. We need 'im. This is a great country, Smoke, I don't have to tell you that. We gotta keep it that way. If people like me an' you don't stand up to the communists and the unions, they'll take over, take over sure as I'm talking here.'

Cal Grundy's eyes began to water. Whether the tears were from the booze or his pep talk I couldn't say. He concluded as best he knew how.

'If they take over, Smoke, they'll take away everything our forefathers fought for – everything George Washington fought for. They'll wreck America. Smoke, we can't let 'em do it, we can't.'

He buried his head in his hands and sobbed alcoholically.

I was unmoved by Grundy's sales pitch. I would rather have bought the Buick.

He pulled himself together a few minutes later and began telling me about things more interesting. He said Sinclair was in LA for a rally and a couple of boys from the Committee were going to attend as part of a reconnaissance operation. A meeting was scheduled for later in the day in which the entire cadre would be let in on what he called the 'coming events'. I pumped him for information about those events, but even Cal Grundy knew when to dummy up. He said only regular initiated members were allowed to participate, but he told me he would speak to the Executive Board after the Sinclair rally and argue my case. If they agreed, I could attend the evening meeting.

'I'd hate for you to miss this meeting, Smoke,' Grundy said excitedly. 'It's gonna be a humdinger. Mr Mason himself will be doin' the speakin'. This is the first time one of the big boys has made a public appearance. They thought it would be a a good idea, sort of give the fellas the feelin' they have friends in high places. Maybe I shouldn't be tellin' you all this, but I'm so excited I could bust, just bust.'

All I could utter in response was a very sincere 'Holy Cow'.

McArthur Digges Mason was big. He was bigger than big. He drew his pay as a Congressman from Orange County and had been spending recent weeks traveling up and down the state campaigning very hard for Sinclair's opponent. In fact he was the point man leading the opposition's attacks on Sinclair and was responsible for producing most of the dirt this campaign was becoming famous for.

Mason had a list of credentials that ran from here to there and back again. As California's most prominent conservative, he was one of the architects of the Red Scare back even before the war and was the captain of the Congressional cheer leaders who huzzahed Douglas McArthur's routing of the Bonus Marchers from Washington year before last.

But he was probably best known for his service in the Harding administration, where he had been an under-secretary in the Interior Department. His name had been linked to the Tea Pot Dome scandal, but he came through it without a scratch. At least I don't remember him being indicted for anything. In fact for years afterward his enemies called him 'fish', as in 'the fish that got away'.

Yeah, Mason was big all right. My mind clicked back a few frames and remembered something about Mason and Berg getting a shoeshine at Blinky's.

After picking Grundy's brain I knew that I was onto something that smelled like one of the biggest and shadiest political double deals in California history. But who could I go to? The cops? That would be like the rancher asking a cattle rustler if he had seen his missing cows. Who would believe me, anyway? I doubt Joe Stalin would swallow a story about a nest of Nazis and Kluxers who had their hearts set on stealing an election and lifting the scalp of every liberal and unionist in the state. Mason, Lane and Berg, 'the men who made America great', involved in such a slimy escapade? Who's kidding who, Kovachs? I whistled through my teeth. I was sitting on top of a volcano that was set to erupt, but everyone who could do anything about it was passing out corks.

22.

Yes, I had the goods to a scam so ugly it would have started a revolution on a desert island, but I still didn't know who killed Ira Blodgett. Since I was the prime suspect in his and most probably Blinky's death, and because LA and Frisco cops were sniffing up every strange pant leg looking for me, and because if Milo Buhl and Smoke Bellew ever met, they might find themselves cooling their heels as well as their brains in a downtown morgue vegetable cooler, I decided it was time to blow LA and not take my chances with the Committee's meeting.

I made Grundy believe he had persuaded me to make Los Angeles my new home. I told him I was going to march right over to United Studios and take that job nailing up sets. I gave him a telephone number where he could reach me; though if he ever called it, he would be speaking to a fat man in an undershirt and a dirty kitchen apron at a coast diner who would only be interested in how he likes his eggs.

I left Grundy about noon. I counted on being at least one step ahead of the others who had recently put a price on my skin.

I know I should have taken the rented car back to the agency on Wilshire, but I had worn thin my welcome in the city of Angels and the sooner I gave the joint the needle the better my chances for remaining in relatively good health.

I headed north from Grundy's Used Automobiles, sniffed out highway 101 and put a lead foot to the throttle. My plan was to get to Bakersfield, where I would trade the car for a train ticket and safe passage back to Frisco.

It was stoplight driving for a couple of miles. I picked my way through Hollywood and Burbank until I made the junction of highway 99 which ran straight up to Bakersfield.

I turned on the car radio for some music to accompany me on the long journey. I started the dial at fifty-five and worked my way east. I picked up some crowd noises around ninety-three. At first I thought I had pulled in the Series, but I was wrong. I picked up a live broadcast of the Sinclair rally from Griffith Park. The candidate had just been introduced and was delivering his opening remarks.

The man did have a way with words. His style was unassuming and anti-bombastic in the epoch of bombast. The newspapers both pro and con agreed that he had great appeal and didn't chase after the masses like so many of the political hucksters. The masses, they said, chased after him. He always spoke plainly about the problems everyday people faced and just as plainly about his plan to end poverty in California.

I couldn't say that I supported him, or anybody. Some on the left called him a fascist, and although he did have a hint of Huey Long's populism running through his veins, I think they were wide of the mark. He was no Bolshevik either, as the Hearst syndicate claimed. I don't know where Upton Sinclair stood in the left–right ferris wheel but something about him was catching on and everybody in California knew it.

He came to a part in his speech that had immediate meaning for me. He was talking about the film industry's threatened pullout:

> That's the biggest piece of bunk in this entire campaign. They couldn't move if they wanted to. It would cost them too much. Their investment here is too great. Besides, think of what those big Florida mosquitoes would do to our film sirens. Why, one bite on the nose could be a $50,000 production loss.
>
> I might put the state into the moving picture business. If I do I'll ask Charlie Chaplin to run the show.

The crowd roared with delight. There were a few scattered boos, probably from the Committee's reconnaissance team. The spring in Sinclair's voice seemed to indicate that he was having a swell time running for governor. I wondered how much he knew about the extremists in the opposition's camp. The candidate went on to speak about the economics of poverty and his plan to turn things around. I turned the dial and looked for the fifth game of the Series, which by my watch was already twenty minutes old.

I tuned into a station at the far end of the dial that was carrying the hookup. I almost swallowed my tongue when I heard Ted Husing say, 'Two out in the bottom of the first. Ole Diz is throwing a lot of heat out there today. It's like yesterday's beaning never happened.'

How could that madman be pitching the day after he had nearly been granted a posthumous berth in the Hall of Fame? But he was out on the mound chucking for St Louis as if yesterday's concussion was no more than a teenage pimple. If past performances were any indicator, there was no way the Tigers would get to Dean, beaned noggin or no.

The only reason I didn't turn the game off and concentrate on matters more substantial was geography. I was driving through the heat of California's San Joaquin Valley. It was the hottest part of the day and I felt like a pan of just-baked hot cross buns. The mirages all had little mirages. Blue lakes dotted the middle of the road at every horizon. And the tinder dry staw-colored hills did a hula dance to the undulating waves of heat you could hold in your hand. Listening to the ball game made me think of green outfields. The memory of green outfields brought on thoughts of cool grass, cool dirt, cool worms. It helped a little.

I pulled into the dust-choked, oil-smelly road apple they call Bakersfield around 7 p.m. The Tigers surprised everybody, including me, by touching Dean for three runs while Bridges stopped the Cards with one. Gehringer's homer in the sixth was the difference. The Detroits had a three game to two lead and that made me happy. The irascible sun had pulled in its fangs for another day and that, too, pleased me. I made a beeline for the train station as soon as I crossed the city limits.

I parked the rented crate in the depot lot and placed the keys between the sun visor and the roof. I made a mental note to call the rental agency first thing in the morning and tell them where to pick up their car.

I bought a ticket for the next through train to San Francisco. I had a two-hour wait. I grabbed a couple of cheese sandwiches and some station coffee. A half dozen smokes helped kill the time. I found a copy of the *Telegram* someone had left on a bench in the waiting room. I scanned the local news stories, looking for myself. Section 2, page 2 – there I was – a ten-inch story. Not bad. The twenty-four point headline read – 'Movie Shoe Shine Man Murdered'.

It was a standard piece of sensationalism filled with blood-chilling particulars. The article made sure nobody missed the fact that the body was discovered 'in the room of Riley Kovachs, a private investigator from San Francisco'. There was more.

> Kovachs is currently a fugitive from an arrest warrant issued last Friday by the District Attorney's office in San Francisco. Police there are seeking Kovachs in connection with the 2 October killing of Ira Blodgett, a local dock worker.

> Los Angeles police Lt Joseph Huckleby, who received an anonymous telephone call leading police to the motel where Mr Rizonetti's body was found, said, 'There doesn't seem to be a connection between the two murders at this time, but we aren't ruling out anything.' Lt Huckleby also stated to reporters that 'a dragnet has been laid out in Los Angeles County' in an attempt to apprehend the fugitive Kovachs. He warns citizens to be on the alert for him and to report any suspicious looking characters to local authorities.
>
> 'Do not try to apprehend this man by yourself,' the Lt cautioned. 'He is assumed armed and should be considered dangerous.'

A small mug shot of yours truly accompanied the article. I was lucky; it was a bad likeness. On the other hand, the *Telegram* had done everything short of rounding up a posse to come riding after me. Despite the words of caution from the lieutenant, I don't think he, Chandler Lane or their respective colleagues would have been too terribly disappointed if some John Doe cut me down with a face full of buckshot. I just hoped that not too many of the good people of Bakersfield took the Los Angeles *Telegram*.

It was dark when I boarded the train. It was almost an hour late and that made me a bit jumpy. My imagination had me believing that everyone on the train was sizing me up and the conductor had already been called ahead to Delano where the police would be waiting to nab me. Scenes from *I Was a Fugitive From a Chain Gang* kept running through my mind.

The train loaded its passengers at 9.10. Fifteen minutes later it was chugging into the night. I went to the club car where I had two very quick and much needed whiskeys and ice. I returned to my seat and tried to think about sheep. A man across the aisle who was traveling to San Francisco promised to nudge me when we got to San Jose. I planned to get at Palo Alto just to play it safe.

I pulled my hat over my eyes for a couple of reasons and began counting lamb chops. The train hooted through the valley. I stopped with the arithmetic at two thousand and slept until the man pulled on my coat ten hours later.

23.

I stepped off the train at 7.30. A pleasant little fog crawled into my pores, reminding me I was back in the Bay Area. After coffee and a sinker at the station, I called Steve Busby in San Francisco and pleaded with him to come to Palo Alto and pick me up. He argued against the idea, saying he would have to miss work. I told him I would make it up to him, though I didn't say how. I was desperate. He agreed after a great deal of persuading. He told me to give him an hour or so to get ready and drive the thirty miles. I couldn't complain.

I called the car rental agency and told them about their car and were they sore. Then I walked over to the Stanford campus to do some nosing around.

The fall term had just begun and even at eight in the morning the place was a beehive of cute coeds all looking like Jean Harlow and grouping about the elbows of blond Apollos wearing red 'S' sweaters. I don't know when I've seen so many well scrubbed and groomed people in one place. I wondered if anybody had the nerve to tell them about some of their fellow citizens who weren't doing as well; like those who hang around rear doors to restaurants waiting for the cook to toss out the day's garbage so they can shop for their dinner. I doubt even if they knew they would understand what it means. Stanford is a place to escape reality, responsibility and the present.

There were others walking the campus. Real students, the kind that lug thirty-pound satchels stuffed with books and pack lunches, the latter to be eaten between pages of some tome in a dark and dusty recess of the library stacks.

Stanford is a big beautiful hunk of real estate masterfully landscaped with low Spanish style architecture and thousands of aromatic eucalyptus trees. Standing outside the library I felt very far away from murder and political skullduggery. Yet, most people knew that Stanford was not exactly a garden of priestly virtue. More than a couple of government and industry's major-domos who were on the take, gouging prices or plundering the national resources, once walked these hallowed grounds and cheered the Indians to victory in the 'Big Game'. McArthur Digges Mason, for one, matriculated from Leland Stanford's 'Farm'.

I walked through the portals of the library and into the main reading room of the first floor. I picked out a book called *Prominent California Families*. I thought I might like to know something about the big shots who were causing me to spend more time in the shadows than Paul Muni.

I started at the top with Chandler Lane. Unlike so many of California's moneybags, Lane's antecedents did not come here during the gold rush. In fact, they didn't come to California at all. It was actually his wife's family that came west in 1849 and struck it rich. Mrs Lane's granddaddy was no miner either. He made his loot speculating in flour and eggs and eventually branched out, controlling nearly all the food and its distribution in the Mother Lode. When the big veins ran dry, granddaddy pulled out of Sacramento with a trainload of boodle and moved south, where he bought desert land and started up a newspaper.

He was quite a hit with the railroad tycoons and wheat barons for his outspoken opposition to labor unions and his vigorous support of open immigration for Orientals. By the time he died he owned a third of Los Angeles County.

The newspaper passed to his son in 1883 when the old man croaked. But junior wasn't cut from the same pioneer cloth and the paper went into decline. The son was more interested in land and its speculation and raked in one of the great fortunes in California history.

He bought quantities of land in the San Joaquin Valley where he planted grain. He then sold some of his acreage to the railroads at top dollar, while at the same time being compensated by the government for lost production. Next, he drove the price of wheat through the roof by withholding it from the market and storing it free in railroad warehouses which sat on land he once owned.

This was in 1893 when the country was in a deep Depression.

The author of *Prominent Families* quoted the newspapers of the day which said junior's eventual sale of the wheat was 'an act of great human compassion' as it 'alleviated the suffering of millions who were starving from lack of bread and grain products'. It helped in getting good press if you owned a newspaper.

To make a long story short, the exploits of Mrs Lane's father caught the fancy of the young Chandler Lane, who was working as a $25-a-week bank clerk in Philadelphia. One day in 1901, Lane packed his toothbrush and an extra shirt and headed west to meet the great man he had read about. Lane went to work on the newspaper and the grain speculator's daughter at about the same time. Within eighteen months he had risen to assistant editor with the newspaper and husband to the daughter. The rest, as they say, is history.

The bio on Lane was about as flattering as facial hair on a beauty contestant. But then the book wasn't published by the LA *Telegram* or the Hearst syndicate. It was clear to all who read it that Chandler Lane was initially a cheap gold digger on the make. You had to read the chapter carefully to learn that he was also a philanderer.

When he left his $25-a-week job in Philly it seems that was not all he left. There was a Mrs Lane and she had seven months' worth of child in her stomach at the time. It was only a single sentence and was buried beneath the more important details of Lane's rise to power.

I closed the book and stared up at the library's high-arched ceiling. I spent a few more minutes tapping the cover of the book with my index finger, trying to release an idea, before I was abruptly lifted out of my concentration by the sound of chairs being scraped along the reading room floor. It was time for classes to change. I looked down at my watch. It was 9 o'clock. If Steve Busby was on time he would just be getting to the station, and I couldn't morally afford to be late. I raced out of the library, through the campus, across El Camino and on to the depot.

Steve was out front. His motor was running and he looked unhappy. I apologized for being late. He grumbled something about the time and started for the Bayshore Highway.

I stopped him before we reached the first corner. He yelled at me, but I ignored his protests and dashed from the car back to the station and up to the Western Union desk. I sent two cables to Los Angeles and a dozen-word wire to Philadelphia. I gave Steve's address for the replies.

On the way back to the city, I told him some of the things that had happened the past six days. We had been friends for a long time and I thought I owed him that much. He shook his head, whistled and oohed at points where a murder took place or a kluxer popped up. After that he didn't grumble any more.

I spent the rest of the trip enjoying the scenery. Somewhere near Redwood City I laid my eyes on a small colorful stand of orange flowers growing on the side of a hill next to the highway. Although it was late in the season I knew them to be *mimulus longiflorus* – sticky monkey flower in the vernacular.

Steve dropped me off downtown on Market near the Sinclair headquarters. I was indebted to him for his favor. It's awkward when friends thank each other. It has always made me feel uncomfortable whether I was the helper or the helped. But true to form, I found myself stacking thank yous on him like they were Aunt Jemima's flapjacks. I told him I would call about the cables before the day was out and he told me to be careful. I slid out the door and we said so long to each other.

The sidewalk near the campaign central was littered with paper. Most of it was the same size and shape and looked like it had recently taken up residence there. I fished one from near the curb. It was a handbill announcement of the Sinclair rally scheduled for the following evening.

I continued a half block through the morning foot traffic to the Sinclair office. Inside I observed more of a madhouse than the first time I called. Last-minute preparations for the rally gave the place the frantic appearance of two hundred people fleeing a bomb. I doubted there was much chance of finding Dexter Hall in the reigning turbulence, but I tried the receptionist again.

'Honey,' I roared above the din, hoping to catch her ear, 'you got a customer.'

She jumped in her seat. Then she became testy.

'Just a moment, sir! I can only do one thing at a time.' She pulled and threw half a dozen more phone plugs before pausing and looking up at me. She smiled faintly. 'Now, what can I do for you, sir?'

'I'm here to see Dexter Hall and no, I don't have an appointment.'

She got superior with me. 'Well, then, I'm afraid it will be impossible to see Mr Hall, *especially* today!'

The way she said 'especially today' was to make me feel like I had just asked the Lindberghs how their children were. I cut her off without being angry.

'No lectures, doll, just tell him Mr Kovachs is here. I think he will want to see me.'

The receptionist did a double take, almost losing her headset.

'Riley Kovachs?' she shrieked.

'*The* Riley Kovachs,' I corrected.

'Oh, I am terribly sorry, Mr Kovachs, I didn't know.'

'That's all right, I've been this way for years.'

'No, I mean for being so rude to you. Mr Hall has been trying to reach you for the past two days.'

'So have a lot of other people, if you keep up with the funny papers.'

She ignored my comment. Maybe she wasn't a reader.

'Mr Hall left instructions for you to call him at this number the moment you walked in.'

She gave me a slip of paper with Dexter hall's phone number written on it. I tipped my hat and smiled.

'Thanks, doll. Keep up the good work. Sinclair needs people like you.'

I pushed my way through a small pride of young campaign workers coming through the door. I walked over to the Bay City Grill on Turk to make my phone call in private. I knew the owners and could count on using their personal line.

I pushed by the narrow glass door and went to the counter where I parked everything on a red vinyl stool. Mrs Bolde was taking short orders. Hagen, her husband, was shoveling the hash. She spotted me and began casually working her way in my direction, pouring coffee in every customer's cup as she went. She got to me, turned up the cup in front of me and started filling it slowly.

'Riley,' she whispered, 'what are you doing here? The papers say the cops are looking for you.'

'You mean it isn't just a bad dream?' I smiled. 'Helvitica, I need to use your back room for a couple of hours. I'll understand if you'd rather not.'

Mrs Bolde, a rotund Nordic matron with faded yellow hair wound tightly on the top of her head, was pure gold.

'Sure, Riley. Why don't you take your coffee and go in right now. I'll bring you some ham and eggs when I get a minute.'

'Thanks, doll, you've saved what's left of my hide.'

She was embarrassed and turned the color of a Rome Beauty apple. Come to think of it, she looked a little like one, too.

'Gowan with you,' she said, going back down the counter, refilling cups as she went. She spoke briefly to Hagen, probably informing him of their fugitive guest.

I picked up my cup and slipped into the back room which was behind the toilet. I went immediately to the phone and dialed Hall's number. It rang four or five times before someone picked it up.

'I want to talk to Dexter Hall,' I said.

A cautious voice which I recognized replied, 'Who is this?'

'Hall, this is Kovachs. We've got to talk.'

'Good God, man, what happened to you? I read in today's paper the police in LA want you for murder.'

'Forget that for the time being. We need to talk, but not over the phone. Where can I meet you?'

Hall hesitated. There was, to be sure, a lot on his mind.

'You can't. Not now anyway. If I met you and anyone found out, I could be considered aiding and abetting. Do you realize what that would do to the campaign?'

'If you don't talk to me and I mean right now, you won't have to worry about the election because there may not be one.'

'Make sense, Kovachs.'

'Not over the phone, old buddy. What I have to say takes a face-to-face. A lot happened in LA. I learned some things about your boy Jackson Berg that I think you'll want to know. And that's just the tip of a very large iceberg, if you'll allow the pun.'

'What about Lana?' he asked.

'Actually, I was hoping you could tell me.'

I heard a long sigh coming from the other end of the line. I imagined Dexter Hall had been sighing quite a lot during the last several days. Two or three deep breaths later, he began seeing things my way. He was obviously reluctant to see me, but knew he didn't have another choice in the matter. His enthusiasm matched that of a young boy making his own dental appointment.

'Very well, but we can't meet here.'

He wasn't home, that much I knew. The number was different from the one he had given me the first time we met. I didn't ask him where 'here' was.

'I have a friend up on Russian Hill,' he offered. 'We can meet at his place.'

'Meaning no disrespect to you, Hall, I prefer we meet out in the open. My health demands it. Too many unpleasant things happen to me in hotels and other people's houses.'

Hall didn't go for the idea.

'Are you out of your mind? I can't be seen with you in public. I'm taking a great enough risk seeing you at all.'

'I didn't intend for us to be holding hands on the steps of City Hall. I know a place, an outside place, where no one will see us.'

'I must be insane. Where?'

'Bay View Park.'

'Bay View Park? Where in the world is that?'

'Just hang in there a little longer, Hall, I'm going to tell you. It's out off Third Street – in Hunter's Point – near Candlestick Point.' I followed with precise directions and made sure he wrote them down so there wouldn't be any slip ups. 'I'll meet you on the road at the top of the hill. It's a small loop road so you shouldn't have a problem.'

I didn't see it, but I could tell Dexter Hall was shaking his head, trying to figure a way out of this. I didn't help him.

'You've got too much at stake to stand me up, Hall. In ninety minutes.'

'All right,' he sighed, and clicked our connection dead.

I returned the receiver to its proper place and walked back into the diner. Helvitica was ringing up a bill at the cash register. Hagen was turning hotcakes on the grill. I walked past Mrs Bolde on my way to the front door.

'No time for eggs, sweetheart, but keep a pot of your best grounds warm. I just might be back before you close.'

She gave me half of her attention and smiled. She looked puzzled, but said, 'yah, yah, yah', while counting out change to a paying customer. It was a few minutes past eleven. Once again I took my chances on the street. I headed down Seventh to where it crossed Third.

24.

The bus ride was longer than I remembered. The docks were busy. I could study them all the way from China Basin past Army Street and out to Hunter's Point. If I didn't know better, I would say prosperity had arrived. But then one can't tell a whole lot about the economy from the back of a Muni bus. Just appearances.

I got off at Jamestown, just before Third swings to the right and becomes the Bayshore, and walked over to Key. From there I began the ascent of the narrow asphalt road that climbs for a third of a mile to Bay View Park.

I puffed up the steep incline, all the while being reminded that I was a smoker of cigarettes in a way I'll probably never forget. I reached the top, or rather the loop road, after fifteen minutes. I sat down on a guard-rail post to catch my lost breath. It took a while.

It had been several months since I had visited the newest park in the city's system. I remembered last May being treated to small stands of Clarkia and Farewell-to-Spring hugging the loose soil of its delicate slopes. I used to go there before it was a park. Then it had been only a rugged windblown wilderness covered by the trees John McLaren had planted before the war. I would go there regularly during fatter and quieter times when I studied geology and botany on my own just because I wanted to.

On a clear day the view from the 600-foot high outcrop of naturally polished Franciscan sandstone was 50 miles in all directions. Sometimes I lugged my geology books up its slopes and tried to come to terms with the Bay Area's antideluvian past.

The day was clear and crisp. I walked along the loop road for a quarter of a mile – Hall wouldn't show up for fifteen minutes at least – and turned my peepers on my favorite view – the southern panorama. From a spot near the edge of the little meadow, the only open and flat space on the entire hill, I could forget murder, political corruption and arrest warrants for a few moments.

Stretched out before me were two old friends – the Bay and San Bruno Mountain. The Bay was as soft and quiet as I had ever seen it. Almost asleep. The sun danced on its surface. An immense blue diamond with a hundred thousand facets.

Climbing out of the water on its western shore was San Bruno Mountain. It rises quickly from the mud to about 1,200 feet and becomes a rippling ridge, wriggling west toward Daly City. It commands the southern skyline and I am thankful for it. Its fuzzy brown cover was a place to go and be alone, and many times I had done just that. From where I stood I could see several of the trails above the little town of Brisbane that I had climbed when I stalked wildflowers instead of killers. But those days were gone.

I walked back to the beginning of the loop road and waited for Hall. The odor of eucalyptus and fennel made everything seem worthwhile.

The park was virtually deserted, as it is most of the time. Maybe it is too far out of the way or too small, but for some reason few people visit Bay View Park. A couple of young lovers passed me, but they didn't see anything but each other. The three of us made up the park's human population.

Ten minutes later Hall's car hesitated up the hill. He pulled alongside me. He was upset. I could tell he wished he were somewhere else. He parked his car and eased himself out and came over to me.

'Mr Kovachs, is there a tree where we can go?'

'Lots of trees.' I gestured, pointing to the obvious.

'I mean where we can talk – out of the way. God, Kovachs, this is dangerous. If the opposition were onto this, it would just about finish us.'

He spoke in short, quick chops like the kind I had been taking on the back of my neck. His eyes darted from side to side. I tried to calm him, but that was like trying to get the rain to fall up.

I pointed south and told him we could find seclusion there. Again I tried to get Hall to relax. He was beginning to make me feel uncomfortable – that is, more uncomfortable than I already felt.

'Three weeks from Wednesday,' Hall declared belligerently, 'that's when I'll relax. This ordeal will be over and we'll be on our way to Sacramento. But until then it's twenty-four hours of nerve-wracking hell each and every day. I don't expect you to know that or care very much, but I've been drinking so much coffee the last forty-eight hours I feel I could run all the way to Oakland without getting my feet wet. Everything, the coffee, the rally, and now you have got me wired up like a telegraph office. I'm ready to pop my cork, I really am.'

I think he was, too, and what I had to tell him wouldn't help him keep it in the bottle. But I had to take charge.

'You're going to have to pull yourself together, man. There's still a month to go before the election, and believe me, the worst is in front of you. And here it is. As you suspect, I don't give a damn for your political career or anybody else's for that matter – Sinclair's included. But I don't like dirty politics, the kind where innocent people get bumped off by brown shirts, black shirts, white sheets, or any other slack-jawed bozos running wild in this state. To put it politely, my sensibilities become offended. Put another way, it makes me retch.'

Hall was disoriented. Disbelief was written in every line of his face. He seemed almost reluctant to listen to what I had to say. But he was a politician, and I knew he would demand every crummy detail, however unpleasant.

'Once again, Mr Kovachs, I find it difficult to get your meaning. Could you explain to me in English just what it is you are driving at?'

I did just that. I told him about Moody Pugh and Cal Grundy

and the swamp they presided over under the cover of a fraudulent real estate company. I told him their idea of fun was to beat up trade unionists and pinkos, and that they weren't too fond of Sinclair people either. I informed him of my meeting with Chaplin and learning about the phony newsreels and extortion campaign Jackson Berg was running. I told him of the Committee's meeting the previous evening and their guest speaker. And by way of conclusion I pointed out that we wouldn't need a bloodhound to find both Berg and Chandler Lane with highly concealed, but nevertheless direct links to the Committee.

I stopped there and allowed Hall to let it sink in. He looked flabbergasted. He sat across from me with glazed eyes for a time, trying to sort and catalogue what he had just heard. Then he cleared his throat and began forming words.

'If what you are saying is true – and I don't mean to doubt you for a minute – if what you say is true, then it's a brand new ball game.' His eyes went into orbit, contemplating the possibilities. 'I mean we can expose them and cut their legs right out from under them. The Klan, Nazis, why the American people won't stand for it. We've got to get to the papers! We've got to go to the police!'

Dexter Hall floated out across the Bay with a flock of cumulus clouds. I tried to reel him back to earth.

'Who's going to print this story?' I said. 'Hearst? Lane? It wouldn't make the comics, not with your only sources being me and two dead men. Take it to the cops? Same story. Ed Simmons? The man who would drown cats if he knew their tongues were pink. More red propaganda, that's what it would mean to him. That and maybe giving him the excuse to make raids on your organization to root out the fellow travelers.

'The same applies to the bulls in this town. They bloodied some people pretty badly just for wanting to have their own hiring hall. What do you think they're going to do if you go to them with a story about a plot to take the election away from the one politician who is for giving the longshoremen what they want? Hell, they might just run out and join Grundy's outfit themselves. That is if they haven't done so already.

'No, Hall, there aren't too damn many places you can take this and hope to get results.'

Dexter Hall searched his political intellect, looking for an angle. He must have gathered up and snapped twenty eucalyptus leaves to assist his pondering. I got up and walked a few yards to a clearing that returned me to the southern skyline. I doted on San Bruno Mountain for a few minutes and watched a kestrel riding the air currents scanning the ground for his lunch. Somewhere in Visitacion Valley a dog was barking. I walked back to Hall. He had an idea.

'We've got to go to the President,' he said pounding his fist into a palm.

'Roosevelt?'

'Of course, Roosevelt, who did you think I meant?'

I didn't say anything. He went on.

'Mr Sinclair met with him last week at Hyde Park. We believe the President is planning to come out and publicly endorse him before election day. In fact, just a few days ago Mr Sinclair received a very positive letter from Mrs Roosevelt.'

I threw a bucket of water on his fire.

'Suppose FDR buys the whole package. What can you expect him to do about it? If he does anything he runs the risk of laying himself open to a charge of tampering with a state election. The opposition would love it.

'Let's suppose he doesn't jump in directly, but proposes a Congressional investigation. First, it would probably take until the governor's second term came up before it would be completed, and second, he'd be up against Mason, Lane and Berg and all the weapons they possess. Do you suppose that with Mason's influence in the Congress and Berg and Lane's domination of the media that even a President-initiated investigation would get very far?'

Hall's lungs collapsed with disappointment. I wasn't through.

'That's your negative argument. Now for the other side. You don't have anywhere else to go. Hell, man, you can give it a chance. There must be an honest politician somewhere in this land. If there isn't, well, who knows, in forty years some college kid will stumble across the election of 1934 while doing a master's thesis on 'The

Integrity of Political Institutions in the 1930s – A Decade of Drought'. It will probably even make the headlines in the big eastern newspapers. People will be so shocked and ashamed that something like this was allowed to happen in a country they all love so dearly. The newspapers will decry it, politicians will stand up in Washington and Sacramento and denounce the past, but most of all people will be persuaded to forget it. "That was then and this is now," the pundits will say. They will talk about it as our Dark Ages the way we talk about the robber barons today. It will become nostalgia. "It can't happen today because it's already happened and we're far too enlightened to ever let it happen again." Then everybody will be told to go back to sleep and forget the whole damn thing.'

'That's the positive?' Hall said, knocking me from my soap box.

'Yeah,' I said backtracking, 'maybe some good can come from taking this to Washington. What do I know? But you and I have a problem that's even more pressing.'

Hall looked puzzled again. Then I dropped the main course in his lap.

'Pitts Langley, a little man who traded his life to give me some information, told me that the ninth of October is a date the Committee has circled on its calendar. It's the day they have planned some special activities probably designed to give you Sinclair people some second thoughts about the campaign. All anybody knows so far is the date. Four people outside the Committee know about this date and two of them are dead.'

Hall swallowed his Adam's apple, 'And the other two?'

'Sitting under a blue gum tree in Bay View Park at this very moment.'

He gulped audibly.

'Maybe the punks are just planning to celebrate Columbus Day a little early,' I said, 'but I think we would be closer to the mark if we believed it had something to do with tomorrow's rally.'

Hall must have made the connection the moment he heard the date, but until the possible scenario was verbalized for him, he just sat there staring dumbly at his shoes. Then beads of sweat popped out on his forehead. I could detect a mild hysteria welling inside him, but he kept his presence of mind, such as it was.

'What can we do, Kovachs? We can't cancel the rally. We've got to go to the police!'

'I'm telling you to forget the police. We've got to concentrate on tomorrow and what may happen. We have to find out what is going to come off. When we know that, we might be able to nip it before it turns ugly. And this is where I need some information from you.'

'Me? What sort of information could I possibly have?' he snapped.

I couldn't tell if he was angry or just surprised.

'Where is Lana Birdwell?'

'You don't think Lana's mixed up in this, do you?'

'Everybody is mixed up in everything. I start with that. When was the last time you heard from her?'

'Really, Mr Kovachs, I don't see how Lana fits into this.'

'You're not supposed to. That's my job and I can't do my job if you don't help me. She may know something about Ira Blodgett's death. Don't forget he was bumped off for knowing just that much more than we do.'

I held my forefinger an inch from my thumb to illustrate the point.

Dexter Hall stood up and sat back down again before he found the words to speak.

'I've been very busy as you might guess, what with the rally and all. I've been working eighteen to twenty hours a day. Well, I didn't hear from Lana until Sunday. She called late, around 1 a.m. She sounded strange again like the time before. I tried to talk about us – our relationship – but she wanted to know about you. She asked me if you had gone to Los Angeles. I told her I hadn't the faintest idea. I guess I was pretty rude to her. Anyway she got angry and accused me of lying. Me!

'I reconstructed the conversation you and I had Friday and gave her the message you told me to give her – you know, about Jackson Berg and Antelope Investments. She got very nasty and became abusive. Then she hung up on me. I don't know what's got into her, Mr Kovachs. What is going on? Please tell me!'

'I wish I knew. I wish I could. Things would be a lot simpler, wouldn't they? Maybe she doesn't know anything and maybe she's just a confused dame trying to get along in the big league, like she says. On the other hand, she knew Ira Blodgett and was in his room the night he was killed. She arranged for the Committee to kidnap me and do unnatural things to my body and she has lied to both of us more times than I care to count.'

Still the gentleman, Hall rushed to her defense, but I could sense he had other things on his mind.

'I know it doesn't look good for her, but I think she must have very good reasons for what she has done. Perhaps she is in some deep trouble and needs help.'

'Don't think I haven't thought of that angle myself. This may come as a surprise to you, Hall, but I like Lana Birdwell and I wouldn't want to see her get into something she doesn't deserve.'

Hall's eyes dilated. 'You don't think they would murder her, do you?'

'They are capable of anything. My concern is that Lana Birdwell isn't a "they".'

I leaned on Hall for some more about the slippery femme, but he didn't have much. He told me that, when he insisted upon seeing her, she said she would be out of town for a few days. More than that, nothing.

Hall agreed with me that the executive leadership directing Sinclair's campaign in San Francisco should be the only people in the organization to share the information I had given him until it could be determined what, if anything, the Committee had planned for the rally. Though time was growing short, it was important that at least the leaders be prepared for any contingency.

Hall also thought he should try to feel out the White House through some of his contacts and see if it would respond to what we had. I didn't think it could do any harm.

The rally was only thirty-two hours away; Lana Birdwell was out of town; the cops were surely staking out my office and flat waiting to make a pinch, and I still didn't have a lead on what the Committee had cooked up for the ninth. But I did know where to look. I only hoped there was time.

Dexter Hall walked back to his car alone. I told him to make himself available to me at all times in case I should turn up anything. He got into his car and a moment later rounded the curve in the loop road and disappeared from view. I returned to the meadow and stared out on the southern skyline before going back to solve murders and insidious plots.

25.

The world for me during the next several hours was the back room of Hagen and Helvitica Bolde's diner. I returned there about 2 p.m. to make more calls. Hagen brought in a radio so I could listen to what was left of the sixth game of the Series.

It was a 'white knuckler' as the sports writers would say. St Louis hung on for the victory – 4 to 3. What bothered me more than the loss was Durocher. That little, wise-mouthed *kaposzta*. I liked him about as much as a plate of liver and onions. I wasn't the only one either. He has whole cities full of detractors. He had only two hits in the first five games. Couldn't have happened to a nicer guy and all that. Then – down the stretch – he gets three key hits and scores a pair of runs to beat the Tigers. Detroit could now be added to the list of towns whose fans would like to see 'the Lip' smeared with honey and tied to a small tree in grizzly country. With the win the Cards tied the Series at three games apiece. I found a touch of irony in the fact that the decisive game was to be played on 9 October.

I called the number Lana Birdwell gave me the night we nearly divided my pajamas. I didn't expect anyone to be there. I wasn't disappointed.

Next I called Father Windy's mission and was told that the backwater Barrymore in black cloth had gone to LA and wasn't due to return until evening or early the next morning.

My last nickel went to Harry Bridges. I wanted to see Tom Mooney. I had a fifteen-minute go-around with one of Bridges' associates, trying to make an appointment to see the president of the longshoremen. The man was suspicious of me and I couldn't blame him, considering what those boys had been through. But I hit for extra bases when I mentioned the names of Blodgett, Windy and Chaplin. I dropped Hall's name, too. The man said he would check me out and call back in a half hour.

It was almost an hour before he phoned. He said Bridges would meet me at 4.30 at the union headquarters. I felt I had to warn him that the cops were looking for me and it might be risky for anyone seen with me.

'Hell,' he laughed, 'just being a working stiff in this town is a risky business these days. Four-thirty. Harry'll be waiting for you.'

He hung up. I liked his attitude. A hundred thousand men like him and you could turn things around in this country in a very big hurry.

It was 3.15 when I finished with the phone. Mrs Bolde brought me a plate of Swedish meatballs, a cup of coffee and the afternoon *Examiner*. Those meatballs were a gift from heaven itself – tender, juicy and just the right amount of spices. The right ones, too.

I scanned page one while shoveling the delicious nutriment past my teeth. The world seemed to be caught up in the flames of revolution and it was only 1934. Civil insurrection had broken out in Spain and Catalonia had declared its independence. Another article trumpeted that Leon Trotsky was expected to arrive secretly in the US sometime during the next week. And if that weren't enough to start another run on the banks, there was news of a general strike in Havana. So much for the Platt Amendment.

But I wasn't in the mood to analyze the international situation. I left that job to Gabriel Heater and Woody Broun for the moment. I was hoping to find something else.

On page six, beside the story about the killing of a soldier at the Presidio, was an article about Blinky and me. It was a virtual reprint from the *Telegram*. Nothing new.

I was killing time browsing through the rest of the sheet when I came across a little four-inch story that made me forget about the Swedish meatballs. 'Mooney Ill' the headline read:

Early this morning prison guards found Tom Mooney lying unconscious on the floor of his cell. The former San Francisco socialist and labor leader, convicted for the 1916 Preparedness Day bombing in San Francisco in which twenty-three people were killed, was taken to the prison hospital where he spent the night.

Prison doctors said he was suffering from a mild case of food poisoning.

It is not believed that Mooney is ill enough to warrant his transfer to a hospital outside the prison.

Warden B.W. 'Big Ben' Hogue dismissed the seriousness of Mooney's condition.

'Tom just got hold of some bad food, that's all,' he told reporters.

Everybody knows how bad the slop in the joint is, but it was just too much of a coincidence to believe that Mooney had eaten a bowl of moldy oatmeal.

I ripped the article from the paper and stuck it into my coat pocket. It was nearing 4 o'clock. I gathered up my dishes and put them in the sink near the rear door. I put a match to a Chesterfield and walked out the door into the alley behind the diner and headed for the Embarcadero.

26.

It wasn't a short walk and I could have taken the bus, but I preferred to walk. Even the specter of cops on street corners holding up my mug shot next to the face of every passing male didn't deter me. It took twenty minutes to reach the Embarcadero.

It is a different world down on the docks. The waterfront begins at the foot of Market and runs like a bent horseshoe for seven miles – from Fisherman's Wharf to Hunter's Point. There were forty-three cargo piers at last count.

The Embarcadero is the waterfront's main thoroughfare. A broad cobblestone boulevard with tracks of the state-owned Belt Line Railroad running down one side, it stretches from Aquatic Park in Fisherman's Wharf to Berry where it continues south as Third Street. It is a perpetual hiss and clang of locomotives tugging an endless number of freight cars loaded with sweat and cargo for and from ocean-going ships. Teamsters in big rigs rumble across the cobblestone competing for the abundant freight. Longshoremen, scalers, warehousemen, sailors, pedestrians and tourists straying from Fisherman's Wharf swarm about the thick forest of steam and gas driven transports.

Across the Embarcadero – which is wide as the Russian River in spots – on the side opposite the piers, is a long row of ramshackle buildings. Those that still have paint are faded or peeling badly. There are pool halls, cafeterias, saloons, tattoo parlors, cheap hotels and cigar stores where men talk politics, the union, lottery tickets and the ponies. Behind are the financial districts' skyscrapers, topped with flashy electrical signs that lie about prosperity. They dwarf the waterfront slum and serve as a nasty reminder that wealth has its privileges.

I walked into the ILA headquarters on Steuart Street. It and Father Windy's mission had the same architect. The offices in the back looked smaller, but other than that, there wasn't much difference. The outer area of the single-floor building was a large hall. Several dozen white caps were milling about smoking cigarettes and talking among themselves. Some others were sitting on benches reading newspapers. Neither the floor nor the walls seemed aware that paint had been invented years ago. However, the walls were decorated with posters, hand bills, picket signs and other memorabilia from the big strike. It was a museum of contemporary history.

I went up to the window at the back of the hall and announced myself. The man behind the glass told me Bridges was in a meeting and would see me when he was finished.

I started up a smoke and decided to give myself a tour of the walls. I began with several front pages from city dailies. Their ninety-six-point type headlines would have chilled the bones of even the most stout-hearted citizens. 'Seventeen Maimed in Red

Battle' said the *Examiner*. 'Communist Army Marching On City', hooted the *Call-Bulletin*, not wishing to be outdone.

I moved on to the pictures. There were a hundred or more photographs hanging on the wide gray walls. One was taken from a skyscraper or maybe Coit Tower. It showed a long snaking picket line of a thousand longshoremen stretched out for the better part of a mile.

Under a hand-made sign in large red letters reading 'Know Your Enemies' were two items. One was the text of a particularly provocative statement issued by the president of the Chamber of Commerce and published in the *Chronicle*.

> The San Francisco waterfront strike is out of hand. It is not a conflict between employer and employee – between labor and capital – it is a conflict which is rapidly spreading between American principles and unAmerican radicalism.
>
> The longshoremen are now represented by the spokesmen who are not representatives of American labor and who do not desire a settlement of their strike, but who desire a complete paralysis of shipping and industry and who are responsible for the violence and bloodshed which is typical of their tribe.

Next to it was a statement, a proclamation issued by the acting governor, whose sympathies during the strike were never in doubt.

> Among us is a horde of irresponsible, professional agitators, mostly aliens trafficking shamelessly in the agonies of these stressful times. They are seeking revolution, not reform; to make conditions worse, not better.
>
> These public enemies deliberately provoke demonstrations and incite alarms at a time when peace and civil tranquility are the supreme requisites in our battle for national recovery; a battle calling for all the energies of our people. Their alien creed of violence and sabotage strikes venomously at the heart of constitutional democracy.

With that kind of hate coming from such high places, it was a wonder anyone dared to support the longshoremen. But support them they did. I won't forget marching up Market Street, one of 40,000 mourners in the funeral procession of the two men slain on Bloody Thursday. That day – the day of the funeral – the longshoremen and the working class ruled the streets of San Francisco.

Forty thousand men and women from all trades and occupations marched slowly up the city's main stem like poured molasses. Nothing else moved on the streets. Hats were carried over breasts and those on the sidewalk who didn't abide were given stern warning. It was a show of strength, a demonstration of defiance, and it was a day when there was enough electricity in the air to light up every table lamp for fifty miles.

A finger tapped me on the shoulder.

'Harry'll see you now,' said a voice. 'Come this way.' I followed the man past the dispatcher's cage to an unmarked office door. 'He's in there,' the man pointed. 'Go on in.'

I entered without knocking. Bridges was with two other men. He was much younger than I expected. He looked to be in his early thirties. He rose from his chair to shake my hand as did the other men. Bridges was tall and unbelievably lean. His face was twice as long as it was wide. A prominent bony nose divided it. He introduced himself and the two men, who were members of the union's Executive Board.

Harry Bridges was a living legend or the devil incarnate, depending on who you talked to. He had risen from practically nowhere during the strike as a member of the Rank-and-File Committee to succesfully lead a challenge against Joe Ryan, president of the ILA and Bill Lewis, the west coast longshore boss. They had tried to push the men back to work without a hiring hall or any of the other things they were striking for.

Bridges was crucified in the press as a red and a foreigner. Ryan and Lewis used a lot of the same tricks to discredit him, but the longshoremen protected him physically as well as politically. Since the strike Harry Bridges has become bigger than life, winning the presidency of the local, and is now being treated by the government, the WMA and the AFL crust as one of the most powerful labor leaders of our time.

Evidently he hadn't read his own press clippings, for I saw none of the typical window dressing that accompanies so many of the AFL bosses today. Bridges is a working stiff just like the rest of the boys. He is one of them. And that is quite a novelty, given those bejeweled and tuxedoed craft leaders meeting uptown, who in recent decades have taken to hobnobbing with politicians and millionaires.

The man I talked with on the phone, the one introduced to me as Jimmy, told Bridges that I was working on Ira Blodgett's murder.

'This is the guy, Harry. He's got some pretty good recommendations. Father Windy and that guy Hall from the Sinclair campaign. Chaplin, too. They all say he's on the level.'

Bridges looked me over intently while Jimmy was running down my recent biography. When his colleague finished, the longshore leader spoke.

'Jimmy says you want to see Tom Mooney. How does that connect with brother Blodgett's murder?'

At first I didn't understand him – the words, not the question. He seemed to be speaking in a foreign tongue, one I felt I should know. But after his first half dozen utterances I began a successful simultaneous translation. It was then that I remembered Bridges was a native of Australia.

I told the whole story as economically as I could. Bridges stopped me at several points, insisting on detail. He wrote some of the things I said on a piece of paper. The other two men also asked me to elaborate here and there. Twenty minutes later I had completed the story. There was an overly long period of silence before anyone spoke. Bridges was first.

'You know,' he said scratching his chin, 'I thought we'd seen just about everything down here on the docks in the last two years. We've been threatened repeatedly, lied to and lied about, clubbed and gassed. They steal our labor from us and even our lives. Now they want to steal our elections!' His tone changed from one that suggested irony to outright wrath. 'These bloody capitalists will stop at nothing!' he accused, intiating a two-minute oration against the captains of industry that would have brought any gathering of class-conscious proletarians to its collective feet.

He paused a moment then asked, 'And you think Tom can tell you about the ninth?'

'I don't know that for sure, but Chaplin thinks Mooney knows a lot more about the underside of this campaign than he lets on. Maybe that's why somebody tried to poison him last night.'

The faces of the three men turned the color of jack cheese. They stared at me with disbelief and demanded I repeat myself and identify my sources. I pulled from my pocket the article I had ripped from the *Examiner*.

'It was in today's paper. A tiny filler buried on page ten. Says Mooney has a mild case of food poisoning. My guess is it is a strong case of something a lot more lethal. I could be wrong, but I don't think so. We've got to reach him before they finish the job.'

No one doubted that, if Mooney had indeed been poisoned, it would not be the last attempt on his life.

Bridges was the first to recover from the initial shock. In the flick of an eye the blood was pouring back into his cheeks.

'Jimmy, call Davis and tell him to be ready to go to Quentin in an hour; contact the *Worker* and tell them to hold the front page of the next issue, but don't tell them why. Frank, get a hold of Boyd at the *News* and tell him the same thing. Then start calling the members of the Executive Board and set up an emergency meeting for tonight. Do you think 9 p.m. is a good time? Talk it over with the others. I'll call the warden and insist we see Tom right away.'

It was that kind of decisiveness and efficiency that made Bridges and the longshoremen's union so formidable during their long struggle. The little office where the four of us were meeting had in a moment been energized and the great longshore machine was again in high gear. A sanguine Harry Bridges grabbed the telephone and began dialing. Jimmy and Frank left to carry out their assignments.

'That bloke better not give us any trouble,' Bridges crackled, referring to San Quentin's warden. He pointed to the back wall of the office. 'Get yourself a cup of coffee,' he said.

I walked over to a little table that had pots of both coffee and water sitting on a hot plate.

'And fetch me a cup of tea, will you, mate?'

For the next fifteen minutes I nibbled at a liquid that Maxwell wouldn't let in his house and listened as Bridges lectured the head jailer at Q. The warden was resistant to any suggestion that Mooney receive unscheduled visitors. The prisoner was in the hospital and wasn't to see anybody. But Bridges wasn't buying it.

'I don't care what your rules say,' he snarled into the receiver. 'We've got a court order that permits us to see Tom when anything relevant to his case develops . . . You better bloody well believe this is relevant to his case . . . Do you mean to tell me that you're willing to stand in violation of a court order? . . . I didn't think so. That's much better. We will be there no later than 7 p.m. Myself, Davis and a Mr Kovachs . . . He's with legal defense – from Chicago.' Bridges winked at me.

A minute later he terminated his conversation, if you could call it that. He rose from his chair smiling and began pacing the floor anxiously.

'We're in, mate. You just have to bully the warden a bit, that's all. Say, you've never met Tom have you? How much do you know about the case?'

'Not much. Just that he was sent up for a bombing about twenty years ago. I was only a school boy in Ohio then. It never got the play it did out here on the coast. I guess it was a pretty rotten thing.'

'As the hold of a slave ship!' Bridges added. 'Tom was the first victim of the red raids and this was even before the October Revolution in Russia. He was nailed to the cross because he was a socialist and a militant unionist and because San Francisco had a reputation as a union town.

'Every corrupt boss and politician from the trial prosecutor all the way to the governor fought to send Tom to prison. He's been in stir eighteen bloody years rotting for a crime he didn't commit so the ruling class could have its sacrificial lamb and teach the working class a lesson it wouldn't forget.'

Bridges went back to the phone as he talked. He dialed a

number and raised a hand to excuse himself as he spoke into the receiver.

Ten minutes and several calls later he had arranged for a launch to meet us at pier sixteen at 6 o'clock sharp to take us to the Marin county prison. Jimmy came into the room and informed us that Davis would meet us at union headquarters in forty-five minutes. He also said that he and Frank had contacted most of the Executive Board members and the meeting was set to go off at 9.00.

Bridges leaned forward, elbows on his desk, and continued talking about Mooney. It was not hard to tell it was one of his favorite subjects. He began the story of a legal conspiracy that caught and convicted San Francisco's socialist iron molder, but he stopped short. Without saying anything he reached into a desk drawer and pulled out a thick bound volume. He patted it knowingly.

'It's all right here, mate,' he said with a wide smile. 'The Wickersham Report. Hell!' he spit, rapping the tome with his fist, 'even the government says he was framed.'

He went on to explain that the Wickersham Commission had been appointed by Hoover a few years ago to study 'lawlessness in law enforcement'. Its sub-committee chose the Mooney–Billings trial as its primary case study. He said that the Commission report appeared two years ago, but the study of the Mooney–Billings case was missing.

Bridges sliced the air with a long sharp forefinger. 'It was suppressed, politically suppressed! And do you know why?'

The question was rhetorical.

He threw open another drawer and rifled through some papers, coming out with a small handful. He examined each one until he came up with the one he was looking for. He took it in his hand and read it out loud.

It was a statement by Senator Burton Wheeler in which he accused the Commission of suppressing its own report for the principal reasons that the President was a Californian and that 1932 was an election year and the report would prove embarrassing to him. Bridges put the paper aside and returned to the bound report.

'And listen to this. This is a summary of its conclusions.' He read verbatim from the Report.

Witnesses were coached in their testimony to a degree that approximated subornation of perjury. There is a strong inference that some of this coaching was done by prosecuting officials and after the trials, the disclosures casting doubt on the justice of the convictions were minimized, and every attempt made to defeat the liberation of the defendants, by a campaign of misrepresentations and propaganda carried on by the officials who had prosecuted them.

A lot of people in America felt Mooney had been railroaded – Billings, too. But their reasons for saying so differed greatly. Some saw it as a despicable outrage against justice while others believed it was the best thing that had happened to the mother country since the Haymarket hangings. Still, I was surprised that a government commission would put its official stamp on what everyone knew unofficially to be one of the classical frame-ups of the century.

Not only could such a report have embarrassed Hoover, but it could have destroyed the careers of some of the people responsible for putting Mooney in stripes. I wondered out loud.

'Who was the trial prosecutor?'

'A man named Charles Fickert,' Bridges answered.

Strike one.

'Who was the judge?'

'Griffin.'

Strike two.

'Well then, where was McArthur Digges Mason during all this?'

Bridges's eyes narrowed. He stared right through me. I hadn't mentioned Mason in my earlier rundown.

'Mason,' he repeated. 'He was there all right. Funny you should ask. As far as we know he didn't have official status with the prosecution. But we do know he headed a team of lawyers and eyes – pardon me, mate – private investigators. All this was on the sly. We know that this team coached, bribed and shook down witnesses to make an ironclad case against Mooney.

'In my opinion Mason was the architect of the whole bloody frame-up. Wickersham mentioned him and questions his activities, but the man was too slippery, too far behind the scenes to be linked with any foul play.'

I rubbed my nose and dug into my pocket for a Chesterfield. I went over in my mind what Bridges said about Mason. It was like I had tried to lay down a sacrifice bunt and ended up belting a double. I tried for the score.

'Harry, if I'm right, Mooney does know something. He may know without realizing what he knows. Let me ask you another question. I want to be sure this train is an express and makes no stops. Chandler Lane and Jackson Berg – were they involved in the Mooney case?'

Bridges had any number of names and facts at his fingertips and he didn't hesitate calling them up.

'The Wickersham Report is vague about them, too. But there was a strong criticism of the *Telegram* for its inflammatory editorials and biased reporting of the trial proceedings. There were rumors that Berg paid a large portion of the expenses for Mason's gang. The Defense Committee is checking on it right now. We think we can prove that Mason's people planted false news stories that were printed in the *Telegram*.

'You know, Kovachs, until this minute I didn't make any connections, but if you are thinking what I am thinking . . .'

'Could be dynamite if you'll allow a bad pun. These three men have a lot to lose in this election. If Sinclair wins, heads will roll. He will go after them. They must know that. That's probably why they seem ready to go to great lengths to prevent Sinclair from being elected. And that includes murder.'

Things were now beginning to make a whole lot more sense. It was like one of those flicker books the kids play with. Three murders, extremists on the prowl, fake newsreels, Tom Mooney and big shots with shady pasts – they didn't mean much separately, but when you thumbed them like a giant flicker book you got a very interesting story. It was still incomplete and some things were out of sequence, but the Mooney 'still' was the one that turned a baffling murder case into something I could bite into.

Sinclair had stated early in the campaign – I remember reading about it – that the first thing he would do as governor would be to pardon Tom Mooney. At the time I thought that was a pretty bold and foolish statement with which to kick off a campaign. The Mooney case was a first-rate hornets' nest that had plagued all of California's governors since the 1920s. The late 'Sunny Jim' Rolfe went to his grave with the pardon on his desk, too afraid to act.

When I heard Sinclair wanted to spring Mooney, I thought it was just a matter of old 'Uppie' trying to stir up some controversy and grab a few headlines. I don't think anyone could have realized the chain of events that statement must have touched off. It gave weight to my suspicions that Mooney's food poisoning was a little more than a belly ache.

It was fifteen minutes before 6 and time to go. Bridges and I talked as we walked across the Embarcadero to pier sixteen. Jimmy told us before we left that Davis – Mooney's lawyer – called to say he would meet us at the dock instead of the union hall.

The hot afternoon sun was hanging above a slim milky-white rope of fog that was being pulled through the Golden Gate. It was on its way to Oakland.

Both the launch and Davis were waiting when we arrived at the pier. Davis looked upset.

'What's going on, Harry? Jimmy wouldn't tell me anything.'

Bridges grabbed the lawyer by the shoulders.

'Tom's been poisoned.' Before Davis could react, Bridges qualified his statement. 'He's okay, as far as we know. I talked to the warden less than an hour ago. Tom's in the prison hospital, but he is all right.'

Davis's legs began to wobble and the color left his face. All he could manage to utter was an incredulous, 'My God!'

Bridges told me earlier about the young lawyer who had joined the Mooney defense just last year. He said he was a cracker-jack attorney with thirteen acquittals in fourteen murder cases to his credit. 'He believes in Tom's innocence with all his heart,' the longshore chief told me proudly.

Davis recovered sufficiently for Bridges to introduce us. He was still dazed but managed a weak smile as we shook hands. A moment later the three of us were in the launch cutting through the fog toward San Rafael.

The noise of the small motorboat was too great to allow a normal conversation. We passed the time studying one another. I wondered where we each would have been at that moment had there been no bomb explosion at that parade so long ago and if there had never been a Tom Mooney. But that was foolish. Every society must have its Tom Mooneys.

As the boat pulled farther out into the Bay, fighting against the swift ocean current, Telegraph Hill, Coit Tower and a dozen tall buildings poked through the fog. The sun was low in the western sky. In fact, it was not to be seen. Only a yellow-red glow lingered above the horizon. The tower and the tops of the skyscrapers were floating apparitions. The fog had obliterated everything for a hundred vertical feet. Chunks of concrete hung eerily in the sky, unrooted and moored like great airships by some invisible tether.

We passed Alcatraz. The tan walls of the prison fortress were patrolled by heavily armed guards. This was visible even from our considerable distance. It brought on literary memories of Devil's Island and Château d'If. I had no real notion what either of those two impregnable dungeons loked like, but if they existed at all, they could have been no more forbidding than the place they call 'The Rock'.

Sausalito and Tiburon were putting the wraps of a cool night around their fancy shoulders. Lights were flickering on in the sprawling Marin hills and valleys. Ten minutes later it was dark.

In the distance I saw a menacing beacon pouring light across the water of Richardson's Bay. It was Quentin's main searchlight. It threw daylight to all corners of the upper bay. Another five minutes and we could read matchbook covers. Davis leaned toward me, cupped his hands to his mouth and shouted in my ear.

'I've been here fifty times and the place still gives me the creeps.'

He didn't have to explain. I turned up the collar of my coat and clutched it around my neck. The real and imagined chill of Quentin could have frozen a tube of toothpaste. Bridges spread his arms before the massive penal colony and smiled sarcastically.

'Behold capitalism's monument to justice! Comes the American bastille, I want to be the first one here to open the gates.'

Davis and I nodded, but our minds, like Bridges', were on just one thing – prisoner number 31921.

27.

Two surly-looking guards with wry necks met us at the small boat ramp just south of the prison's main gate. Both cradled shotguns in their arms. One held a flashlight on us while the other grunted at us to identify ourselves. As we each called out our names, the bull with the flashlight put a pencil to his lips and made a mark on a piece of paper. When they were satisfied, they allowed us to get out of the boat.

'Come with us, the warden wants to see you,' said the one that talked.

We were escorted the two hundred yards to the main gate. The guards followed us with their weapons at the ready. A small spotlight from overhead picked us up and threw a blinding light into our faces. When I was able to look up, I could see the slim silhouettes of men with rifles positioned on the catwalk on top of the wall. The sharpshooters in the gun galleries had their high-powered artillery trained on us and, if called upon, could pick a wart off a knuckle at a hundred and fifty paces.

I'd never been to Quentin at night. It was more frightening than it was during the day. You had the feeling they weren't going to let you leave.

We walked through the yard to the 'porch' where the warden's office was located. I was at Quentin about a year ago to see a con named Chicago. Then the porch was a plain two-story mud brick job the color of a man with jaundice. It had a wood canopy supported by a half-dozen wood poles. In front was a tiny plot of ground in which sat a couple of sickly agapantha, two veroe plants and a dozen or so unweeded geraniums. Low bush ceanothus grew in the back at the edge of the 'plot'. I wouldn't have called it a garden. It was dark and I couldn't see anything which didn't have artificial light, but I don't think anything had changed much. In fact almost nothing had changed at Quentin since it was built in the 1850s.

We were led into the warden's office. 'Big Ben' Hogue was pacing the floor smoking a cigar large enough to string a fence from. He looked like a cattle rancher from the Pecos. A long string tie with a turquoise horse head clasp and sharp-pointed hand-tooled boots were a couple of the more obvious indications. He was more than six feet tall and by the great weathered furrows in his face which looked like the badlands following a flash flood, I guessed his age to be around sixty. He started talking – yelling would be a better word – even before the door had closed behind us.

'Bridges, this is going to go mighty hard on both Mooney and your damn committee if this is some kind of trick. I've bent the rules on this until they're ready to break.'

'That would be a bloody shame if one of your rules were to break, now wouldn't it, warden?' Bridges taunted.

Hogue, however, didn't seem to notice. His mind was one tracked and he was plenty steamed.

'You think you're so damn smart, don't you? You and your goddamn unions and communists and all that garbage about justice and cruelty and political prisoners. Hogwash! Bridges, you and this wet-nosed pup of a lawyer don't know the first thing about prisons. It's a hard business looking after 6,000 cons; making sure they get food in their bellies, a place to bunk and trying to stop them from carving up each other every time more than three of them get together. It's hell running a joint like this, but I run it and I run it well. Better than any of you reds and crybaby reformers could.'

Bridges wouldn't let up on Hogue.

'You're not running for re-election, are you, warden? You sound like a campaign speech.'

'Hummphh!' snorted the cowboy jailer. 'If it weren't so close to the election I wouldn't be standing here wasting my time on you. Don't want no bad publicity. That's the only reason I'm letting you see Mooney.'

He spit a chunk of tobacco out of his mouth and started up again.

'It's rabble like you that give the prisons a bad name. If politicians and newspaper reporters would get behind the prison system, we wouldn't have half the problems we got. But no, every time a con stubs his toe the radicals start hollering he was tortured. Every time . . .'

I took it upon myself to step in and remind the warden we had come to see Tom Mooney, not to listen to a lecture on penology. Big Ben didn't take to me or my suggestion.

'Who the hell are you?' he barked in my face, giving me a look like I was something that had backed up in his sink.

'This is Mr Kovachs,' Bridges said, 'and he's right. We came here to see Tom. Is he back in his cell?'

'Nah, he's still in the Old Hospital.'

'Well, that's where we want to go.'

Hogue finally realized we weren't going to stand around and listen to him harangue us any longer. He went to the intercom on his desk and called for a guard to come in. The bull reported a moment later.

'Take these men to the Old Hospital,' Hogue instructed him. He then motioned us out of his office with a wave of disgust.

Before we reached the door Hogue started up again on the woes of the modern-day warden. Even through a closed door and some fifty feet of distance, Big Ben's voice still nipped at our heels.

The guard took us across the yard to the 'Old Hospital'. It was called the 'Old Hospital' to distinguish it from the 'New Hospital'. The 'New Hospital' was built in 1885, so you can guess what the 'Old Hospital' looked like.

It was a small crowded building made from adobe. The builders hadn't been too careful how they laid the bricks. Gaps in the uneven rows of badly overlapping blocks gave the outside an appearance of impending collapse. The 'pogey', as the cons called it, was a fourteen-bed affair on the first of the building's two floors. The guard led us into the ward. Several small lights burned overhead, giving the place enough light to see but not enough to read.

There were a dozen cons in prison pajamas in the pogey. Some were in their beds snoring. Some others were huddled around one of the beds playing cards. And in the rear of the ward, two old white-haired geezers were sitting on a cot playing checkers – probably their millionth game.

The guard pointed to the bed opposite the checker players. 'He's over there. Warden says you got thirty minutes, no more.'

Bridges mumbled something to him and said we wanted to be alone. The bull went to the door and stood at parade rest. We walked to Mooney's bed. He was underneath a pile of papers and books. His upper body was propped up with pillows and a gray prison blanket. He was dozing quietly. Bridges leaned over him and jiggled his arm.

'Tom! Wake up, Tom, you've got company.'

Mooney jerked awake and rubbed his eyes.

'Harry?' he said with a start.

'Tom, are you all right?'

'Harry, how'd you get in here? This isn't visiting day. George? Hey, what's going on?'

'Tom, this Riley Kovachs,' Bridges said, introducing me to Quentin's most famous prisoner. 'He's a private investigator who's been working on the murder of a brother longshoreman and he's come up with some pretty hot cargo that involves you.'

I shook Mooney's hand as Bridges spoke. His grip was firm, but it was the only physical thing about him that was. He had a square build which had probably once been very solid. Maybe prison had made his flesh go soft or maybe it was the poisoning. Bridges told me before we left union headquarters that Mooney suffered from stomach ulcers. Whatever the reason, Mooney looked only slightly reminiscent of the stocky, dark-haired Irishman with the ruddy defiant face that had been so well known in labor and socialist circles two decades ago. The hair had turned gray and the face, although its eyes retained much of the old fight, was sunken with age and involuntary confinement.

'Glad to meet you, Kovachs,' he said. He was wide awake now and turned to Bridges and Davis. 'I'm sure glad you fellas came here. They tried to poison me!'

'Are you sure about that, Tom?' Davis asked.

'Well, at first I thought it was just that damn ulcer of mine, but one of the con bosses told me the word is out. I don't have hard proof yet, but I've written this press release.'

Mooney searched through the several sheets of paper on his bed and came up with two handwritten pages. He gave them a quick glance before handing them to Davis.

'George, see that all the papers get this. I want the working class to know that someone tried to kill me. I'm working on a longer version that will tie this up with the whole conspiracy against the labor movement in the state. I will have it finished before the election so Sinclair can use it.'

'About the election,' I said, 'I was in LA two days ago. With the help of Charlie Chaplin and a little shoeshine man who turned up dead for talking to me, I was able to uncover a network of Kluxers and Nazis who are being fed through a long straw by some power boys well known in the other camp. Jackson Berg and McArthur Digges Mason are two of them.'

Mooney pulled out a pencil from under his covers and jotted down some things as I spoke, nodding his head like he knew or at least suspected much of what I was telling him. I continued.

'Mason, Berg and, I suspect, Chandler Lane of the *Telegram* are connected in some way through a real estate company called Antelope Investments. Only Antelope Investments doesn't have any land to sell. It is a front to recruit people into an outfit known as the Committee. The Committee is a gang of bullies that goes around making life uncomfortable for anybody who is politically to the left of Calvin Coolidge, if you know what I mean.'

'I like your way of thinking, Kovachs,' Mooney smiled. 'I'm sure Harry has told you the special place in my heart I have for those three. What you don't know – what none of you know – is that our researchers are closing in on them. I just got word Tuesday from back east that we have a man in Philly who says Mason paid him $200 to testify against us at the trial. This man was the prosecution's key witness. He testified that he saw me driving a car and Warren jump out and plant a suitcase where the bomb went off. Now the man wants to tell the truth, the truth being he was in Oregon at the time and was set up by Mason to finger us.

'It will only be a matter of days before we will be able to prove fraud, suborning witnesses and conspiracy. I'm writing it up now for the campaign. That's why they tried to kill me. They don't want this information to reach the people.'

Mooney stopped and wiped his brow with the sleeve of his pajamas.

'But what you're telling me,' he said, lowering his voice, 'means this thing goes deeper than I thought.'

'Yes,' Bridges said, 'they have a bloody private army to make sure Sinclair doesn't get elected. There are fascists organizing all over the state.'

Mooney put his pencil to his lips and scanned his notes before speaking.

'Let's boil this down. An extremist element in the opposition party wants me dead. My guess is their party mainstream doesn't know anything about it. They're being suckered. If it comes out that some of their most trusted and prominent backers were responsible for framing Tom Mooney, the working class would rise up and repudiate their entire party. They would be finished as a political force and they know it.'

Mooney spoke with the fire of an old-time socialist addressing a political rally, not a man who had been behind bars for nearly twenty bitter and frustrating years. The sickly, sallow-looking man I had met less than fifteen minutes before was transformed into a robust lump of energy. He raised a forefinger in front of his face.

'But suppose Messrs Mason, Lane and Berg and their collection of skunks can't bump off Tom Mooney. He's a tough cookie, the wisest con in the pen. They'd have to be awful damn smart to get to him again. Besides, when they bungled the job the first time they let the cat out of the bag. I'll be watching for them from now on. Tom Mooney isn't just any con in stir. He has the international working class behind him and it would know if anyone tried to kill him. The bosses know that workers in this country would go into open revolt if Tom Mooney were the victim of foul play.'

Mooney was in a near trance. I half expected a halo to materialize above his head and for him to rise off his bed. The man was deadly serious in what he was saying. There was no doubt about that. And much of it was right on the money. But twenty years in lockup changes the way a man perceives himself and the outside world and his links to it. He continued with his scenario.

'So the fat cats say, "Mooney can't be got, but we've still got to stop him from getting the goods on us. What'll we do? We'll knock out Sinclair." They'll figure that if Sinclair wins the election, the first thing he'll do is release me, and the first thing I'll do is go after them. And they'd be right on both counts. They'll figure if Sinclair is elected, he will put unionists and progressives in the District Attorney's office and appoint communists to the bench. So it's the natural thing for them to try and stop Sinclair at all costs, even if it takes an army of hired thugs to do so.'

'Suppose all this is true,' I said, 'the $64 question is how? How are they going to stop him. The polls show him leading and the Spring Street bookies in LA are quoting him at seven-to-five. There's something they've planned for tomorrow – the ninth. At least that's what we think. But we haven't been able to put a make on it. Maybe it's the day they're going to throw a monkey wrench into Sinclair's campaign. Charlie Chaplin says you might know something.'

Mooney reached around behind him and punched up one of the pillows that was supporting his back. He gathered up the magazines and pieces of paper that covered his bed. All the while the wheels were turning inside his head. There was a silence while we waited for him to speak.

'Five minutes!' the guard croaked from across the ward. The old boys playing checkers had become embroiled in a heated argument, also probably their millionth, and were squaring off ready to slug it out with each other. Reason or fatigue got the better part of them, for after fifteen seconds, during which time they stripped off their pajama tops and pedaled around the bed like nineteenth-century boxers, they stopped and sat down on the bed and resumed their game without passing as much as a word between them.

'Upton came to see me about three weeks ago,' Mooney said finally. 'I told him he must be vigilant both within his own camp and that of the enemy. I told him he might become the victim of an *agent provocateur*'s rash deed, coming at such a time and manner that it would be extremely difficult to explain that his enemies did it. A provocation could be made to appear that it was done by his supporters.

'Look at the Reichstag fire two days before the election in Germany. Hitler's gang did it and accused the communists. The same thing can happen here. A bomb planted at the opposition party's office or some symbol of wealth like the Bank of America. That's how *agents provocateurs* work. Then again they might not want to do it the roundabout way. They might just put a high-powered rifle in the hands of a sharpshooter and tell him to bump off the "Bolshevik sonofabitch". They're capable of either.'

'But the ninth,' I said. 'What about the ninth?'

Mooney looked up at the ceiling trying to come up with something. I tried to help him out.

'Sinclair is scheduled to address a rally at Union Square at 6 p.m. Do your sources say anything about a rumble?'

'You know, that's funny. My pipeline has nearly gone dry the last four weeks. That might mean something. It might mean that something is in the works and the lid has been clamped down extra tight. Nothing has come down the line about tomorrow, but that doesn't mean nothing is going to happen. Like I said, it might be just the opposite.'

'*Agent provocateur*', Mooney said. The phrase skipped through my mind like a child's nursery rhyme. It had a feel to it, a specific, familiar feeling. I asked the three men if they knew Father James Windy.

'Sure, we all know Jim Windy,' Bridges replied. 'He's the waterfront priest. A good man.' Mooney and Davis nodded their agreement. 'Why do you ask?'

'Father Windy has put in many long hours with the Defense Committee,' Davis said, speaking for only the second time since we entered the hospital ward. 'We've even used his mission for meetings.'

Mooney made it unanimous. 'He is one of the main faucets in my pipeline. Him being a priest, he can go where a lot of people can't. A good man to have on your side.'

They had nothing but the highest praise for the 'tireless worker on behalf of justice for the working man', as Mooney put it – but what did they really know about him? I continued to probe.

'Where does Father Windy come from? What are his credentials that make him rate the kudos with you?'

'What's all this interest in Father Windy for?' Bridges demanded to know.

I had to tread lightly. 'All three of you say Father Windy is one hundred per cent for the Cause. Maybe he is, but I would like to know the basis of your trust in him.'

Mooney glowered at me.

'Why shouldn't we trust him?'

Then I handed them what I had been holding under my hat. I told them of finding the letter from Moody Pugh in Father Windy's office and my conversation with Cal Grundy.

The three men were dumbfounded. I would have provoked the same reaction if I told them mother Mooney herself had planted the bomb that sent her son up the river. Their expressions of squinting disbelief were penetrating reminders of the high regard they had for the priest, in case I had forgotten.

I also felt the heat of suspicion being directed my way. It wasn't said, but I could sense they were thinking, 'why the hell should we believe some peeper we've known only a few hours. Maybe *he* is an *agent provocateur*.' I tried to allay that suspicion.

'Look, I'm not accusing Father Windy of anything. I'm just telling you what I know. I'm telling you three people have been murdered since Wednesday and I've got a fugitive warrant on my head for at least one of them. Your Father Windy knew all three of the dead men and has had secret communication with the leaders of the Committee and Antelope Investments. Conclusions might be pretty easy to draw from this – almost obvious conclusions – but I'm not about to poke my finger into anybody's eye until I have the goods on them.'

The distrust seemed to drain a little from their faces. I felt they were willing to believe I was leveling with them, but I knew they didn't buy the line about Father Windy being a back-stabber and a murderer. Mooney, however, was willing to give it some play.

'You know, I'm the last one to be throwing any stones at Jim

Windy, but he's my one source that has dried up the most. I've only seen him once since the middle of August. It has caused me to wonder. If I believe my own words, I'd say maybe – and this is a big maybe – maybe it's a sign he knows something. Maybe somebody got to him and put heat on him to stop supplying me.'

I disagreed, stating the obvious. 'I think we all know that nobody has enough muscle to make Father Windy do anything he doesn't want to do.'

'Yeah, you're right,' Mooney admitted, 'I was just thinking out loud. I can't believe Jim Windy is a fink. I just can't believe it.'

He hung his head. Bridges and Davis looked at the floor. After a moment Bridges broke the uneasy silence.

'There's only one way to handle this. We'll convene an *ad hoc* committee of longshoremen and go down to Windy's. We'll give him a chance to explain. There is likely a reasonable explanation for all of this.'

'That's a good idea,' I countered, 'but not right now. If Father Windy has turned rat, and I'm not saying he has – just yet – he must know about tomorrow. We've got to trap him and that's something I can handle best myself.'

The three men exchanged glances with each other and then traded some words. They agreed to wait in the wings until I learned as much as I could from Father Windy. With time the main factor, they figured I had the best handle on the situation and were willing to let me stand at the plate and take my swings before they jumped in. They said they would play it my way until noon. After that, the union would go looking for Father Windy.

The screw came over to Mooney's bed and informed us our time was up. No one beefed. The three of us shook hands with prisoner number 31921 and wished him luck. I could believe that after nearly two decades of visitors wishing Tom Mooney luck, the phrase had ceased to mean anything to him. But until a new one is invented, he is stuck with it. The clock on the wall ticked ten minutes to eight as we walked from the pogey. The Sinclair rally was less than twenty-four hours away.

28.

The waters of the Bay were choppy and the night air frigid as we sped back to San Francisco in the tiny outboard. I lit up a smoke to keep warm, but the real chill was not in the air. It was in the atmosphere all right, but it wasn't the temperature. It was the chill men sometimes get deep down in their bones. It stiffens their joints and slows the circulation of their blood. They don't admit to it, but the cold is fear – fear of losing their job, or getting evicted from their home, or the wife running out. The chill I felt, however, was something more. It was a Big Fear – the fear the people of Germany have, the fear that blood-lusting barbarians are taking over your country and there is nothing you can do about it.

Bridges and Davis shivered, too. Maybe they felt the Big Fear coming. We didn't talk about it.

The little boat putted into the shipping lanes south of Alcatraz. Bridges navigated it across the current, dodging a barge and a lumbering freighter with great finesse. He cut the motor as the launch neared land and we drifted the final hundred yards to pier sixteen where we tied up. Somewhere a clock was announcing the hour. It was 9 o'clock.

Davis offered to give us a ride in his car. Bridges was due back at union headquarters to convene that emergency session of his Executive Board. He was already a few minutes late and decided to go with the lawyer. I had other things on my mind and just wanted to get to the nearest telephone.

I walked with them to Davis's car. Bridges climbed in on the passenger's side and rolled down the window while Davis groped for the ignition switch.

'Tomorrow, by noon, Kovachs. If we don't hear from you by then we'll go see Jim Windy ourselves.'

I waved at him and promised. 'If you don't receive a call from me, check the morgue when you have time. I'll probably be there.'

Bridges rolled up the window. He wasn't smiling. Neither was I. Davis turned on the motor, put the car into gear and drove off into the misty dark.

I groped my way around the pier looking for a phone booth. The night was silent save for the soothing baritone baying coming from the lighthouse at Fort Cronkhite. Visibility was just beyond the end of my nose and was changing for the worse. Great billowy wisps of fog snuck along the ground looking for somewhere to hide. I was expecting Bulldog Drummond to step from the night at any moment. He didn't. If the night had the density its appearance implied, it would have wrapped around and smothered those foolish enough to venture into it.

Occasional lamps were beacons that restored dignity to the simple art of getting from here to there. Their small, hazy golden globes poked soft holes in the gaseous dark and guided me to a phone booth between piers eighteen and twenty. I dropped in a nickel and dialed Steve Busby's home. I hoped I had a few telegrams waiting for me.

'Steve. Riley. Have the cables arrived?'

'You got two from LA. One from Philadelphia was delivered this afternoon, but I was out. They're supposed to send it by again sometime around ten.'

'Read to me what you have.'

I heard the crackling sound of paper as he tore open the envelopes.

'Let me see here. Does it make any difference which one I read first?' I assured him it didn't. 'Okay, here goes. "To Mr Riley Kovachs." It's from the Los Angeles County Auditor. It reads – "In response to request concerning Antelope Investments stop Corporation formed 1 January 1934 stop Board directors Berg, J., Mason, M., Lane, C., Rennest, L. stop." That's the end of that one, Riley. You want me to read it again?'

'No, Steve. Let's hear the other one.'

'Okay. This one is from the First National Bank of Southern California. "Account opened for Antelope Investments on 4 January 1934 stop Authorized signature L. Rennest stop Average balance through 31 July 1934 $185,517,32 stop." That's it, Riley. What does it all mean?'

'Don't ask me right now. I'm not sure I could give you the answer. Confirms what I suspected about those big shots I was telling you about. The wire from Philly may put it all together. I'll call you back after ten, probably closer to eleven. But the way things have been going, don't be surprised if you hear from me in the dead of night. I wouldn't do this to you, old man, but I think you have some idea how important this case is.'

'Don't worry about calling me during the night, Riley. I'll be here with the telegram in my hand, glad to help. Just be careful. We've been friends a long time and I don't want to read any more about you in the papers.'

'Thanks, Steve, that makes two of us. I'll call you later.'

'Is there a place I can reach you, Riley?'

'Silly boy,' I laughed. Steve laughed too.

I dug into my pocket for more nickels. I flipped through the phone book and came up with the number of the Pasadena Hotel. I dialed it. My friend the night clerk yawned into the receiver.

'Yeah?'

'Don't fall off your chair, pop, but I want to reserve a room for tonight.' He began cackling uncontrollably as I knew he would. 'Cheer up, junior, things are bound to get better. You have a room or not?'

'Buddy, is this a gag?'

'No gag. I need a room number to give out to a couple of friends. We're having a sort of reunion. We can't have our reunion if I can't tell them what room it is in. You follow me?'

'Sure, sure.' He was still laughing.

I had to agree. Reserving a room at a place like the Pasadena Hotel was funny. Like calling ahead for blanket space at Ocean Beach on a foggy day. The desk man recovered, though he still snickered intermittently in my ear.

'Take your pick, buddy, we got twenty empty rooms.'

'How about one a couple of floors up?'

He didn't have to think much about it. '309 has been empty since a guy got killed there last week.'

'You're a great salesman, you know that? I'll take it.'

'Okay, mister, it'll be here when you are.'

He hung up without asking for my name. But then, that's the way these places do business. You make your reservation in person, pay cash in advance and check out when your luck improves. The tourist season is as foreign to the Pasadena Hotel as salt pork to a Rockefeller.

The fog was unrelenting. I felt like a doughboy in the Argonne Forest during a poison gas attack. The milky vapor had penetrated my clothing and was working its way into the pores of my skin. I had always put myself squarely on the record as a pro-fogger, but something told me I should have taken that ride with Davis.

I dropped another nickel in the box and dialed Lana Birdwell's number. I hoped I wouldn't be connected with the post office. Three short rings found a customer. A woman's voice said hello.

'Lana?'

'Darling,' she breathed sensuously. My ear tingled. 'Where on earth have you been? Oh, my darling, I've missed you terribly. Where are you?'

'Save the sweet talk for later, sugar. I've got to see you. Tonight!'

'Oh, yes, Riley, I'll be right over.'

'Not so fast. I'm not at home. The cops are waiting for me there. I want you to come to the Pasadena Hotel. Room 309. Be there by 10.30.'

There was a silence on the line that could have picked up the sound of plants growing in the next room if she had plants and a next room.

'Did you hear me, sugar? Do you understand?'

'Why there, Riley darling? It sounds like a positively dreadful place.'

'Hate to disappoint you, lover, but romance is pretty far down on the agenda right now. I need to talk to you about something else.'

'Is it about that old Committee?'

'I'll tell you about it when I see you. I've got to go now. Don't stand me up, sugar. I wouldn't like that.'

She responded without enthusiasm that she wouldn't and then hung up.

One more call to make. I rung up Father Windy's mission.

'Jim Windy speaking,' boomed the voice at the other end.

'Father Windy, this is Kovachs. Remember me? I'm the guy the cops have been looking for.'

'Riley, my boy, where have you been? I've been looking everywhere for you. How's the investigation coming?'

'I'll tell you about it when I see you. We've got a lot to talk about, Father. I'll be at the Pasadena Hotel in half an hour. Room 309. We can talk there.'

'That's up in the Tenderloin, isn't it?'

'Yes, on Ellis Street. You will be there?'

'Sure, sure I will. Only why all the mystery?'

'No mystery, Father. I have the cops from two cities on my tail and there are some others who have been unkind. I just don't want to take chances.'

'All right, Riley, it's your ball game. Sign me up to play. I'll see you in half an hour.'

'Oh, Father, one last thing.'

'Anything.'

'Come alone.'

'Certainly, Riley, certainly.'

Father Windy sounded almost too cool and confident. I would have liked to have seen the expression on his face when he said, 'certainly, Riley, certainly'. I didn't like his tone.

All that was left was to catch a bus up Market to Ellis, walk over to the Pasadena and wait for the showdown to begin.

I started heading west toward the Ferry Building. I hadn't taken a dozen steps when two figures emerged from the fog. They were walking directly at me. One was a small creature, a dwarf really. His legs were bowed and he walked by bounding from side to side on tiny feet. He was your normal dwarf except for one thing. I picked up a stray beam of light from something shiny he held in his hand.

As the pair drew closer, the dwarf looked smaller and the shiny object larger and sharper. I knew without asking that it was a dagger and he hadn't come down to the waterfront to clean clams. When I wasn't watching the stiletto, which was pretty hard not to do, I observed the form walking next to the little man. He was as large as the dwarf was small. When they got close enough for me to see their faces, I recognized him. It was Momo, the human redwood with the matching IQ.

'Hi, Momo,' I said, 'who's your little buddy?'

'Shut up, mug,' he snarled. Momo would never get my vote for Mr Congeniality.

'It's such a pleasure to meet you, Mr Kovachs,' said the dwarf. 'Momo has told me so much about you. Please allow me to introduce myself. I am called Cassius, the Blade of Toledo.'

The little man bent from the waits, taking a sweeping bow with the hand that held the knife. Then he took a handkerchief from his pocket and wiped from the blade the beads of moisture deposited by the fog.

'You're cute,' I said returning his greeting, 'but I have the feeling that you boys didn't come down here to swap stories about the good old days.'

'You are quite correct in your observation, Mr Kovachs,' the dwarf answered. 'Our business with you is of a more, shall we say, fundamental nature.'

'I was afraid of that. Well, do you want me to go some place with you?'

The dwarf laughed.

'On the contrary, Mr Kovachs. We can transact our business right here.' He turned to his giant companion. 'Momo, you may begin transacting our business with Mr Kovachs.'

Momo was eager to oblige him. He came lumbering toward me with a stupid leer on his face. He said nothing. He raised a powerful fist that looked like a blacksmith's anvil and swung it at my head. But the beast was slow and that allowed me to make a slight move. It wasn't much, but the extra second enabled me to keep my head from being opened like a coconut. I couldn't claim total success, however. His blow missed my face, but found a yielding shoulder. I went down to my knees like a nail being driven through soft wood. I could hear the dwarf shouting encouragement to the towering evergreen.

Momo moved in to finish me off. I decided to make him work for it. I lunged at him from where I knelt, grabbing him around the legs. I drove forward. He stumbled and fell to the pavement. Momo bellowed in anger.

He rolled over and rose to one knee. But before he could stand up, I rushed him and landed a drop kick in a place that even on him had to be tender. He expelled a howl from his lungs that could have made people forget about that twenty-story-tall monkey in New York.

I could hear the dwarf screeching from behind me. 'Get up, Momo, you big idiot! Get up!'

Despite his condition Momo was doing just that. I turned and glanced at the dwarf before attempting a second punt. A burst of shimmering blue-white steel caught my eye. The hand holding the knife had been raised and was cocked behind a tiny ear.

I dove and grabbed the pavement a split second before the angry metal came hurtling through the air. I could feel it cut open the night as it flew by my head.

The blade might have skidded harmlessly along the ground at some point had it not been for Momo. He had just regained his feet and was focusing his dull eyes when the knife sliced into his neck. Instinctively his hands flew up to pull it out. He was too late. The blade had ripped open the jugular and blood gushed from the gaping wound like water from a broken hydrant. He gurgled once or twice, staggered toward me and fell over dead.

I turned and rushed the dwarf. He was easy prey without the dagger. I picked him up at the waist and hoisted him over my head. Then I stepped in the direction of the Bay. I was close enough so that I didn't have to go far to reach the edge of the pier. I reared back my pint-sized load and flung it as far as I could. His cries of protest came to an abrupt end with the initial splash in the water. Then there was nothing. I don't know if the dwarf could swim. I didn't care.

I sat down on the pier railing to catch my breath. The pain in my shoulder from Momo's blow throbbed like nothing I had ever known. It felt like someone had dropped an unabridged copy of *Anthony Adverse* on it from the top floor of the Fairmont. But that was nothing compared to what Momo and the dwarf got.

I looked at my watch. It was 10.15. I had fifteen minutes to get to the Pasadena Hotel. If the buses were running on schedule, I figured I had half a chance to make it.

29.

I stepped off the bus where Market and Ellis come together and walked the block and a half to the hotel. The Pasadena looked like it had been locked in a time closet since my first visit. The same coughing men were sitting on the same metal chairs in the same dirty linoleum lobby still waiting for things to pick up. The same character I had played footsy with the night Ira Blodgett was killed was sitting behind the desk. He was reading a racing sheet, probably the same one. Only the absence of cobwebs from him and the others allowed me to believe that life, as routine as it might be in the Tenderloin flop house, had inched forward in time. The desk man looked up from his paper. He recognized me.

'Well, if it isn't Mr Wiseacre of 1934.'

'You remembered. I'm touched.'

'Gowan, beat it before I call the cops.'

'Now just a minute, junior. I didn't come here to pull your tongue. Tonight is business. I want room 309 for a couple of hours.'

I reached into my pocket for some change. The night man's mind began working.

'Say, you're the drunk who called about the room! I knew it was a gag.'

'This is on the level. I need the room. A couple of friends are dropping by later.'

He wasn't convinced. He looked hard into my face, trying to remember something. He remembered.

'Say, ain't you the fella the cops is looking for? A mug named Kovachs?'

'No, you've got it all wrong, junior. My name is Joe Doaks and I have a little business deal cooking tonight.'

'Doaks. Ha! Who you tryin' to kid? I should call the coppers right now.'

He reached for the phone sitting next to him. I placed my hand on his.

'You know, I get the feeling you don't care for me anymore, junior. I don't know why, I still like you. That's why I want to help. If you pick up that phone, better dial an ambulance. I want you to have the best medical care available.'

'Say, what're you talking . . .' He got the message just before he completed his sentence.

'Why don't you just be a good scout and give me the key to 309.'

He grabbed the money I had placed on the counter and reached behind him to the key rack. He pulled one off and tossed it at me. If looks could kill, I would have been under fifty pounds of freshly turned earth.

I picked up the key and leaned over the desk. I looked from side to side and spoke to him in a whisper.

'And don't go getting any funny ideas about calling the cops while I'm upstairs. See that building across the street?' I motioned with my eyes. 'You might not see anything, but there is a guy watching this place with high-powered binoculars. He's not the brightest guy in the world, but he knows what to do if anybody picks up that phone.' I pointed to the phone. 'That's the phone.' I pointed to him. 'And you're the anybody he is watching.'

'What's he liable to do?' said the night clerk with a shiver.

I drew even closer to him.

'Inside his coat he carries a heater big enough to bring down a runaway cable car. And he's the kind of guy who gets cranky and hard to live with, if he doesn't pop it at least once a day.' I pulled back the sleeve of my coat and looked at my watch. 'He's been shut out so far today and there are less than two hours to go, so I guess I don't have to tell you how jumpy he is. If I were you, I'd sit here like a good little soldier and not make any moves you might be real sorry for.'

I patted his shoulder. The scowl which had been stitched into his face became unraveled with fear. The story I told him wouldn't have been purchased by a certified idiot, but the night clerk had no trouble digesting it, no trouble at all.

'I won't budge, mister. I promise.' He shifted his eyes to the building across the street without moving his head. 'Tell him I won't budge, will ya?'

I turned to the street and held up three fingers as if to signal.

'I told him that you want to cooperate. Now don't disappoint me, junior. I'm counting on you.'

I turned away and walked for the stairs.

30.

The only thing different about Ira Blodgett's room was Ira Blodgett. He wasn't in it. Oh, there had been other changes, too, I guess. The bedspread had been changed, most of the blood was gone from the floor, and the overhead light bulb had been replaced. All else remained as it was – the dirty vinyl floor with blue and brown triangles; the cheap night table chipped and scratched from years of being banged by half-pint bottles of muscatel; a lamp with a yellowed shade the color of vanilla wafers; a chest of drawers. On the wall hung a mass-produced painting of Jesus, but it failed to break up the monotony of the wall's color, which reminded me of old flamingos.

As for the rest of the furniture, there was a green fake leather chair that looked like all the troops from the Presidio had bivouacked in it at one time or another. The bed and stiff-backed desk chair were the only other places to sit.

I lay down on the bed and pulled on a cigarette while listening to the buzzing neon sign outside. Down the hall a man was still coughing. Everything else was quiet. The smoke from my cigarette trailed lazily upward to the glass bowl covering the overhead light. I tried to blow smoke rings, but I never did have the knack. My rings always looked like strands of limp vermicelli rather than circles.

One and a half smokes later there was a knock on the door. It was Lana Birdwell. I had barely opened it when she came bursting into my arms.

'Hold me, my darling,' she puffed. 'This place frightens me so.' She placed her warm lips on mine. I couldn't say that I hated it. We parted. 'Riley, darling, why are we meeting in this, this place?'

'Take a look around, sugar. Anything look familiar?'

She was startled by the remark and backed away from me.

'Riley! Do you think I'm in the habit of frequenting transient hotels?'

I brushed a hand between us and walked to the window and looked down on the street. 'Skip it,' I said.

'Riley, dear, what is all this about? Are you expecting someone else? Why are you being so mysterious with me?'

I came away from the window.

'You ask too many questions, sugar. Stick around and you'll get your answers.'

The second caller was rapping at the door. I let him in. Father Windy grabbed my hand and gave it a squeeze.

'Good to see you, Riley.'

He stopped when he noticed Lana Birdwell. I introduced them, but I almost had the feeling it wasn't necessary.

It was time to get down to business. I spoke to my bewildered guests.

'Well, ladies and gentlemen, boys and girls, it's time to take your seats. The show's about to begin.'

I escorted Lana Birdwell to the green chair. Father Windy deposited his powerful frame in the straight-back. Both protested mildly at first, but I hushed them with the announcement that I was about to deliver the solution to the Ira Blodgett murder.

There was an unnatural silence as I began. If their palms were as sweaty as mine they could have lathered soap. I stood between Father Windy and Lana Birdwell and began, once again, to play poker. The stakes in this game were the highest yet.

'I think it's best to start at the beginning. Last Wednesday afternoon Ira Blodgett was murdered in this room.'

Lana Birdwell gasped and stood halfway up in her chair. Father

Windy's eyes moved about the room, studying every object with the scrutiny of a building inspector looking for cracked beams. He mumbled something under his breath. I waited for order to restore.

'Since that day I have had some pretty nasty luck tracking down the killer. Yours truly has been slugged, kidnapped, drugged, punched around by the cops, had a body sent to his room in LA and has just come from a run-in with a dwarf who thought I was a dart board. Also, four more men have died. And that's the good news. The bad news is that lurking behind all this murder and mayhem is a private army of thugs and social derelicts who are being bankrolled by some of the wealthiest and most powerful men in the state of California. Their aim is to prevent Upton Sinclair from being elected governor. And the cost in terms of money and human life doesn't seem to matter much to them.'

Father Windy was on his third cigarette and chewing his nails like they were nickel candy bars. Lana Birdwell was desecrating another linen handkerchief and crossing and uncrossing her legs in a way that was most distracting.

I told them in sparing detail the events from finding Ira Blodgett's body in the Pasadena Hotel to the meeting with Tom Mooney at San Quentin. Certain things I left out on purpose, but not much. Then I started playing hardball.

'The reason I'm telling you this story is to let you know that I've been on the job and have nearly every angle covered. But there are still some open ends that need to be closed.

'Now both of you are no strangers to some of what I have said. Father Windy, you, for instance, knew that Ira was investigating the murder of his friend killed during the longshoremen's strike. You know that it was his investigation, or, more to the point, what his investigation turned up that set this whole thing off. And you, sugar, know about the Committee and something of its capabilities. I have a crushed shoulder you can look at in case you have forgotten.

'The point of all this is that neither of you are outsiders to the case. In fact, you both know a lot more than you have told me and that's the reason we are here – to share our information. I've shared mine, so now it's your turn. Who's going to be first?'

Lana Birdwell protested. 'Riley, darling, I don't know what

you mean. I've told you everything. I really know so very little. What more can I tell you?'

'For starters, sugar, you can tell me what you were doing in this room the day Ira Blodgett was murdered.'

She was horrified. She squeezed her handkerchief into a ball of sweaty wet cloth. She stood up and moved toward me, attempting an embrace.

'Darling, if you are implying . . .'

I stopped her and held her at arm's length.

'No kisses right now, sugar. Just answers will do. What were you doing here? Don't say you weren't. Your perfume gave you away.'

Her head drooped and her eyes covered the floor. She began to sob slightly.

'I went to his room because he asked me to. He called me and said he was ready to make a deal. My money for his silence. He instructed me to meet him here in this room, but he was dead when I arrived. Please believe me.'

She tried to tie up my mouth again, but I turned her away.

'Control yourself, sugar. As for believing you, why should I do that? You haven't leveled with me since the first time I laid eyes on you. You lied about Chandler Lane. You lied to Dexter Hall about your past. Or maybe it was me you lied to. And your story about being coerced by the Committee to set me up for the kidnapping rates a big horse-laugh.

'Now maybe you had a good reason for all those lies. Maybe you are in some kind of jam. I don't know, but I think I will have the answers to a lot of things about you in just a few minutes. I'm going to pick up this phone and dial a number. So you take a load off your heels, sugar, and think real hard if there isn't something else you want to tell me.'

Her face was red and she was sniffing into her overworked hankie. I picked the receiver off the hook. As I dialed Steve Busby's number, I studied my guests. Lana Birdwell was a distraught wreck, but then I hadn't known her any other way. Father Windy was somewhere behind a cloud of yellow-gray smoke. The ashtray at his elbow had more butts in it than the chorus line at

Radio City Music Hall. He appeared calm, but puzzled. His silence was unusual.

I reached Steve. The telegram from Philadelphia had come twenty minutes before. I waited while he opened the envelope. He read the cable twice. It was short and to the point. I thanked him and returned to the party. I smiled at Lana Birdwell, although I didn't have a reason she would have liked. Her eyes melted some.

'Ever been to Philly, sugar?' I asked.

'Why, no.' She coughed an artificial cough.

'Come, come, sugar. Think back, way back. Their Hall of Records says you've been there. In fact, they say you were born there.'

She must have known the game was over because she shed her former self like a locust in a tree. She grew hard and combative where before she had been soft and vulnerable. The nervous, stumbling ingenue had turned into a shrewd and savy lady familiar with the ways of the world. The transformation was as smooth as twenty-weight oil. The expression on her face changed only slightly, but her eyes gave her away even before she spoke.

'Yes, yes, it's true I was born there. I suppose being from Philadelphia makes me a murderess?'

'No, that doesn't make you a killer, but let me go on. Your mother moved you to California to be close to the father who had deserted you before you were born.'

Lana Birdwell didn't go into handkerchief shock as she might have done earlier. Nor did she try to bury me with affection. She knew I had plenty on her and decided to take me head on.

'That's right, Mr Riley Kovachs. My mother moved us to southern California so she could claim the birthright for her daughter, the birthright her father had denied her when he ran out. You and I both know who that man is, don't we?' She turned to Father Windy. 'We might as well make it unanimous. My father is Chandler Lane!'

Father Windy raised his eyebrows and whistled slightly through his teeth. There was more, only some of which I knew for sure.

'And your mother put the bite on Lane to keep hushed the fact that he skipped out on a pregnant wife and an unborn child. Am I right?'

Lana Birdwell didn't disagree. 'My mother devoted her life to seeing that I had the best of everything – clothes, education, culture. Making my father provide those things was a small price to ask.'

'You should have hated Lane for what he had done, but you didn't, did you, sugar?' I didn't wait for her answer. 'You admired him, or rather you admired his power and wealth and when you learned he was your father, which I suspect was only recently, you went to him yourself to collect all the financial and social privileges that come with being a Lane.

'Lane was only too happy to see his daughter – his own flesh and blood – but he couldn't acknowledge her existence and provide her with the social amenities she had expected. But Chandler Lane is nobody's fool. What he couldn't give his daughter publicly he gave privately. Even more than the money he gave her a position, a career in the Lane empire. All she had to do was change her name, which she did gladly.'

I stopped only long enough to light a smoke and change grammatical case before continuing.

'Changing your name was no problem, you just assumed your mother's maiden name – Rennest. How am I doing so far, sugar?'

'Fine, darling, just fine. You *are* a detective, aren't you?'

'That's what it says on my office door.'

'But I don't see what my past has to do with anything. I admit I worked for the Lane Foundation as an executive director. Hardly a criminal offense, I'd say.'

'The Lane Foundation? Maybe, but I know of another of daddy's outfits you served – Antelope Investments. Now there's some kind of stink.'

Her eyebrows jumped up into the orange locks on her forehead. It was the one thing I had carefully avoided mentioning in my earlier chew about the Blodgett case. Father Windy reached for a fresh pack of squares. I connected Antelope Investments to the puzzle, hoping it would light up the Christmas tree. I told them about Moody Pugh and Cal Grundy.

'So Antelope Investments is the transmission belt that makes the machine purr. It is the link between the big shots and the mugs of the Committee. Without Antelope Investments, there would be no threat to subvert the election, and three good men would be alive today.'

Father Windy was eager to help put the collar around Lana Birdwell's pretty neck. He gave me a verbal nudge.

'So the fascists are being outfitted through this dummy corporation. Where does Miss Birdwell fit in?'

'Miss Birdwell fits in very nicely, I'm afraid. She is one of the four directors of Antelope Investments.'

'Liar!' she shrieked, leaping from her chair and rushing me with fingernails in the fixed position. She had it in mind to shred my face. I grabbed her wrists before she could do so.

'Take it easy, sugar. This hurts me, too.' I pushed her back into the green chair. Her anger, having nowhere to go, subsided, for the moment anyway. 'Yes, L.Rennest is a director of Antelope Investments and keeper of its money. That's you, sugar. I might have figured it out myself from the cute little twist of the name, but the telegram from Philly with your mother's maiden name was the clincher.'

She glared into my eyes like she had just found out I had been spreading rumors about her in the boys' locker room at Kezar Stadium.

'You haven't proved a thing, Mr Private Eye. I quit Antelope Investments when I found out what it was doing behind the scenes. My father was afraid I would talk and kept me under lock and key at one of his houses. I escaped and came to San Francisco. Even you should be able to figure out why I wanted my identity kept from him. I was fleeing the whole sordid affair. It's that simple. You can't send me to jail for that.'

'You're absolutely right, sugar. All I have proved so far is that your skirts are soiled; that you are the daughter of a power-hungry newspaper publisher; and that you are an inveterate liar. That's so far.'

'So far?' she repeated.

'So far. But let's put you on the shelf for a minute, sugar, and hear what Father Windy has to say.'

The priest poked an eye through a nicotine cloud.

'Me? What do I have to say? Looks like we've got our murderer right here.'

'Let's look before we leap, Father. Cast not the first stone and all that malarky. For instance, I'd be real interested to know what you can add to my knowledge of Antelope Investments.'

Father Windy shook his head. The look on his face was not pleasant.

'You're barking up the wrong tree, Kovachs.'

'Father, are you trying to tell me that you don't know anything about Antelope Investments?'

He nodded weakly. I reached into my pocket and pulled out the letter I had been saving for that moment. I held it out in front of Father Windy's face.

'This letter says you're a liar. Moody Pugh says you're a liar, and a used car salesman named Grundy agrees with him. In fact, Grundy says your services to the Committee are indispensable.'

Father Windy's neck turned purple. The color rolled north toward the top of his head. When it reached the hairline he exploded. He rose from his chair and heaved his great shoulders. He stretched out his arms and held them taut and curled as if he were holding a giant invisible boulder. His hands clenched and unclenched nervously.

'Kovachs, you idiot, you don't know what you are doing.' I tried to interrupt, but he wouldn't allow it. 'Just what the hell are you trying to prove? I was Ira's friend. Why would I want to kill him? You've got your killer right here.' He pointed an angry finger at Lana Birdwell. 'She had motive and opportunity.'

Father Windy wheeled forward and bent down, sticking his boiling face into hers. He slammed a fist into the table next to her chair. I can't say why it didn't shatter into a hundred pieces. Lana Birdwell didn't bat an eyelash.

'You killed Ira!' the priest screamed at her. 'Admit it, you bourgeois wench!'

Lana Birdwell took a cigarette from her bag, lit it and blew a defiant puff of smoke into her accuser's face.

'This isn't confession, Father. So don't expect anything from me unless you are prepared to do more than shout.'

The dame was cooler than the tip of a polar bear's nose.

'Bitch!' was Father Windy's invocation. He turned away from her and returned to me. 'Kovachs, don't be a sap. She's the killer all right, and if you don't get her out of here I may do something I will regret later.'

I put my hand on Father Windy's shoulder. I admit it took some nerve.

'Slow down, Father. Why are you in such a rush to put a noose around Miss Birdwell's neck?'

'She's guilty, damn it. Everything points to her. She killed Ira and she must be made to pay.'

'That may be true, but remember I work with facts, not appearances.'

'Damn your facts!'

'Oh yeah? These "damn facts" say maybe Lana Birdwell killed Blodgett, but you can't hang a murder rap on somebody with a maybe.'

'Kovachs, you're a damn fool. What do you want – a signed confession?'

'It wouldn't hurt.'

'You take yourself too seriously, shamus. You're nothing more than a cheap hustler on the make. I was willing to go along with you while it looked to me like you were trying to find Ira's murderer. But you're not interested in finding the killer, are you? I'll answer that one for you. It's the case and all its cheap thrills that interest you, not the killer. Prolong the case. Make it exciting and daring. Accuse innocent people of murder. Concoct wild plots to make your blood race. Anything to keep it going with you in the driver's seat, pulling all the knobs. Nice work if you can get it – making your fantasy world come alive.

'Well, look here you petit-bourgeois fake, I am getting out of your daydream. I'm getting off the boat right here, understand me?'

The priest moved up on me. We stood toe to toe. A cat's whisker kept our noses from bumping. Father Windy clenched his teeth. His words came out low and hard, pushing their way into my face. 'I've a mind to turn you both in. As much as I hate the cops, I hate your kind even more. At least the police have their class reasons for what they do to people, but to you the murder of longshoremen and right-wing plots are all part of the big game. People's lives are nothing more to you than chessmen to be moved around your stinking game board.'

He turned and walked to the door as if to leave. I beat him to it and stood in his path. I knew if he didn't want to stop he could walk right through me.

'Stop right there, Father,' I shouted in his face. 'Speaking of games, that was quite a performance you just gave. But I don't buy it any more than you do. You've been on a soap box so long you think you can change mountains into monkeys just by talking. Well, talk all you want, it won't change a thing. Go to the cops, too, if you like. I'm sure Cahill would like to hear what you know about Blinky Rizonetti's murder. When I tell him you were in LA over the weekend and saw Blinky, he just might be able to put two and two together and come up with something that resembles four. And knowing how bad the cops would like to bag a big bad Bolshevik like you, I'm sure they can come up with something and make it stick.'

Father Windy's bluff had been called. He backed away from me and returned to the center of the room. He reached for his smokes and savagely tore open a pack of Camels, pulling one out. He lit it and in a moment was back in a yellow cloud. He started to pace the floor. He spoke as he paced.

'Kovachs, don't try to scare me.' He shook his head. 'You are a stupid fool.' Then his voice dropped to a whisper. 'You don't know what you are doing.'

'I thought we established that several minutes ago.'

Father Windy's voice resumed its normal bellow. 'Don't crack wise with me, peeper. You know, I think you want to pin Ira's murder on me, though I don't know why. Is it the girl? Did the other side buy you out?'

Sometimes Riley Kovachs, master of the controlled emotion, logician extraordinaire and the coolest cucumber in the jar, loses his grace, and now and then, his temper. It was something Father Windy said that had thrown such a low blow that I couldn't let it pass. I reached back and planted a haymaker to the right side of the cleric's jaw. It was a stupid thing to do, for reasons too obvious to enumerate.

He was taken by surprise and stumbled backwards, knocking over the stiff-backed chair, and crashed into the wall. Father Windy was stunned, but that was all. He reached inside his black coat and produced a steel-gray heater – a police .38. Lana Birdwell screamed. I did too, only mine didn't make any sound.

He could have easily dropped me from where he stood, but he chose to charge me instead. Then everything slowed down. It seemed like hours before he reached me. I glanced at Lana Birdwell. She was cowering in a far corner. Her lips were taut against her teeth and her mouth was open. I think she was screaming, but I didn't hear her anymore. In fact I didn't hear anything. I had this vision – call it a vision brought on by mortal fear – that I was hog-tied to a railroad track. There was a big superchief rumbling toward me, though all I could see was its bright headlight. It grew bigger, slowly bigger, as it chugged toward me. Finally, the light grew so large and so intense that it was a blinding flash. Then nothing.

I saw the flash, but I couldn't tell whether it was the vision or the fire from the talking end of Father Windy's roscoe. All I remember was going down under superior force.

I woke up minutes later. It might have been hours, except the cops hadn't arrived and even they would have been on the scene if shots had been fired. My head was throbbing violently as if something trapped inside was trying to get out. The room was dark and I was alive. Other than that I couldn't be responsible for much else. I crawled around on the floor until I got up enough steam to stand.

I turned on the light and tried to focus my eyes on the room. Slumped in the corner where I had last seen her was Lana Birdwell. My stomach wanted to climb out through my windpipe and my heart was pounding louder than Gene Krupa's drums. I walked to where she lay and bent down.

There was a small purple gash high on her cheek, but it wasn't put there by the business part of a gun. She was breathing. I applied my handkerchief to her wound and tried to bring her around by patting her face. She began to moan and then opened her eyes. They rolled around a couple of times before focusing on me.

'You're alive, sugar,' I assured her.

'Oh, I'm not so sure that's good. What happened?'

I helped her sit up and then to her feet. I carried her to the green chair.

'I was hoping you'd be able to answer that one,' I said in response to her question. 'The last thing I remember was a flash. Then I guess Father Windy pounced on me.'

'He shot you, Riley darling. And he shot me, too.'

'I don't think so, sugar. Both our heads have been through batting practice, but no bullet holes anywhere. And I don't think the good Father is that poor a shot. He didn't intend to kill us, just rough us up a bit. How are you feeling now?'

'I feel terrible, but I think I will survive.'

I rubbed the lump on my head demonstratively.

'Well, I'm glad to hear that at least one of us will pull through.'

She got the message and began playing nurse.

'Oh, you poor darling. Here you have taken such good care of me and I haven't even as much as inquired about your wounds. I am so sorry.'

She pulled my head to her breast and kissed my battered forehead.

'I should be angry with you,' she continued in mocking anger. 'All those nasty things you said about me. But I'm not. You're wild and impetuous, Riley Kovachs, and I have the misfortune to be hopelessly cast under your spell.'

I could have rested my head on her bosom a whole lot longer, but I sensed Lana Birdwell was trying for a comeback. I stood up and lit us a couple of cigarettes.

'You never give up, do you, sugar?'

'Never give up what, Riley?' she breathed with that sensual something that does something to a guy that makes it extremely difficult to stand up if he were sitting down.

'You're still on the hot seat, sugar. You're still a suspect for murder.'

She became indignant. I couldn't say I blamed her.

'How can you say that after what has happened? I didn't try to kill you. That phony priest is your killer. Even I can tell that.'

'Maybe you're right, but I'm not ruling out anything.'

'Riley, dear, I may have been a shameless liar to you in the past, but I am not a murderer. You do believe that, don't you, darling?'

'I believe everything and nothing. Now let's get out of here. I can't believe the cops aren't swarming all over the place.'

We left room 309 and walked down the two flights of stairs to the lobby. The night clerk was sitting behind the desk, motionless, facing the front window. His hands were clasped together on the top of his head. He caught sight of me out of the corner of his eye as we approached.

'Say, what's going on up there?' he asked.

'Just celebrating, junior.'

'I didn't call no cops, mister, honest! You think you could call off your boy now? My arms have been asleep for hours.'

'Sure, sure I can. You stay the way you are for five more minutes. It'll take me that long to convince Lucky to go home. He won't like it, but I think he'll listen to me.'

'Thanks, pal,' he said, greatly relieved.

Lana Birdwell and I walked out onto Ellis Street. A clock in the window of the cleaners next to the Pasadena read ten minutes past twelve. What it didn't say was that it was 9 October.

I hailed a cab for Lana Birdwell. I had no idea if she would go straight to her hotel, but I knew I didn't need her tagging along to confuse me. I had enough troubles.

I told her to get a good night's sleep and that we'd talk in the morning. I also tried to let her know where she stood with me.

'Now don't go and do something foolish like leave town, sugar. I'm trying very hard to believe in you, so don't let me down. I can be real nasty, you know.'

She looked like she understood. She puckered her lips and closed her eyes. 'Kiss me, darling. You know you can trust me from here on out.'

It was easier to kiss Lana Birdwell than trust her. Much easier.

I shut the door to the hack and watched it speed up Ellis until it turned north on Leavenworth and disappeared from sight. I lit a butt and walked across the street to the Kit Kat Klub to use the phone.

I got the Boldes out of bed and asked them to unlock the door to the back room of the diner. Mrs Bolde said they would be happy to oblige. She didn't ask any questions. That was good because I was short on answers.

31.

I spent the night on the cot Mrs Bolde fixed up for me. It would have been just swell if there hadn't been so much on my mind, but I kept running over the showdown at the Pasadena. I thought cases like the Blodgett murder were always brought to a successful conclusion by rounding up all the suspects, placing them in a locked room and questioning them until the guilty one cracked under the withering pressure of indisputable logic. Neat and simple. Worked for Nick Charles, anyway.

But what happens when two of the suspects are tripped up and neither cracks? That's what I had on my hands. Each had been working both sides of the street and had the opportunity as well as the motive to commit one or more of the murders. They could be working together, against each other, or for some third party not yet in the picture. I lay on the cot wishing I had until Thanksgiving to figure what the Committee was up to, but I knew without looking at my watch that 9 October had been here for hours.

My head was pounding. I would have preferred to blame it on the pain emanating from my most recent bruise, but the tangled condition of the caper had to take most of the credit. I thought to myself, if a woman in Canada could give birth to quintuplets, why couldn't I bust open this case? It seemed like a much simpler thing to do.

I began to dote on it, but just at the right moment an angel entered the room. It was Helvitica Bolde and she was toting a tray full of relief. A pot of steaming coffee, a plate with a double order of scrambled eggs, toast, bacon and a mountain of hash browns. The morning *Chronicle* was there, too, fighting for space on the brown tray. Mrs Bolde set it down on the desk.

'Who do you like in today's game, Riley?' she asked knowingly.

I had nearly forgotten that 9 October was also the day the World Series would be settled. I reached back into my mind to conjure up the starting pitchers. It seemed so long ago. Dizzy Dean was taking the hill for the Redbirds with that lump still on his head and only one day's rest. For the Bengals it was the sinker-baller Eldon Auker. I cleared the night from my mouth and offered my analysis.

'You know I like the Tigers, but you won't catch me putting up real cash money against Dean.'

'That's the way I feel, too.' She smiled and cupped a hand to her mouth. 'I have fifty cents riding with Hagen that St Louis will win.'

'Smart bet.'

She walked to the door. 'I know you must have scads of things to do today, Riley, so I'll just scoot and leave you to your breakfast. It's just about time for the second morning rush to begin.' She opened the door and turned to leave.

'You're a doll,' I called after her.

I could see her ears take on a scarlet glow as she left. With her back to me she waved me off with her hand. 'Oh, gowan with ya,' she said without turning.

I climbed out of the cot, which wasn't as easy as it sounds if you've ever been on played-out canvas. I put on my pants and poured a cup of hot black. Sinclair was on the front page of the paper. The rest was standard stuff – rebellion in Spain, Roosevelt denouncing the unions and the government trying to come up with a scheme to stabilize a 'wobbly' currency. That one was a pip.

I made the eggs and their tray mates disappear in double-quick time and washed it all down with a full quart of Helvitica Bolde's Depression brew. The clock sitting on top of the filing cabinet inched toward 9 a.m. I had three hours before Harry Bridges expected my call.

It was no use trying to pick up Father Windy's trail and I thought I had just about come to the end of the road in my search for information from Lana Birdwell. I told myself that from here on out, it was going to be purely a matter of instinct and hunches. As if I had been following a plan before.

I called Dexter Hall to bring him up to date. I reached him at Sinclair headquarters. He was agitated as usual.

'Mr Kovachs, what did you find out? What is the Committee planning? Does it have anything to do with the rally?'

He would have jabbered on indefinitely if I hadn't cut him off.

'Not much; I don't know; and probably,' I said.

'What?'

'I said, not much, I don't know and probably – the answers to your first three questions.'

'Please, Mr Kovachs, this is no time for joking.' His voice was quick and jumpy. He sounded as nervous as a cat in a room full of rocking chairs. 'I don't know if we should cancel the rally on the basis of what we know or take our chances and proceed as scheduled.'

'What does your executive board say?'

'Why, I, I haven't told them.'

'I thought we decided to clue them in. Take them into our confidence.'

'I changed my mind. I was afraid it would create a panic situation and that's something we can definitely do without. If only we knew what is going to happen. Did you learn anything at all?'

'Not about the Committee, but I got some high-powered dope on your girlfriend.'

His voice changed in a way that's hard to describe.

'Oh, what did you find out?'

'Get yourself ready for this, Hall. Lana Birdwell is Chandler Lane's daughter. She has been working for him and is the treasurer for Antelope Investments.'

I waited for a vocal denial of what had just passed my lips or at least a convincing rationalization, but nothing came from the other end of the line, not even a Dexter Hall sigh.

'Hall, did you hear me? I said Lana Birdwell is working for the other side.'

'I heard you, Mr Kovachs. Did she say anything about the murders? Did she have anything to do with them?'

'I don't know for sure. That's as much as I got from her last night. But I've got a pretty good hunch about the identity of the Committee's head waiter here in northern California. Find him and I'd say we've got our killer. I'm going to dump a little firecracker in Lana Birdwell's pretty lap this morning. If I'm right, she'll sing sweeter than Ruby Keeler and we'll know both the identity of the murderer and the Committee's plan of action for today.'

'When are you going to see her?'

'In about forty-five minutes.'

'At her place?'

'No, here at the Bay City Cafe.'

'I'd like to be there, Mr Kovachs. Lana may need me. I feel I have a right.'

'Maybe you do, but it's best if I go this alone. I will call you the minute I turn up anything.'

Dexter Hall whined a bit about being denied permission to meet with Lana Birdwell and me, but it wasn't much of a whine. He said he would be standing by for my call.

Next I called Lana Birdwell. I found her in, which was terribly encouraging. It was a short conversation.

I told her to get away from her hotel and go to the park or to a movie and not to speak to anyone. I emphasized the anyone. I told her Father Windy might be gunning for her. I also instructed her to meet me at the Powell Street corner of Union Square – Powell and Geary – fifteen minutes before the rally was scheduled to kick off.

She was puzzled by my instructions, especially the part telling her to make herself thin and button her lip to anybody but me, but she said she would follow them to the letter. Perhaps she was moved by my subtle hint about alerting the cops to her connection with the Blodgett murder at 5.50 if she failed to make our rendezvous at 5.45.

She called me darling a few times and made me feel like I wanted to take a big bite of that soft and yielding flesh of hers. She let me know the offer was still open.

I told her once again that I was counting on her and she replied once again that I had nothing to worry about. I wondered how much we believed each other.

I finished dressing and downed the last of what had become lukewarm coffee. It didn't matter, it still tasted good to me. I noticed for the first time since I returned from LA that my clothes smelled like the Berkeley mud flats at low tide. My socks were stiff with grime and felt like licorice that's stood out in the sun too long, while my underwear was too dirty even to run for Congress. I dreamed about a hot bath and a clean set of duds. Then I called Harry Bridges.

'I've been waiting for your call, Kovachs,' he said anxiously. 'What did you get from Father Windy?'

'A lump on the head the size of a golf ball.'

'What are you talking about?'

'I'm talking about last night. And that was after two hoodlums insisted on showing me the bottom of the Bay. But that's another story. I met with Father Windy and the Birdwell dame up at that fleabag where Blodgett was iced. I faced Father Windy with what I knew about him and the Committee.'

'Yes, and what did he say?'

'Well, it wasn't so much what he said. He pulled his heat and blackened my head with it.'

'He shot you?'

'If there were any shots fired, they missed. All I got out of it was a purple strawberry on my noggin.' I stopped a moment to consider what I had said. 'Get me,' I said out loud, though not particularly for Bridges's benefit, 'like getting your head crushed is a case of pimples or something. I must be getting hard-boiled.'

Bridges wasn't concerned with my self-awareness.

'I am afraid it looks like Father Windy is our man, doesn't it?' he said with a sigh.

'Harry, I wish I could say one way or the other, but I can't. I've got a strong case against him, but I can't go to market with it.'

'Look, shamus, we don't have the time to wait for you. We've got to talk with him. He's got to tell us what he knows. Have any other suggestions?'

'I wish I did. But you're right about not waiting. I think whatever Father Windy is up to, he knows about tonight. You can try to find him before 6 p.m., but I'm afraid that's not going to be easy.'

'Do you think he's left town?'

'No, I think he's probably lamming it somewhere until tonight. But I'd bet the rent he'll be there for the fireworks.'

'I'll send some of the boys to look for him. Oh, and about tonight. Our Exec decided to send two hundred of our men to the rally as sort of an unofficial safety committee.'

'Good! That's the best thing I've heard since the score of the fifth game of the Series. Have you told Hall about it yet?'

'The chap with the Sinclair campaign?'

'Yes.'

'No, I was waiting until you called. I had hoped you would have better news.'

'You and me both. Harry, do me a favor and don't tell Hall about the safety brigade.'

'Why not? Don't you think he should know?'

'He's pretty spooked by everything and I think if he were told two hundred longshoremen were going to show up, he might just burst. You know what I mean?'

'I really can't say that I do, mate, but that Hall chap is a squeaky beak, he is.'

'What do you mean by that?'

'Nothing that I can be specific about, but the bloke does strike me as an unstable sort and all that. He's been asking a lot of questions about you, too.'

'Oh, what kind of questions?'

'The snooping kind if I had to call it by name.'

'Well, I'm not surprised. I'm sure a lot of people are asking questions about me, including you. Am I right?'

'You are not above suspicion, if that's what you mean. We've been checking on you.'

'I'd be disappointed if you hadn't.'

'We haven't found anything that disputes what you have told us, but don't let that go to your head.'

'You don't have a thing to worry about on that account.'

'Let's hope not.'

I told Bridges to call me if he found Father Windy. He assured me that I would have a front-row seat at the proposed 'hearing', should the priest be found.

I had just hung up the phone when I heard a commotion out in the diner. A dame was shrieking. It sounded like bloody murder. I went to take a look. It was Mrs Bolde. She had a spatula in her right hand and was waving it menacingly at two men. The men I knew – Cahill and Leery. They were fighting about me.

Mrs Bolde was swatting at Leery like he was a 200-pound shuttlecock and crowing into Cahill's face that I wasn't on the premises and they had no right to search the place.

It took everything those two flatfoots had to restrain her. Hagen tried to step between them, but she flicked him out of her way like a long ash on a short cigarette. Then a couple of customers joined the fray, each grabbing one of Leery's legs in an effort to drag him away from Mrs Bolde. A small gal in a pill-box hat and a plain cloth coat jumped from a stool onto his back and spiked him in the side with her heels while at the same time covering his eyes with her hands.

Cahill reached inside his coat for a gun, but was caught between the eyes with a couple of farm fresh eggs thrown by one of the cafe patrons. I would have preferred to stick around and watch the donnybrook, or better still, have entered the mêlée with a cast-iron skillet or two. But I decided that discretion was the better part of the rumble and exited through the rear door into the alley.

I could see a couple of squad cars pull up in front of the diner as I was making my getaway. It was one free-for-all I regretted having to pass up.

The circle was drawing tighter. I felt like Atlanta the day before General Sherman dropped by – no place to go and not much time to do it in. There was no one to call, no one to see and no more meetings to be arranged that would shed one extra kilowatt of light on either the murders or the bake sale the Committee had planned.

I had come to the end of a very unpleasant road. I felt like it had been a long ride to nowhere. That's the place you end up when you don't know where to look for what you're trying to find, and when you find what you're looking for – if you find it – you haven't an idea of what you found. I did have my hunches, however.

Maybe Bridges would find Father Windy before it was too late. Maybe Lana Birdwell would bump into me on the street and confess everything. Maybe Cal Grundy or McArthur Digges Mason would call the whole thing off. Maybe. But unless and until that happened, there was nothing I could do, absolutely nothing. Until the rally, that is.

I hopped on a bus and rode it all the way out to the beach.

32.

I spent an hour or so kicking the ocean and looking for seals. After that I crossed the Great Highway to Playland and watched two small children and their mothers terrify themselves on the ferris wheel. The laughing lady outside the Fun House cackled in my ear. I tried not to take it personally.

I lunched on a bowl of something thick – a burgoo the counter man said was chili – and one of those ice cream cookies I get every time I go to the beach. I shouldn't have eaten either, since what I really wanted was alcohol to give me an edge until the rally.

I walked down the Highway from the lights, the buzzers and bing-bong sounds of Playland's penny arcade to the Flame Bar. It wasn't yet a dump, but it didn't have a whole lot of class either.

I was well into my third drink – I was alternating between whiskey and soda and whiskey straight up – before I realized the game had begun. The bartender turned up the volume so the three customers in the back by the door might hear the broadcast.

I got serious for a time. I peeled away the cellophane and paper from a dog-eared pack of squares to get at my last Chesterfield. I got a clean bar napkin so I could score the game. I could feel the tension in the air. The seventh game of the World Series is no small potatoes. Only wars and some elections command as much attention from the American people, and maybe that's the way it should be.

Consider the drama involved. Two teams from rival leagues, leagues that hate each other's guts, facing each other from dug-in trenches. Like well-disciplined armies they have mowed down their respective adversaries systematically and without compassion through five long months of bitter and protracted diamond warfare just to earn the right to slug it out with each other. If that isn't excitement, then Tunney and Dempsey were rag salesmen. Napoleon *vs* Alexander the Great; Tamburlaine against Caesar – that's what a World Series is like.

In the 1934 version of the autumn spectacle, the two great armies of the Midwest had dueled through six games to a spine-tingling standstill. Each team had won three games. The Series, in fact the entire season, had come down to one final and decisive engagement. There would be no draw here, only a victor and a vanquished. Game seven would be a painful Waterloo for one. At stake was perhaps not civilization as we have come to know it, but something almost as vital. To the winner went baseball's royal crown, signifying purpled supremacy in the sport of champions. Few things in the twentieth century approach such lofty distinction.

My palms sweat as Ted Husing called out the starting lineups. There were an undetermined number of chills racing up and down my spine as the maestro of the microphone announced, 'The Detroit Tigers are taking the field.' I wiped my hands on my thighs, waiting for Eldon Auker to throw the first pitch. I ordered another drink to even my count.

The hometown crowd shattered the October air in thunderous approval when the umpire cried, 'Strike one'. It was one of the last times the Motor City partisans were given an opportunity to voice their satisfaction.

St Louis scored in the second. In the third inning the irascible Dean led off with a double to left that started a Cardinal rally. Thirty minutes later, when the proverbial dust settled on the diamond, the 'House that Greenberg Built' was a burned-out shell. The Cardinals had hammered across seven fat runs. So much for drama and history.

I called Harry Bridges before the fourth inning got under way. Father Windy was still in a closet somewhere and wasn't likely to come out.

I left the bar and spent the rest of the afternoon at the beach, playing tag with the surf and looking at my watch.

33.

The fog pedaled its strong legs just off the horizon for most of the afternoon. Around five it came crashing down like the curtain to a bad play. In a matter of minutes the coast was socked in and foghorns and seals began barking at each other. Ships whistled in the white dark.

When the fog rolls in at the beach, or anywhere else in San Francisco, it is accompanied by a ten to fifteen degree drop in temperature. When that happens, a wet chill owns the streets and smart people stay inside.

I rolled up my collar and blew on a pair of whitened hands. I could barely see Playland from the beach. The omnipresent cackling from the Fun House lady guided me across the Great Highway and to the stop where a bus was catching its breath before making the return trip downtown. I hopped on and five minutes later the coach was under way. It outraced the fog as it lumbered down Geary, past the sand, through the avenues, the Fillmore and Western Addition.

A great snarl of cars and buses slowed the coach to a standstill around Taylor. It idled through two lights like an elephant treading water. I pulled the cord and got off. The sidewalks were worse than the street. The tail end of rush hour traffic and rallyers made the going slower than a bicycle in loose sand.

I put my head down and did some fancy broken field walking

toward a Geary and Powell goal line. Ten minutes later I was standing on the corner where I was to meet Lana Birdwell. So were eight hundred other people.

Floodlights turned night into noon. A local high school band was belting out tinny campaign tunes from a large elevated platform. Unshaven drunks were having a field day, touching middle-aged couples for dimes. Seagulls circled overhead, not knowing what to make of the human swarm below. And young men with megaphones hollered for people to move to the center of the square, while girls pinned Sinclair buttons on helpless bystanders.

I picked my way through the peopled plaza looking for Lana Birdwell. Through a din of voices and brass horns I heard a female voice call my name. I turned and focused my eyes on Lana Birdwell, fifteen paces and seventy-five people behind me. She was waving a gloved hand. I peeled away the people between us like so many leaves from an artichoke to reach her.

She threw her arms around my neck and kissed me on the lips. It felt warm, like a belt from a bottle of twelve-year-old Scotch, and tasted just as good.

'Oh, darling, I thought I would never be able to find you in this crowd,' she uttered breathlessly into my chin.

'We're just a couple of lucky so-and-sos,' I answered. It was hard to think of anything even politely romantic to say with a thousand people elbowing their way between me and my overcoat in an attempt to get somewhere else. My shoes were like strategic military targets – everyone made a point of stepping on them. At some point I had a good idea what a white sale at the Emporium was like.

I took Lana Birdwell by the arm and marched her to a small clearing in the square the masses had not yet swallowed. The band had stopped playing and only an occasional direction or announcement, flowing over the public address system, broke the night air.

'I'm sorry we have to meet like this, sugar,' I said in a voice that carried over the general buzz, 'but we still have some work to do.'

'Work? Whatever do you mean?'

'In case you have forgotten, sugar, there is still an unsolved murder or two, and those creeps working for your father are just bound to show up here tonight.'

I looked around the swelling crowd, scanning it for signs of Cal Grundy's brutes. If they were in Union Square, they weren't in uniform. Maybe they had canceled out, I thought. I was anything but convinced of that. Also I noticed the great absence of white caps. 'Where's Bridges's boys?' I muttered under my breath.

I returned my eyes to Lana Birdwell. She appeared disappointed with me, but I'd given up trying to read faces, so I couldn't really tell what was going on behind those shimmering green eyes.

'I wish all this would just go away so we could be alone together,' she said. 'The world is such a dreadful place to spend one's life.'

She started pawing me again. I pushed her away.

'Plenty of time for that later. Right now we've got to put our heads together.'

'I'd like that,' she purred, moving closer to me.

'I mean we've got to come up with answers to some very difficult questions.'

Her lips drooped. 'Oh, that.'

'Yeah, that. Like why did you come to me in the first place with that hokum about being Chandler Lane's girlfriend?'

She tried to control her impatience.

'I thought if I made you think I was involved in some kind of lovers' quarrel you would be more likely to take the case without asking a whole lot of stupid questions. I thought you private detectives worked exclusively in the area of domestic problems.'

I generally handle cracks like that in the usual way – swiftly and with a drop of acid from the tongue. However, on those rare occasions when I'm at a loss for words, I have been told that it is my wont to take out a smoke, light it and take a long, thoughtful first drag. I was on the second long and, I assume, thoughtful puff before I got my gums working again.

'Why have you kept Dexter Hall in the dark about all this?' I said finally. 'If you two have been as thick as oatmeal, I would think you would have taken him into your confidence. The sap doesn't even know who you are, does he, sugar?'

She closed one eye. It was more of a squint, really. Like she had just received an eyeful of grapefruit juice. Her head rolled slowly back and to one side.

‘He knows more than he lets on.’

‘You know, that’s what I think, too. At first he protected your honor at every turn. Quite loyal he was. You would have been impressed. I know I was. But when I talked to him this morning, he was humming a different tune.’

Lana Birdwell was very interested. She took a pastel-colored cigarette from a gold case and put it to her lips. I supplied her with a light. I had to raise my voice to keep ahead of the band, which had just struck up another chorus of ‘Happy Days Are Here Again’.

‘Yeah, he was a different Dexter Hall this morning. I think if we both didn’t know better, I’d say he was trying to start a real serious whispering campaign about you, sugar. Said he’d been covering for you from the beginning. I think he wanted me to believe you killed Ira Blodgett. He implied it was his love for you that made him dummy up about it. You know, I think he’s ready to send you over.’

Lana Birdwell’s face turned the color of her hair. She threw her cigarette to the ground and stomped on it with a vengeance.

‘That louse! That dirty little insect!’ She was trembling with rage. ‘Dexter Hall is your man, you poor dumb darling. He’s your murderer! And he is behind everything else that is going on. I was used by him just as I was used by my father. I covered for that worm because I thought he loved me. A fat lot of good that has done me.’ She tossed her head back and laughed sarcastically. Then she began to weep. She threw her arms around my neck again. ‘Help me, my darling. I’m so confused, so terribly confused.’

I comforted her some. It’s a man’s prerogative.

The rally was starting. A familiar voice introduced the first of several preliminary speakers. It belonged to Dexter Hall. He was the master of ceremonies. Over his voice, I resumed with Lana Birdwell.

‘I’ll help you, sugar, but first you’ve got to come clean with me.’

Tears poured from her eyes down her Greek face. Red-brown rivulets of salt water mixed with mascara cut shallow paths in her cheeks. Teardrops tumbled from the tip of her nose. I wiped her face with my handkerchief and told her to blow, but women just don’t blow their noses, not in public anyway. She would only pinch her nostrils with the cheap cotton mouchoir and exhale gently. I offered her one of my smokes but she turned it down. She coughed once or twice, then spoke.

'I thought I was in love with Dexter Hall, believe me darling, I did. He was a good-looking man with plenty of ambition. I thought he was going places and I liked that combination. When I found out what he was really doing, I mean all those nasty, criminal things, it broke my heart, but I didn't leave him. I couldn't.'

I asked the obvious, 'Why?'

'Why? Why didn't I leave him? Because I wanted fame, fortune and position, the things most girls want, but never have a ghost of a chance of getting.'

'What about your father? He could give you all those things a dozen times over.'

'Yes, he could and he did. But there was a catch to it.'

'A catch?'

'Dexter Hall. He was the price for regaining my birthright.'

'Hmmm.'

'Two months ago, father introduced me to him as his "blue-eyed boy", his chosen heir and successor to the Lane empire. Everything was to go to him, I mean everything. Father wasn't actually cutting me out; he wanted me to become Mrs Dexter Hall and he put it in a way that was hard to refuse. Oh, it didn't sound like a bad proposition to me at first. I mean I actually fell for the guy. Then I found out what a loathsome and despicable creature he really was. But by that time it was too late.'

'Loathsome? Despicable? Are you sure, sugar? He looks like such a harmless boy scout.'

'I'm sure, all right. I found Mr Dexter Hall to be cut from the exact same mold as my famous father. They were both ruthless, scheming, vengeful men obsessed with their own importance. Hall was the perfect man to do my father's bidding here in San Francisco. He is like the son he never had. The whole thing makes me terribly ill.'

I don't mind admitting that the information flowing from Lana Birdwell's luscious lips made my eyebrows jump up and down. I felt like someone had just taken their finger out of the hole in the dike. I started rowing with everything I had.

'You're telling me that Hall is working for the other side? A spy? An agent?' Lana Birdwell sniffled her runny nose and nodded affirmatively. 'A moment ago you accused him of murdering Ira Blodgett. You were upset and angry and maybe just said that to get even, I don't know.' I took her by the shoulders and looked squarely into a pair of large, green dilated dots. 'I'm going to ask you again, sugar, and this time I want you to be positive. Nothing but a big white sheet will do. Did Hall kill Ira Blodgett?'

She didn't answer right away. She had a distant look in her eye. It wasn't fear or hate or anything other than distance. A great distance.

'Did he kill Ira Blodgett?' I repeated.

She came back to earth. Her eyes filled again.

'Yes! Yes! Yes!' she choked out through her tears. 'He killed that poor man and had another man in Los Angeles killed, too. I was there when he made the phone call. He is an evil man, a very evil man.'

'Why didn't you go to the police, sugar?'

'He told me I would go to jail as an accessory to murder.'

'Why did he kill Blodgett, do you know the answer to that?' Lana Birdwell went to pieces. She began weeping uncontrollably, almost hysterically. I took her by the shoulders again and shook her firmly. 'Don't fall apart on me, sugar. You've still got some more things I have to know.' I shook her again, but she just continued to bawl like a child. Someone tapped me on the shoulder. I turned to look.

'Hey, buddy, why don't you leave the little lady alone.' It was the voice of an interested citizen who had appointed himself the defender of Western Womanhood.

'I shrugged my shoulders. 'It's my wife, pal. I just told her our cat died. How'd I know she'd take it so hard.'

He wasn't a big man, just wide. He had a round fat face that Porky Pig couldn't have improved on and was wearing a thin cotton jacket that gave away a pair of arms that looked like telephone poles with elbows. I don't think he bought the story about the cat, for he wound up one of his beefy limbs and took a poke at me. I doubt chivalry had anything to do with it.

I sidestepped the blow, but Lana Birdwell, still mewling into my handkerchief, did not. The punch didn't catch her full, but then it didn't have to. The fist of the fat-faced man glanced off her wet cheek and she went reeling into a crowd of people. She was more shocked than hurt, but she produced a wailing sound that could have been picked up by most of the ships sailing this side of the Farallones.

A man in the front of the crowd who saw at least part of the incident pointed a long finger at the fat-faced man and cried out, 'Hey, he hit a woman!' The people in the vicinity turned to stare at the offender. He became horrified and began pleading with an unsympathetic citizenry.

'It was a mistake. I meant to sock that guy over there,' he pointed at me and prayed. I didn't help.

'This beast came up to my wife and without the slightest provocation belted her in the chops.'

The fat-faced man held out his hands to halt two dozen people who were moving menacingly in his direction.

'No, no, please,' he begged. 'He's lying. I was trying to help the lady, honest!'

But like the crew of the *Bounty* stalking Captain Bligh across the deck, the crowd would not be influenced.

'Let's show this guy what we do to people who beat up helpless ladies,' shouted one man. A woman several rows back cupped her hands and hollered to those even further back, 'Some man is beating a woman to death.' Several hundred rally-goers from all directions converged on the fat-faced man.

I grabbed a dazed Lana Birdwell and pulled her to safety. From the center of the throng I could still hear the fat-faced man pleading for his life. Several arms holding clenched fists waved above his pitiful wailings. Then the pummeling commenced. Placards praising Sinclair were ripped from their wooden stakes and transformed into clubs. Fists began to fly. They clunked against bone and tissue. Clubs sliced the air, landing with dull thuds against the unsuspecting craniums. The mêlée had outgrown the fat-faced man and the protection of female kind. It was a free-for-all that promised riot.

I dragged Lana Birdwell along the edge of the crowd towards the speakers' platform. We worked our way to a spot about twenty yards from where the main event was taking place.

We were close enough to get a good glimpse of Dexter Hall. He was approaching the microphone. The great majority in the square, a number which reached into the thousands, were unaware of the commotion on the Powell Street side of the square.

Hall took the microphone from the previous speaker.

'Who do we like?' he challenged.

'Sinclair!' the multitude replied.

'Who do we want for governor?' Hall shouted.

'Sinclair!' cheered the people.

'Who?'

'Sinclair!'

'Who?'

'Sinclair!'

A thunderous pandemonium obtained. It was a full five minutes before the roar subsided. Hall was wearing a broad smile.

'It is with great and rare privilege,' he said, 'that I bring before you the man unique to California and the nation.'

I relaxed my grip on Lana Birdwell's arm. An instant later she jerked forward and broke away and went scurrying toward the steps leading to the elevated speakers' platform. My shouts for her to stop were smothered by Hall's voice praising the candidate.

I ran after her. It wasn't easy. Picking my way through the tightly packed crowd was about as simple as lugging a sofa through an alder thicket. I was a good ten feet behind her and wasn't gaining much ground.

Dexter Hall was wrapping up his introduction. I could see Lana Birdwell approaching the steps at the rear of the platform. I could also see that the steps, in fact the whole platform, was ringed by a human chain of men wearing white caps – Bridges's boys!

I continued pushing my way through the throng. An unintentional shoulder was swung from a jostled front-row Sinclair enthusiast and caught me in a good eye. It was all my fault, but the stars that eye saw for the next few minutes didn't care who was to blame.

I regained my sight in time to see Lana Birdwell burst through the thin and surprised cordon of stevedores. She scampered up the steps to the rear of the platform.

I was still at least ten paces away from her. Out of the corner of my smarting eye I saw one of the safety monitors throw down his cap and light out after her. It was Father Windy! In his right hand I saw the muzzle of the .38 service revolver he had pulled on me the night before.

I reached the cordon an instant later. The longshoremen closed ranks on me. One jabbed a finger in my chest.

'Sorry, mac, nobody gets through without a pass.'

'The woman!' I shouted into his entire face. 'She may have a gun!'

'We'll take care of her, don't you worry.'

I pushed against him, trying to gain the step. Two of his buddies came to his side, making my efforts meaningless. I tried a different approach.

'Harry Bridges knows me. I'm Kovachs, Riley Kovachs. Doesn't that name mean anything to you?'

'Look, buddy,' said the longshoreman, who was growing visibly irritated by my persistence, 'I don't care if you're a "ding dong daddy from Dumas", you can't go through without a pass. Now scram, before we have to escort you to the first aid wagon.'

I didn't miss his meaning.

'You're right,' I said, 'absolutely right. No pass, no get through.'

I turned back toward the crowd. I took one step, wheeled hard and fast, put my head down and charged the momentarily relaxed monitors. I hit the three of them like a bowling ball slams into the pins on a Brooklyn side strike.

Once through their line I charged the steps. I landed on the third one and stumbled up the remaining two. My momentum was such that I was almost a quarter of the way across the dais before I regained my balance.

I saw the colorful backs of the twenty-piece band sitting to my right. On the left were a dozen people sitting on metal folding chairs. They were also facing the front of the platform. In the middle was a large floral display, mostly carnations. In front of the flowers was the speakers' lectern with wires and cords snaking up its four-foot height.

Beyond was the charged assembly. Large floodlights beamed down from overhead. The glare was intense, and unless I held my head a certain way, everything on the speakers' platform was thrown into black silhouette. The golden glint forced me to divert my eyes and move to the far side of the platform.

Dexter Hall had just finished introducing Sinclair. Both men stood side by side facing the cheering crowd. The candidate raised his arms and the multitude exploded with approval.

I moved out of the light's glare. Everything became as clear as Steuben glass. Lana Birdwell was racing down the platform between the flowers and the people on the folding chairs. Clasped in her hands was a small caliber pistol. Behind her some eight to ten paces and racing at an angle, knocking over band members and most of the floral display, was Father Windy. The revolver in his right hand looked large and very deadly. After plowing through petals and people he came to an abrupt halt some dozen steps from Hall and Sinclair. Lana Birdwell had stopped halfway in between.

The band and the guests in the folding chairs shrieked and grabbed the deck when they saw the weapons.

The commotion caused the two men at the speakers' stand to turn away from the admiring masses. Hall wheeled forty-five degrees in the direction of the candidate and like a Red River cowboy drew steel from inside his coat.

The crowd, that portion which could see what was happening, collectively mouthed a groan of fear and anticipated grief. They were too shocked to do more. Someone yelled, 'Oh no!' Other than that, no intelligent sound drew breath.

In a moment it was over.

At least three shots broke through the night, their sound reverberating off the tall buildings that box Union Square. Maybe there were more, I don't know. A blue-gray smoke rose ever so slowly from the front of the dais. The floodlights caught it, dissected it for purposes of examination, and found death in each particle. The vapor was then picked up by a confused breeze and pushed out over the heads of the rally-goers to inform them of the tragedy.

I was the first one to the fallen bodies. The only survivor among them was the candidate. In the moments before the platform was crawling with police, ambulance drivers and thrill seekers, I tried to reconstruct the events as best I could.

When Hall had whirled toward Sinclair with a drawn gun, he stepped in a way that partially concealed the candidate from the approaching Lana Birdwell and Father Windy. Lana Birdwell had fired first. She was the closest and had been set a split second longer than the priest.

Father Windy's weapon was the next to report. Hall's gun was fired a micro-second later. Or maybe before, I couldn't tell.

Hall had been the first to go down. He fell on top on Sinclair. This may have saved the candidate's life. Lana Birdwell and Father Windy both crumpled where they had fired their fatal shots. I didn't see either one fall, but the point is not debatable.

I went to Lana Birdwell. She was stirring slightly. Her hands clutched a massive stomach wound. I took off my coat and bent down to place it under her head. Her eyes were open but they were very far away. Yet she recognized me.

'Riley, darling,' she whispered. She took my hand and gave it a squeeze. She asked me what had happened to her and why she was in such pain. I told her about the shooting and it all came back.

'Can you ever forgive me, my darling?' Her voice grew fainter with each word she breathed. It could have been drowned out by a yawn. 'I'm no good,' she struggled, 'I lied to you from the very beginning. It wasn't that I wanted to, but I was hopelessly trapped by a way of life you will probably never understand.'

She choked on the blood that trickled down the corner of her mouth. 'Ambition and greed blinded me to everything else, Riley, dear. My whole life has been driven by them for so long, I don't know anything else. You were right about my connections with Chandler Lane and Antelope Investments, but what you didn't know was that my father sent me up here to work with Dexter Hall. Hall was in charge of the Committee here. When Ira Blodgett found out Hall killed him. He stabbed him that night at the Pasadena Hotel.'

The sound of sirens filled Union Square. Men in white coats and blue-suited cops swarmed over the platform. A photographer's flash went off every other second. I put my ear to Lana Birdwell's mouth. It was almost over.

'You wanted to know about 9 October. I was 9 October, my darling. I was to assassinate Mr Sinclair. In return I was to be paid $100,000 by my father, and he promised Hall and I safe passage to South America. Until last night I was planning to go through with it. Yes I was.

'It was Hall who knocked us out at the hotel last night, not Father Windy. Hall betrayed me. Why, I don't know. Maybe he thought I was falling for you and couldn't be trusted anymore. And when you told me he wanted to turn me in to the police I knew I had to even the score and kill him instead of Mr Sinclair.

'Call it poetic justice or revenge, but I would do it again a thousand times. My only regret, my darling, is that I won't be able to be with you. I am afraid I won't be able to keep our date, but we will always have that night at your apartment.'

A look of fear overcame her ashen face. Life was all but drained from her body. She squeezed my hand again and began speaking in short, spurting breaths.

'Everything is growing dark, but I'm not frightened with you here, Riley, darling.' She smiled for the first time. Then surprise.

'Kiss me, Riley Kovachs,' she said, rallying the very last breath she had.

I placed my lips softly on hers. They had already become cool to the touch. I closed my eyes.

The embrace lasted only a moment. When we parted, Lana Birdwell was dead. Her Nile-green eyes were locked open and fixed on some distant star in the blue-black heavens overhead. With two fingers I pulled her eyelids down, closing her eyes forever. It seemed like the right thing to do.

Medical attendants kneeled down and took Lana Birdwell's pulse and listened to her still heart. I got up and backed away. They unfolded a white sheet and placed it over her before lifting her onto their stretcher. I felt someone grab my arm. It was Cahill.

'We got a letter from the dame this afternoon explaining everything. You're in the clear, Kovachs, but I'll want to see you in my office in the morning for a statement.'

I heard his words clearly and I'm sure they were in a regular grammatical order the way words are supposed to be, but I didn't comprehend a thing he said. I shook my arm loose from his grip and walked up to the speakers' lectern and looked out over the plaza. The crowd was dispersing slowly and quietly at the insistence of the police. The rallyers, who moments before had been a cheering, chanting, whooping throng were mute as they methodically snaked their way out of the two Geary Street entrances to the square. They looked like pilgrims passing Lenin's tomb.

The amber haze streaming down from the floodlights amplified the somberness of the spectacle. It was as if the gaseous radiance had a purpose in the bizarre drama and that purpose was to halt the film of life at the frame the shooting occurred.

I am told that all tragic situations are like that. Movements before and during a calamity are caught and rerun endlessly in the mind. They never move forward beyond that point.

That's how I felt standing at the speakers' lectern, gazing out over the shock-stricken remnants of the once jubilant political gathering. I had to force my thoughts from a circular replay of the last thirty minutes. The mood was overpowering. I pulled a Chesterfield from my pocket and lit it. It tasted stale.

I turned around to look at the platform. Hall's body had already been removed. Lana Birdwell's lifeless form was being lifted onto a stretcher by two ambulance attendants, to be taken to the morgue. Father Windy was being photographed by news wolves, shoving each other to get the best angle that would most sensationalize death. The right picture would sell an extra 50,000 newspapers. At any rate, Father Windy didn't care. His subscription had run out twenty minutes ago.

I felt sick to my stomach. I knew I wouldn't throw up but I wanted to very badly. I walked slowly across the platform to the steps. I turned for one last look at the grisly death scene. I was no different from the rest. The lights overhead bored into my eyes.

Everything was plunged into shadow and silhouette, but nobody had to explain to me what had happened. I knew, I would always know.

I threw the stub of my cigarette at a bush and descended the steps of the platform. I walked into a hostile night where I hoped to lose myself, maybe for good.

34.

The night can only hide you so long. In my case it wasn't long enough. I walked the waterfront that night – that 9 October night – from the Ferry Building out past Army Street and back again.

First the thinning of the bituminous black sky and then the initial blades of light slicing through the valleys of the Oakland hills exposed my cover.

I continued to walk in the post-dawn hours, trying to give the raw nerve endings of my mind time to mend themselves. It was one of things that only time and being alone can help, and sometimes even that's not enough.

I called Harry Bridges about 8 o'clock to find out about Father Windy's funeral. He told me more than that. Some I had suspected even before Lana Birdwell's death-bed confession. Some I had not.

The longshore boss said Father Windy had called him late the previous afternoon and told him the whole story. Bridges relayed the gist of that conversation to me.

Father Windy knew that someone in the Sinclair organization had killed Blodgett. He learned from Ira that the person was receiving funds through Antelope Investments to outfit a vigilante army to throw the election. When Blodgett was killed, Father Windy continued with his work. He decided to infiltrate Antelope Investments and the Committee and was doing quite well until I went to LA and nearly queered it for him.

Father Windy told Bridges he was afraid I had blown his cover at our meeting at the Pasadena Hotel and that it might have been disastrous had not Dexter Hall showed up and tipped his hand. Hall, the priest told Bridges, knocked me cold and slugged Lana Birdwell. Hall told Father Windy that he had been tipped off that Blodgett's murderer had set a trap for him at the hotel. He wanted Father Windy to believe that he had rescued him from certain death. He was counting on the notion that his false heroism would divert any suspicion Father Windy might have of him.

'Jim Windy might have bought Hall's play except for one thing,' Bridges said, drawing his story to a close. 'He told me he might have believed him if it weren't for the fact that he trusted you. He knew you were no killer and would not have set him up, no matter what you might have thought of him.'

I gulped and felt knee-high to a very small salt shaker. Father Windy had trusted me all the way. I would have been a liar if I said the same thing about him.

The rest I could have figured out myself. Father Windy probably knew Blodgett's killer to be Hall. He also must have suspected that Hall had a part in the plot to assassinate Sinclair. Tom Mooney's apocryphal words about *agents provocateurs* placed the idea in my mind, and Mooney and the priest were much closer. I guess he wasn't sure about Lana Birdwell's role in the whole thing and that's why he played it so close to the vest, right up to the end. When he saw her break through the monitors at the speakers' platform, he must have believed that the assassination attempt was under way.

He had both Lana Birdwell and Hall within range of his revolver in those fateful seconds before the shots were fired. It is unlikely he had time to pull the trigger twice so the only question that remained was – which one did he shoot?

Police ballistics will tell the story, but I'm not sure it makes any difference.

Bridges told me Father Windy's funeral would be that Friday, with services to be held in the union hall. I assured him that I would be there. I said goodbye to the longshore leader. I still had some walking to do.

A light mist was floating down from a fat cloud. It washed the night from my face. It was one of those mists that brings with it a pensive mood that is inescapable. It was the kind of mood everyone sometimes needs. I boarded a streetcar and rode it to Golden Gate Park.

I entered the Arboretum at Ninth Avenue and Lincoln Way and walked past the magnolia trees, past the Port Orford Cedars, down through the native California garden to the small Redwood forest. Besides its wetness, it was dark and green. The nasturtium and large swatches of sorel offered a soothing contrast to the brown fuzz that covers most of the Bay Area in October.

I thought about Lana Birdwell as I walked. I thought of the person she was and how she lied to me at every turn. I thought of the time she almost got me killed and the way she tried to pin Ira Blodgett's murder on me. And I thought about that night we almost touched the stars.

I couldn't say I loved her. I didn't know her – not the real Lana Birdwell/Rennest/Lane. I'm not even certain how much I liked her. To be sure, I was attracted to her, but I've been attracted to many women. Yet, Lana Birdwell was different. I knew that the first day she walked into my office. I also knew then she could prove to be as poisonous as nightshade.

Lana Birdwell – murderer, liar and greedy adventuress. I couldn't help feeling sorry for her, though. There's no question that I would have turned her in had she lived – she was in it too deep. I would have done just what the detective in Hammett's novel did, but I would have done it with a great deal more remorse. Hammett's character was the true hard-boiled type. I was more like a three-minute egg.

But I'm no bowl of mush when it comes to the opposite sex. Love is a word I kicked out of my vocabulary some time ago, and the mixed feelings I had about Lana Birdwell convinced me I had done the right thing. Love, Jack London once wrote, is nothing more than the disorder of the mind under the stimulus of passion.

The gentle dripping rain which softly tickled my face was responsible for the philosophy. It felt good.

My face was totally bathed in the atmospheric refreshment. I hardly noticed the slight salty taste on my lips. I stared blankly at the yellow skunk cabbage in a small pond and watched it grow.

Sometime later the mist called it quits and I emerged from the forest. I lit a Chesterfield. It tasted good.

The Tigers had lost the big one, but there was always next year. The election was less than a month away and Sinclair was leading in the polls. The Depression – well, when you thought about people like Harry Bridges and Tom Mooney and Father James Windy – men who had devoted their lives to fighting for the little guy – then the world didn't seem like such a bad place to be, in 1934.

I caught the streetcar back downtown. I was looking forward to getting back to my flat and taking a long hot bath, and just maybe this time I would be able to brew a decent cup of coffee.